"W... ...?"

Norma... ...would have answered with a well-rehearsed spiel. But she knew it wouldn't fly with Matthew. He was too perceptive. "A cop helped me once when I was in trouble. I guess I admired her and I wanted to help other women like me."

"What kind of woman would that be?"

Angel refused to allow anyone but her very close friends and her superiors to know she'd ever been that vulnerable. A victim.

"You know all you need to know about me, Matt." She stood and headed for the bathroom. Stopping in the doorway, she glanced over her shoulder. "Except that you really don't want to get in my way."

"What about the game?"

Angel wasn't sure if he referred to the Scrabble game she'd abandoned or the dangerous personal game developing between them.

Dear Reader,

If you enjoyed my first romantic suspense,
The Secret Wife, I suspect you'll become immersed
in *Secrets in Texas.* As the titles suggest, both books
involve (family) secrets. They also contain twists and
turns and complex emotional entanglements.

The idea for *Secrets in Texas* was born of news articles
I read about the Fundamentalist Church of Jesus Christ
of Latter Day Saints–polygamous sects prevalent near
the Arizona/Utah border, among other places.

I contemplated how hard it must be for men and
women raised in this culture to adjust to living in the
outside world. So I gave my hero, Matthew Stone, just
such a challenge. I tested him to the limit and sent him
back to the polygamist group, this time with a faux wife
who is anything but submissive. Problem is, there are
secrets in Angel Harrison's past that have her wondering
if she might be more vulnerable than she thinks.

While I did research fundamentalist sects, I didn't try
to factually recreate their lifestyle in my book. Instead,
I created my own sect, Zion's Gate.

Please join Angel and Matthew on their journey of
discovery at Zion's Gate.

Yours in reading,

Carrie Weaver

P.S. Carrie enjoys hearing from readers
by e-mail at www.CarrieWeaver.com or snail mail
at P.O. Box 6045, Chandler, AZ 85246-6045.

SECRETS IN TEXAS
Carrie Weaver

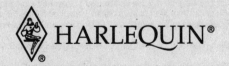

HARLEQUIN®

TORONTO • NEW YORK • LONDON
AMSTERDAM • PARIS • SYDNEY • HAMBURG
STOCKHOLM • ATHENS • TOKYO • MILAN • MADRID
PRAGUE • WARSAW • BUDAPEST • AUCKLAND

ISBN-13: 978-0-373-71387-5
ISBN-10: 0-373-71387-8

SECRETS IN TEXAS

Copyright © 2006 by Carrie Weaver.

www.eHarlequin.com

Printed in U.S.A.

ABOUT THE AUTHOR

With two teenage sons, two dogs and three cats, Carrie Weaver often feels she lives in a state called Chaos (not to be confused with Dysfunction Junction, a place she's visited only once or twice). Her books reflect real life and real love, with all the ups, downs and emotion involved.

Books by Carrie Weaver

HARLEQUIN SUPERROMANCE
1173—THE ROAD TO ECHO POINT
1222—THE SECOND SISTER
1274—THE SECRET WIFE
1311—HOME FOR CHRISTMAS
1346—FOUR LITTLE PROBLEMS

HARLEQUIN NASCAR
NO TIME TO LOSE*
HIS FATHER'S SON*

*Coming in 2007

This book is dedicated to my editor, Laura Shin.
Thank you for having confidence in me even
when I sometimes don't.

PROLOGUE

ANGEL OPENED HER eyes, trying to focus. What started as a fuzzy recollection of violence morphed into full-blown terror.

She stifled a whimper as she rolled onto her stomach. *Must be quiet.* She knew her survival depended upon it.

Drawing her knees beneath her, she bit her lip as her legs slid in opposite directions. It was like a grotesque combination of Twister and Slip 'N Slide. Only the splotches were red instead of an assortment of colors, and the liquid was too slimy for water.

It was blood. Hers? His?

Her knees stabilized, gaining traction. Slowly, deliberately, she placed a palm on the once-pristine tile floor. Then she put her other hand next to it.

Sweat rolled down her face. This should have been so simple.

But nothing had been simple for a long time.

She bit back a hysterical chuckle.

Must be quiet.

By slowly tilting her head, she was able to survey much of the kitchen peripherally without expending precious energy.

Kent wasn't in the room.

She had already registered that fact on a subconscious level, but caution had served her well in the past. Otherwise she'd be dead.

Inching forward, she focused solely on the cordless phone that had skittered beneath the table. Frowning, she tried to remember holding it, making a call.

But it was like a recurring nightmare. The phone was just out of her reach. And so was the memory.

Angel smiled grimly.

The phone might be out of reach, but the butcher knife wasn't. It was a foot or two away, probably dropped in haste.

She forced back the hot saliva pooling on her tongue as she moved forward and grasped the handle. It was slick with blood from hilt to tip. The blade was coated with the stuff. And she was pretty sure it was her own.

Bones crunched. Pain radiated up her arm. The knife dropped from her numb fingers.

It took precious seconds for reality to register. A size-twelve work boot pinned her wrist to the floor. Jeans brushed the tips of the brown boots, jeans she'd laundered so carefully earlier that morning.

Angel's scalp burned as her head was jerked backward. Her long, dark hair had once been her pride and joy. Now it was simply a handy leash, snarled in Kent's fist, as he forced her to look evil in the face.

She struggled to get away, an effort so ineffectual it made him smile. A cold, triumphant smile that told her she would die today.

The sound of splintering wood barely penetrated, as did the shout to freeze.

That confused Angel. It was a bright, beautiful Sunday afternoon. No frost or snow on the ground.

But something about that weather report seemed to enrage Kent even more. Or maybe it was the jumble of DPS officers arriving uninvited into his home.

He glanced at the cordless phone lying a few feet away. Fury burned in his eyes.

"Bitch." He swung her just far enough away so he could reach the knife and still keep her within his grasp.

She saw the knife arc into the air, then sweep toward her.

Waited for the fatal thrust that never came.

Flinched as shots echoed in her sunny kitchen.

Stumbled to the floor, still tethered to Kent. Saw him writhe once, twitch, and then lay still.

Sighed when her hair was cut from Kent's grip. And focused on the hank clutched in her husband's fist.

Even in death, Kent had refused to let her go.

CHAPTER ONE

Nine years later
Brownsville, Texas

ANGEL HARRISON squared her shoulders and entered the conference room. One look at her new assignment and she wanted to puke—the man and all he represented sickened her. But he was one of the good guys now, she reminded herself.

Or so she was told.

Realizing her supervisor waited for her to make nice, she forced herself to step forward and shake the visitor's hand. She also forced herself not to break all twenty-seven bones in his pale hand. Just apply enough pressure so he knew she meant business. "I'm Agent Harrison."

To his credit, he didn't flinch. And he didn't try to one-up her by resorting to force. He just held her gaze, his green eyes serious as he acknowledged her greeting. "Ma'am. I'm Matthew Stone."

"So when are we getting married?"

He shrugged, not a golden hair out of place on his conservative head. Nodding toward the suit and the ranger entering the conference room, he said, "Whenever they decide."

To give him credit, he was a cool one. And better-looking than his photos suggested. Definitely not Brad Pitt-perfect, more like Matthew McConaughey masquerading as an overgrown, utterly serious Eagle Scout. His crooked nose was the only feature out of the ordinary.

Angel's inspection was interrupted by the ranger, Javier Perez. He was legendary in the law-enforcement community as tough but fair.

Ranger Perez took the lead while the man in the suit positioned himself in an unobtrusive corner. He had *federal agent* written all over him.

Angel struggled to keep her expression impassive as her supervisor went to fetch coffee. Women of her rank shouldn't fetch coffee. Women of *any* rank shouldn't fetch coffee.

Perez took his place at the head of the table. "Please sit down, Mr. Stone, Agent Harrison."

Angel longed to defy the command. But today compliance served a purpose. She sat stiffly on the edge of the chair.

Ranger Perez slid a file folder to Stone, then one to Angel. "Here is the identity we've created for Agent Harrison. Since she works undercover with the Department of Public Safety gang unit, there will be no paper trail to refute the identity we've set up or cast any doubt on the whirlwind romance you two are about to begin. It's the best cover we could devise to get an agent inside."

"Is it really necessary? The Vegas wedding?" Stone asked, crossing his arms over his chest.

Perez frowned. "We think so. It's likely Jonathon Stone has been keeping tabs on you in recent years, possibly even the entire time you've been away from the sect. Marriage records are in the public domain, precluding a more long-term union. Hence your new red-hot romance with Agent Harrison resulting in a quickie marriage. The more public, the better."

Angel winced. This was so not her idea of a decent cover. How would she be able to act lovey-dovey with the Eagle Scout? Eyeing him, she decided even a bottle of tequila wouldn't do the trick.

Perez cleared his throat, as if sensing she wanted to bolt for the door. "We've shaved a few years off Agent Harrison's profile because ATF surveillance indicates your stepfather, um, uncle, might be more…receptive to a daughter-in-law on the easy side of thirty. Fortunately Agent Harrison appears much younger than her age."

Thanks, asshole.

Matthew's lips twitched as if he'd heard her thoughts loud and clear. And agreed with her.

Angel revised her earlier assessment of Matthew white-bread-bland Stone. He might seem quiet and un-perturbed, but beneath the surface he was razor-sharp.

Angel's cheeks warmed with an unfamiliar wave of shame. Surely he couldn't see inside her with that steady gaze of his? Couldn't see all she'd endured and sacrificed to rejoin the human race?

He averted his head, but not before she'd seen pity flash in his eyes.

Damn. Did he know? There was nothing to tie her to the news reports detailing the bloodshed nine years ago.

But Matthew Stone somehow *knew* her shame. And pitied her.

Angel did what came naturally these days—she came out swinging. "Let me get this straight, Ranger Perez. You want to serve up my well-preserved-for-an-old-broad-of-thirty-one body to Jonathon Stone? That's how I'm supposed to protect the women and children at Zion's Gate?"

"Certainly not, *Agent* Harrison. Your job is to observe and report back. You will *not* have a weapon. You will not confront anyone at Zion's Gate. You will secure information, nothing more."

"You say one thing, Perez, but your actions say another. You are putting Agent Harrison at risk." Matthew's voice was deceptively quiet, with an underlying edge. "I won't be a party to prostituting any woman to get in my uncle's good graces. And, yes, as my father's brother, he is my uncle. His marriage to my mother was not legal and was not sanctified in any church I acknowledge."

Perez's eyes narrowed. "Point taken."

Angel noticed he didn't deny sending mixed messages. He wasn't going to flat out tell her not to sleep with the perverted old goat to facilitate her assignment.

Instead Perez fell back on the bureaucratic mumbo jumbo so uncharacteristic of a ranger. At least uncharacteristic until the deaths at the Branch Davidian sect and the resulting Waco fallout. "The Rangers are grateful to Agent Harrison for volunteering for this assignment. But, just so you're both crystal clear, she is not working for the Texas Rangers in any capacity. Nor is she working for the ATF or DEA. Our agencies will merely be apprised of any information she gathers that might pertain to the security of our citizens."

"So if anything happens to her, you're not responsible." Matthew's relaxed pose didn't change, but the air seemed to crackle around him. No wonder Jonathon Stone had taken the dangerous gamble of inviting his nephew back into the fold. Matthew had the charisma to shore up his uncle's crumbling position as Zion's Gate lord and dictator.

When Perez didn't confirm or deny the allegation, Matthew continued. "The way I see it, you *gentlemen* are putting Agent Harrison at the mercy of a murderer, in the very core of his highly armed compound."

Perez stiffened, his fists clenched. "We're all adults here, we know what we're up against."

Matthew stood, his movements slow, almost lazy. "I'm not sure you have any idea what you're up against at Zion's Gate, Ranger Perez. And if you do, you will be no less culpable than my uncle."

Only then did Angel realize Matthew Stone was sending a civilized death threat. She got the impression Perez's badge would be little protection against Stone if things went wrong.

Angel understood in that moment how huge her initial error in judgment had been. Not only was Matthew Stone a lot smarter than he'd let on, he was an extremely dangerous man. Her gut told her he wouldn't hesitate to kill if necessary.

And if the way Perez clenched his jaw was anything to go by, he realized it, too. "The fact is, Zion's Gate is in law enforcement no-man's-land. Part of it lies on the U.S. side of the border and is connected by a tunnel system to the rest of the compound. Even if the Texas authorities were magically able to remove their thumbs from their collective Waco-weary asses, Jonathon Stone would still use his tunnel system to move to the Mexican side."

"And if the Mexican government pursued his flock, the same would happen in reverse." Stone's voice held a note of resignation.

"Exactly. Stone leases the Matamoros section of the

property from drug lords, which further complicates the situation. Hence the DEA interest. It's a volatile situation to begin with. Add a large cache of weapons, political unrest at Zion's Gate and reports of Stone's increasing paranoia and we've got a potential bloodbath on our hands.

MATTHEW SUPPRESSED a groan as he glanced around the foyer of the Las Vegas wedding chapel. *Tacky* was the first word that came to mind. *Surreal* was the second.

But he stood quietly to the side as Agent Harrison entered with her parents. The man was tall, stately, distinguished. He cupped his wife's elbow with his hand as his gaze lingered on the woman's face. She was beautiful, an older, more polished version of her daughter. Her bearing was graceful, the line of her clothes clean yet alluring. And when she turned in his direction, her dark eyes searched his face.

Angel stood on tiptoe to whisper something in her father's ear.

The older man stiffened and turned toward Matthew. Angel took him by the hand and the three joined him.

"Daddy, this is Matthew, my, um, fiancé."

Matthew extended his hand. "Pleased to meet you, sir."

"You can save it. I'm aware this isn't a real wedding."

The woman at his side made a censuring noise low in her throat.

"Keep your voice down, Daddy," Angel snapped.

"Princess, it pains me to see you go through another ill-advised wedding, if only on paper."

Princess? She'd impressed Matthew as more assassin than princess.

"It'll be fine. Just do your part today. That's all I ask."

"I'll do my part. But I can't help worrying about you."

"I know. But you don't need to. I can take care of myself."

Matthew observed the interplay with interest. Why was her father so worried? Surely she'd been on assignments just as dangerous. Maybe it wasn't the mission that bothered him but the wedding, fake though it was.

"I'm Isabella Harrison." The older woman extended her hand to Matthew. "We are very protective of our daughter."

He accepted her hand, inhaled her exquisite scent. Intelligence gleamed in her eyes, her carriage screamed old-world class. And the tilt to her head said she'd never accept mistreatment from anyone.

Squeezing Isabella's hand, he murmured, "With good reason."

She tilted her head to the side, frowning slightly.

"Angel is a beautiful, unique woman. I assure you I'll treat your daughter with respect."

Nodding, she said, "Yes, Matthew, I can see that. How unfortunate the regular rules of etiquette don't apply to weddings such as these. Otherwise I would welcome you to the family."

Matthew wasn't sure how to respond, so he simply said, "Thank you."

"And is your family here?" Isabella asked.

"No, my mother's health isn't good. She sends her regrets."

Matthew only hoped his mother didn't learn of his sham marriage. She knew he was visiting Zion's Gate at the government's behest but had no idea a bride had been included in the package. Rescuing his sister from the compound would more than make up for his deception.

Isabella patted his arm. "Yes, Angel said something about chemotherapy? I will be sure to light a candle for your mother at Mass."

"Thank you. She'd like that very much."

The chapel doors opened and a young, radiant couple brushed past them.

"It looks like it's our turn," Angel said, her voice low and tense.

CHAPTER TWO

ANGEL GLANCED AT her watch. They'd been standing near the front of the chapel for what seemed like ages but in reality had only been twenty minutes.

Tucking her hand in the crook of Matthew's arm, she gazed up into his face with adoration. Fortunately Pastor Elvis wasn't close enough to hear the content of their conversation. "What's the holdup?" Angel asked through her fixed smile.

"Only a tiny delay. I asked the pastor's mother to retrieve something for me."

"This was supposed to be a quickie wedding," she whispered.

Shrugging, he placed his hand over hers. "I know this is difficult for you. But please humor me."

He was extraordinarily calm for a man who had never been married. Even a fake wedding was enough to make most bachelors a little psychotic. Or maybe she was just remembering another man who'd made the leap from bachelorhood to craziness so quickly.

Angel was spared further wedding-day reminiscences as Elvis's mother bustled in carrying a florist's box as if it were the Holy Grail. She handed it to Matthew, along with a wad of bills. He accepted the box but pressed the bills into the woman's pudgy hand.

"That's too much," she murmured, and appeared humbled. And this was Vegas, a town where large tips were as prevalent as silicone implants.

"No. It's just right." Matthew's smile was warm. "Would you mind presenting it to my bride? I'm a little nervous and clumsy today."

"Certainly, dear." She removed the lid and drew back layers of tissue paper. Sighing, she presented Angel with a single white rose so perfect it brought tears to Angel's eyes.

The pastor's mother nodded and blinked. "He's such a lovely man. You two will be very happy."

Her words made Angel want to sit down on the floor and cry. Because once upon a time she had believed in happily ever after. Before Kent had twisted their love into a living nightmare.

"It's time, sweetheart," Matthew murmured, pressing his lips to her forehead.

"Would you stop being so damn nice."

The pastor's mother clucked in disappointment and Angel's mother stepped closer.

She grasped Angel's chin. "Are you okay with this, *mija?*"

For a split second, Angel was tempted to call it off. But her mother had raised her to have courage. Angel wouldn't turn her back on the women and children at Zion's Gate.

"Yes, Mama. Very sure."

"Remember, if you need us, all you have to do is call."

"Yes, Mama. I will."

She turned to Matthew. "Take good care of her, Matthew."

Matthew's eyes widened a fraction. He had to

realize there was a threat in her words. Whether their marriage was real or not, Isabella expected much from her son-in-law.

"Yes, ma'am."

Her mother patted his cheek as she walked by. "Good. We are of like minds, I think."

"Yes, we are." Matthew nodded to the pastor. "We're ready to begin."

Those had to be the scariest words Angel had ever heard. Because his voice held a timbre of finality that told her she was in way over her head.

Pastor Elvis stepped forward and cleared his throat, which had his mother scurrying to the boom box to start "Love Me Tender."

But there was no need for a bridal march. The bride was already in position. Her father wouldn't walk her down the aisle. He had guilt-ridden memories of giving her away to Kent. Instead Angel's mother took her husband's arm and led him to the first row of chairs.

The awkward three-plus minutes of Elvis's croon gave Angel too much time to think about her assignment. She'd come a long way from her days as a terrified battered wife, but this assignment still made her uneasy. What if she fell into old ways of thinking?

The song ended with a sudden click and Elvis cleared his throat. Matthew looked composed.

But Angel couldn't seem to keep the damn rose still. It trembled in her hands like a terrified kitten. Or maybe it was Angel herself who felt like a terrified kitten.

Squaring her shoulders, she resolved to be strong. She was a professional. And she knew how to kill a man in at least eighteen different ways. Without a weapon.

The absolute absurdity of being married by an Elvis

impersonator should have reassured her. But glancing at Matthew's solemn face, she started to sweat. The men in his family took "till death do us part" seriously. No one seemed to know how Matthew's mother had managed to leave the man and live to tell about it. Angel figured Abigail Stone held some incriminating evidence against good old Jonathon, though she'd never revealed it.

"Do you have your own vows?" Elvis glanced from Matthew to Angel.

Angel opened her mouth to say no but heard *yes* being spoken in a very definitive baritone.

Matthew grasped her hand, turning her to face him. "Angelina, you are beautiful and courageous. I will love you, honor you, cherish you, protect you till death do us part. This is my solemn vow."

Oh, God, he was laying it on too thick.

Mother Elvis sniffed, dabbing her eyes with a tissue.

Angel opened her mouth. This time she was relieved to hear her own alto. "Um, yeah, what he said."

"I now pronounce you husband and wife," Pastor Elvis intoned. "You may kiss the bride."

"Don't even think about it," she muttered under her breath.

But Matthew took her in his arms and kissed her anyway.

After that it was all a blur. The wedding license was signed, her mother and father left and Elvis and his mother hustled them to the door, stammering something about a lovely honeymoon.

ANGEL'S EYES WIDENED as she entered the Venetian with Matthew, barely noticing the cabdriver leave their bags with the bellman.

The lobby was huge, with crystal chandeliers and a high ceiling. While the wedding chapel had been pure camp, this was close enough to the real deal for her to wish her honeymoon were, too. Wishes that should have died the first time Kent had raised his hand to her.

Angel vowed to remain strong and independent in her heart despite the stupid cover that required her to play a woman disillusioned enough with the outside world to embrace Zion's Gate and all it entailed.

Matthew eyed her intently, as if he could read her thoughts. "Ready?"

She raised her chin. "Yes."

As they approached the registration desk, Matthew wrapped his arm around her waist and pulled her tight to his side.

She suppressed the knee-jerk reaction that would have had her delivering a crushing blow to her hubby's groin. Although if she'd started her first marriage that way, things might have turned out very differently.

"Relax," he murmured in her ear. "You're supposed to look like you worship the ground I walk on."

"Yeah, right."

"Remember, my uncle has eyes and ears everywhere."

He wanted an act? He'd sure get one.

Angel threw back her head and laughed. "Oh, Matthew, this is so wonderful." She stopped mid-lobby, wrapped her arms around his neck and pulled him closer to lay a passionate lip-lock on him.

Pleasure shot through her. Not from the kiss but from Matthew's groan of submission.

Then he nipped her lower lip.

Angel drew back, smiling. She was pleased to note several people were staring.

Matthew leaned close and whispered, "You're acting too aggressive for a Zion's Gate bride. Even for a woman unaccustomed to their ways. You leave me no choice."

He stiffened and his face became stern. "Angelina, darling, you will need to learn your place before we arrive at my uncle's house." He grasped her shoulders, rotated her toward the reception desk and swatted her on the rear end.

Angel yelped and turned, ready to do battle.

"Remember, sweetheart, I am the man and you are the woman. My lessons will be gentle as long as you show a willingness to learn."

This was what he'd meant by "no choice." He felt the need to publicly chastise her. Too damn bad.

"Screw you."

Matthew's eyes flashed. He stepped close, grasping her chin. "Oh, I intend to, *darling*. I intend to." Then he leaned down and ground his mouth to hers, possessiveness evident in every aggressive thrust of his tongue.

Angel felt trapped and small. She broke free. Very deliberately she wiped the back of her hand across her mouth. Stopping short, she suppressed a desire to spit at her new husband. "You sicken me."

"I don't think so, Angelina. Just the opposite. But we'll see. Now go tidy yourself in the ladies' room while I get our key. Then you will show me the proper respect a woman shows her husband."

Angel turned and fled, just as Matthew had instructed.

Once inside, she pressed her back to the door. Her hands trembled violently. Her heart raced.

Oh, Lord, what had she gotten herself into?

MEMORY OF ANGEL'S stricken expression haunted Matthew while he registered at the front desk. His peripheral vision was trained on the ladies' room door, and he saw Angel approach a few minutes later, her manner subdued as she took her place next to him.

Glancing at his bride, he was surprised to see a slightly green tinge to her olive complexion. Was her anguish an act, simply part of her cover? He hoped Perez knew what he was doing.

Matthew accepted the key card from the front desk manager. In turn, he pressed several large bills into the man's palm. "My bride and I expect privacy. We might not set foot out of the room for the five days we're here."

The manager nodded and pocketed the money. "Certainly, sir. I'll see that you aren't disturbed. The bellman will show you to your suite."

Angel stiffened when Matthew grasped her hand.

Sighing, he could have kicked himself for letting her aversion bother him. It didn't matter what she thought as long as they could carry off this charade.

"This way, Angelina," he murmured.

"Yes, Matthew." Though her tone was passive, she held her head high.

When they reached their room, he tipped the bellman. "Thank you. I can take it from here."

Nodding, the bellman pulled their bags from the cart and retreated down the hall.

Matthew swallowed hard when they entered their suite. It was every woman's wedding-night fantasy. At least that's what the flash of longing in Angel's eyes told him.

Too bad there would be no wedding-night, can't-get-enough-of-each-other sex. Or slow, sweet sex, for that matter.

Angel took one look at the king-size bed and laughed. "Looks like I'll be very comfortable." She nodded toward the couch. "You, on the other hand, might be a bit cramped."

"I've slept in worse places."

She eyed him up and down. "Why doesn't that surprise me?"

He set down the suitcases. "Look, Angel, get this straight. We're here to make things look a certain way. If we succeed, my uncle will allow us into the compound and may invite us to stay. If we fail, one or both of us could end up dead."

"You already made your point in the lobby. I know I'm supposed to portray some brainless Stepford wife."

He tucked a lock of hair behind her ear. "I understand it'll be hard. You shouldn't have to disguise your wit and strength. But it's necessary."

She cleared her throat and glanced away.

He wondered if he'd revealed too much. He also wondered why compliments bothered her.

Matthew stepped back. "Fortunately my interest in you is something my uncle will understand, as well as the hasty marriage. As long as I appear to be training you in the ways of our people, chances are good he will accept this impulsive wedding."

"I hope that sexist crap in the lobby was an act."

He nodded, uncomfortable with the half-truth. A part of him wanted to make Angel his own. But not by resorting to trickery.

Angel placed her suitcase on the bed and opened it. "What is this?" she demanded.

Glancing over his shoulder, he couldn't help but chuckle at the look of sheer revulsion on her face.

Angel held the pastel long-sleeved cotton nightgown between her fingertips as if it were something poisonous.

"That's your, um, nightwear."

"No way."

"Yes way. Those are the clothes a good Zion's Gate wife wears. Very conservative and demure."

"Demure, my ass."

Matthew laughed. "No, your ass is anything but demure, Angel. The point is, nobody but me is to have a clue about your, um, attributes."

Angel's face grew pink.

He was intrigued. The tough-talking, independent policewoman was embarrassed by a relatively tame flirtation.

"Maybe this monstrosity is a good thing." She glared at the offending garment. "At least *you* won't get any ideas. It'd take a satellite GPS to find me in this sack. Where on earth did they get this horrible stuff?"

Matthew took a deep breath. "It's my mother's."

Angel's eyes widened. "Oh, God, Matt, I'm so sorry. I didn't realize. I mean, I'm kind of nervous here and I get a smart mouth on me when I'm nervous and say stupid things and—"

Matthew's hurt evaporated. He pressed his finger to her lips. "Shh. Apology accepted. You ought to know the rest of the clothes were my mother's when she lived at the Zion's Gate compound in Arizona. That was before Jonathon moved the group here. Besides being practical, one of the profiler types thought my mother's clothes might strike a chord with Uncle Jonathon. My mother was the one who got away. He probably has a hot button or two where she's concerned."

Angel placed the nightgown on the bed, smoothing the fabric with her fingers. Her tenderness was almost his undoing. She might talk and act tough, but there was a sensitive core she couldn't quite disguise.

Removing a dress from the suitcase, she tilted her head. "It, um, looks like it should fit. I assume it's not supposed to be flattering, uh, show off my figure…um, well, you know what I mean?"

A smile tickled his mouth. There was something so charming about her.

"No, the intention is to avoid inciting impure thoughts."

"It should work then."

Matthew laughed, enjoying her immensely.

"Damn. I did it again, didn't I?"

"Did what?"

"Stuck my foot in my mouth. Your mom was probably wearing these same clothes or something similar when your uncle Jonathon had the hots for her."

"It didn't occur to me exactly that way, but yes, you're probably right. But then again, I'm not sure whether he was attracted to my mother because she was beautiful or because my father loved her with his whole heart." Memories of the bond his parents had shared was one of the few things that had kept him sane in an insane time and place.

"As you said, your mother was the one who got away. But your uncle had something like twelve wives. How could he miss one or two?"

If only she knew. But he hoped like crazy Angel never experienced the depths of his uncle's possessiveness.

CHAPTER THREE

FRESH FROM THE shower, Angel tied the belt of her fluffy, white Venetian-issue robe. She combed tangles from her wet hair as she peeked over Matthew's shoulder, watching him remove a flat rectangular box from his suitcase.

"A board game?" she asked.

"Scrabble. I'm tired of card games. Old Maid pretty much did me in." He smiled, tilting his head. "Are you always this curious?"

"After spending two days in a hotel room with me, you need to ask?"

"I haven't even scratched the surface." His gaze roved over her robed figure. "But I guess I'll have to be content with knowing you are *very* curious. And sleep with a gun under your pillow."

Her face flamed. "You're lucky you didn't get shot."

He raised his hands. "Now I know not to detour on my way to the bathroom in the middle of the night."

"You were standing there watching me. It was a little creepy."

"Creepy is a matter of perception. I was just getting my bearings in a strange location."

"Yeah, right."

His lips twitched. "It was worth a try, huh? I assure

you I'm no Peeping Tom. But I couldn't pass up the chance to study you. You put up a lot of barriers."

"And they're there for my protection."

"I'm sure it's necessary in your line of work."

Angel glanced away so he wouldn't see the uncertainty in her eyes. "Yeah, in my work."

"What about when you get to know someone? Do you relax then?"

"It takes a long, long time for me to trust."

"Why's that?" His voice was low.

"It would mean I trusted you if I told you the story. And I definitely don't."

"Fair enough. So what have you learned about *me?*"

"Who says I'm interested in finding out about you?" No way was she going to admit studying him, even if it was true. Over the past two days she'd learned Matthew meant what he said and didn't hedge the truth.

"It would be only prudent for someone in your situation. I think you doth protest too much."

"Now I know you misquoteth Shakespeare. Which should really shock me, except I guess the Book of Mormon and Shakespeare aren't mutually exclusive."

"So you're starting to see me as a person? Good. I like that."

"Don't get any funny ideas."

He raised an eyebrow. "Do I impress you as a laugh-a-minute kind of guy?"

"You're a lot funnier than you give yourself credit for. As a matter of fact, it's one of the things that surprised me."

"Other than my charm and good looks?"

Angel made a noncommittal noise.

"What's so surprising about my having a sense of humor?"

"Well, I've seen photos of the polygamous sects, and life seems pretty serious. You don't often see some-one crack a smile."

Matthew stiffened. "I haven't lived at Zion's Gate since I was fifteen. I've lived most of my life outside."

"Yeah, but it's still a part of you. In the way you carry yourself, your word choices, the way you see the world."

"Maybe. But my father had a wonderful sense of humor. Gentle but observant. He could always make my mother laugh." There was a wistfulness in his voice.

Angel sat on the bed and curled her legs beneath herself, making sure the robe didn't gap anywhere critical or reveal scars. "I guess I assumed all polyga-mous leaders would be about power and dominance."

"My uncle, certainly. He leads by intimidation. My father led by example."

"Your father and mother were a love match?"

He nodded. "Approved by their parents, of course."

"It must've been hard on your mom, then, sharing your dad with other women."

He frowned. "She never complained."

"Would she? Complain about the system in which she'd been raised?" A system in which dissenting opinions were actively discouraged.

"I think she accepted sharing him as best she could. She was his favorite, his legal wife, sealed to him for eternity. Maybe that was enough."

Angel shook her head. "No way. From what little I've read about your mother, she's a courageous woman. I can't see her settling for a small portion of the man she loved."

"She's a strong woman. You remind me of her in some ways. But she did what was best for the brethren. My father was a wonderful man, but he was still the leader, and my mother respected that."

"Or else?"

Matthew set his suitcase on the floor. "Or she would have had to leave and never come back."

"That sounds very final."

"It was. Always."

"Except now your uncle has invited you back for a visit."

"I imagine he has his reasons."

Angel removed the game board from the box, opening it and placing it on the bed. "How's your mom feel about you going?"

"She never would have suggested it. But once the government approached me for my cooperation, the idea took hold. I have—or had—two sisters. One died in childbirth." He hesitated, picking up a tile holder and rotating it in his hands. "My mother's afraid her cancer is terminal, so she wants to make sure her surviving daughter is happy. And, though she doesn't belabor the point, I think she'd like to see Rebecca one more time."

"Of course she wants to see her. Why would that be so hard to admit?"

"Because there's little chance for it to happen. My mother made her choice when she left Zion's Gate. My uncle made it very clear she would be severing all ties to her daughters."

"Why didn't they go with her, like you did?"

"I was…a liability." He set out a holder in front of Angel and kept one for himself. "My sisters, on the other hand, were beautiful, like my mother. They begged my mother to stay. You see, there were several elders vying for consent to marry each of them, and their futures were assured. My uncle told my mother she and I could leave but my sisters had to stay. It ensured my mother's silence about anything the authorities might have found unsavory."

"Such as?"

"Plural marriages are against the law."

Angel mixed the tiles and set them out facedown. "But the authorities have looked the other way for years. Probably still will with the threat of another Waco."

"Since Arizona and Utah have become more aggressive in pursuing lawbreakers among the brethren, I imagine Texas will follow suit. It's not as easy to look the other way these days. I don't like to see people persecuted for their beliefs, but I also don't like people to get away with crimes against children in the name of religion."

Angel refrained from voicing the zillion other questions she burned to ask. She could tell he was shutting down. As it was, he'd opened up to her more than she'd anticipated.

From what she'd read, the children in polygamist sects were taught to distrust outsiders, to deflect any untoward interest, lest their families be torn apart by raids and persecution.

Matthew sat on the bed a few feet away from her. He selected his letter tiles. "You know my story. Now it's your turn."

Angel shrugged. "Not much to tell. I had a great childhood. I went to college and graduated with a degree in criminology. I've been with the Texas Department of Public Safety for five years and I love what I do."

"Why law enforcement?"

Normally Angel would have answered with a well-rehearsed spiel. But she knew it wouldn't fly with Matthew. He was too perceptive. "A cop helped me once when I was in trouble. I guess I admired her and I wanted to help other women like me."

"What kind of women would that be?"

Angel refused to allow anyone but very close friends and her superiors to know she'd ever been that vulnerable. A victim.

"You know all you need to know about me, Matt." She stood and headed for the bathroom. Stopping in the doorway, she glanced over her shoulder. "Except that you really don't want to get in my way. Now I need to dry my hair."

"What about the game?"

Angel wasn't sure if he referred to the Scrabble game she'd abandoned or the dangerous personal game developing between them.

"Later." Her answer was sufficiently vague to cover the subtext.

When she'd finished blow-drying her hair, Matt was packing his suitcase, placing his neatly folded shirts over the boxed Scrabble game.

"What gives?" she asked.

"My uncle called on my cell. He wants us at Zion's Gate tonight."

"Tonight? That's three days early. Did you tell him we're honeymooning?"

"Yes. But he's accustomed to being obeyed and I don't want to antagonize him. We'll need to leave within the hour. The shortest flight I could find is seven hours including the layover in Houston. Then we'll rent a car or take a cab to Zion's Gate."

"I don't like this. Why the sudden rush?"

Matt shrugged. "It's a power play. Get used to it. Besides, my uncle is a very cautious man, and if there's a question of my loyalty, it would only benefit him to throw me off balance. Me and anyone who might be conspiring with me."

Nodding, Angel said, "I see your point. I'd probably do the same thing if I was in his position. I'll have to clear it with Perez first."

He retrieved her cell from the credenza and tossed it to her. "Then do it."

Frowning, she opened her phone and dialed. Perez wasn't happy about the change in plans but didn't seem completely surprised, either. He again warned her not to take a weapon to Zion's Gate and told her not to be surprised if her cell was seized, at least initially. She was to hide a pocket PC in her luggage as backup communication.

Angel shut the phone. "We'll rent a car in Brownsville. I'd rather have transportation available if we need to leave the compound in a hurry. Fortunately for us, I guess uncle dearest isn't going to pick us up at the airport?"

"No, nor will his elders. They'll want the home-court advantage. We can use the travel time to go over our cover again."

"Yeah, our lives might depend on getting it right."

IT WAS NEARLY midnight when they approached the Zion's Gate compound. Although the design was reminiscent of an old hacienda, a closer look revealed a solid fortress.

They drove up to a guard shack and announced themselves on the intercom.

Halogen floodlights nearly blinded Matthew. A male voice instructed him to pull forward and park on the other side of the gate.

As the car inched forward, he turned to Angel. "This isn't exactly what I expected. How am I supposed to drive with those spotlights?"

"Very slowly, which I'm sure is one of the purposes."

"Yeah, the other is to blind me."

"You were right when you said your uncle was a cautious man."

The guard remained in his shack, and a short, stocky Mexican stepped out of the shadows and waved them forward. Once they were in the gate, he gestured for them to stop.

It was then Matthew noticed the assault rifle.

He rolled down his window. "I'm Matthew Stone. My uncle is expecting me."

"I know who you are," the man said. "Get out of the car slowly. Raise your hands above your head. Then clasp them behind your neck and get on the ground."

"Boy, your uncle really knows how to make you feel welcome," Angel muttered under her breath.

"Do what they say."

She glared at him. "Well, duh."

He grasped her forearm. "It's important you remember your place, Angelina. If you don't think you can do that, I need to know now. We might still be able to say our visit was a mistake."

"I'm sorry, Matthew. Of course you're right. You're always right." Her mouth trembled as she slipped into her role. A tear crept out of the corner of her eye.

But Matthew wasn't fooled. He knew Angel a lot

better than she thought. Though her acting was excellent, he knew she wouldn't go down without a fight. Ever. "Very nice. Let's keep it this way. No mistakes."

She lowered her face. "Yes, Matthew." It was little more than a whisper.

"Get out, now!" the guard commanded.

Matthew opened his door slowly. Angel did the same.

He raised his hands above his head and carefully exited the vehicle. He glanced at Angel. She had her hands behind her head, her face lowered demurely.

"Toss the keys at my feet. Then kneel on the ground. There." The guard kept the rifle trained on them while he jerked his head in the direction of the area in front of the car.

Matthew carefully tossed the keys and twined his hands behind his neck. Were they afraid he might be a suicide bomber, for goodness sake? His uncle had apparently gone from caution to outright paranoia. Or was he involved in something more dangerous than leading a polygamous community?

"Down."

Matthew walked slowly forward and sank to his knees, keeping his hands behind his neck.

"Matthew? What's this all about?" Angel's voice quavered convincingly. "Surely your uncle doesn't want us treated like common criminals?"

"I don't know, sweetheart."

"A thorough search of all visitors is required," the man said. "On your knees next to the man."

Angel obeyed.

A third man came forward and patted down Matthew, stopping to empty his pockets.

Enough was enough. "Where's my uncle?" he asked.

"You will see your uncle soon. We take precautions first."

Out of the corner of his eye Matthew saw a man approach with something that looked like an airport security wand.

Sure enough, the thing set off a tone when they reached his waist. Matthew bit back a protest when the man lifted his shirt to reveal his belt buckle.

"You'll get this back later," the man said. "We'll search your luggage, too. Is it in the trunk?"

"Yes." Sweat beaded Matthew's forehead.

"Get up. Bring out your suitcases and open them."

"Is this really necessary?"

"Si."

Matthew clambered to his feet and went to Angel, extending his hand to help her up.

"Senor," the man warned.

"She's my wife. I won't leave her in the dirt."

The man opened the trunk. "Remove the luggage."

Matthew bit back a curse. He set their suitcases on the ground.

"Open them."

Angel stepped forward. "But—"

The guard trained the rifle on her.

"It's okay, Angelina. We've nothing to hide." Matthew placed the cases one by one on their sides. He unzipped the flaps and peeled them back.

The man pawed through Matthew and Angel's belongings.

One of the men handed the laptop case to the guard.

"We'll hold on to this for you. And we'll take your cell phones, too. There are landlines you can use."

"I need my laptop to conduct business and check on my investments."

The man shrugged. "Talk to Jonathon. Now hand over the cell phones."

Matthew reluctantly complied, as did Angel.

Once the electronics were in his possession, the guard seemed to lose interest in searching further. He said something in Spanish to the other man, who closed the suitcases and set them in front of Matthew. His buddy tossed the car keys to him and he got into the rental car.

"Where are you taking our car?"

"To the garage, where we keep most of the vehicles." The voice came from the shadows to Matthew's left.

A tall older man with a commanding presence stepped into the light.

Matthew sucked in a breath. *Dad.*

But he knew it wasn't his father. His father was dead. And more than likely this man had killed him.

"Uncle Jonathon, what a pleasure to see you."

CHAPTER FOUR

ANGEL KEPT HER EYES downcast, but surreptitiously surveyed Jonathon Stone. Though he was believed to be sixty-four, he was powerfully built and moved with athletic grace.

"This must be Angel." He stepped closer, lifting her chin with his finger. There was a hint of steel beneath the softness of his tone. "What a lovely young woman. I can see why you wanted her, Matthew."

Matthew pulled her close to his side. "I thought she was the most beautiful woman I'd ever seen. And when the vision came, I knew she was the one for me."

"Vision?"

"An angel trumpeting the news of our betrothal. It was ordained by god. A match made in heaven."

Angel sucked in a breath. Matthew's piety gave her the creeps. As did his talk of visions.

But apparently it struck the right chord with Uncle Jonathon. He slowly nodded. "It would certainly seem so."

"Angel has much to learn about being a good wife, but I'm confident she will learn quickly with other godly women to teach her."

"Yes, fellowship with the women of our community

will show her how to be a loyal, loving helpmate. If she truly desires to embrace our ways."

Angel nodded stiffly.

He released her chin. "Good. I'll take you to your quarters. Follow me."

He turned, his loose-limbed stride long.

Matthew picked up their suitcases and followed.

She tried to survey her surroundings as she walked behind Matthew but only had time to commit the immediate arrangement to memory. They passed a group of three homes on the right side of the path. Farther on, they came to eight adobe structures surrounding a large courtyard. All had flat roofs and heavy wood doors. The windows were high, narrow rectangles, protected by wrought-iron bars.

There were no trees or shrubs, just hard-packed dirt. Still, dust rose in plumes from their feet. Angel felt coated with the stuff, grimy from the top of her head to the tips of her toes.

Jonathon took them to the largest of the homes, opening the door without knocking.

A tall woman who appeared to be in her late fifties came forward. A teenage girl of about sixteen followed.

"Matthew, I'm sure you remember your aunt Eleanor. You'll be staying here with her. Ruth helps Eleanor with the children's schooling. The children now live in dormitories and are educated in several of the larger homes during the day."

Angel didn't like the idea of dormitories. Why didn't they live with their mothers? And she'd noticed he didn't give the young woman a title. Where did she fit into the family? She had the sick feeling the young girl was another of Jonathon's brides. The girl kept her eyes glued to the ground and didn't utter a word.

Matthew nodded, his face impassive. "Thank you for inviting us to stay in your home, Aunt Eleanor."

The woman's lips thinned. Angel got the distinct impression it hadn't been her idea. "Of course. You're family."

"This is my wife, Angel." Matthew nudged her forward.

Angel was at a loss how to proceed. Should she curtsy? Shaking hands seemed too confident and contemporary. Raising her eyes, she nodded. "Pleased to meet you, ma'am."

The older woman made a noncommittal noise in her throat.

"Eleanor, see that Matthew and his wife are made comfortable." Jonathon turned to Matthew. "I'll meet with you tomorrow, son."

"Yes, sir."

And Jonathon was gone, exiting the front door, humming what sounded like "Onward Christian Soldiers."

Angel repressed a shudder. His cheer seemed ominous.

Ruth raised luminous blue eyes. She looked like a china doll with pale, porcelain skin and wide, round eyes. "This is for you, Brother Matthew." She held out a flat rectangular object to him.

Matthew frowned, accepting the gift. "It's beautiful."

"I made it. A marker for your Bible."

"Yes, lovely stitchery. Thank you."

Triumph flashed in the young woman's eyes and was gone. "I'm glad you like it." Her voice was low and sweet.

Angel felt for all the world as if she'd been one-upped in a competition she didn't understand.

"I'll show you to your room." Eleanor bustled by them.

Matthew took Angel's arm and they followed the woman down a short hallway and up a flight of stairs. There were several doors on either side. Eleanor opened the last door on the right.

"You have a private bathroom. If you need additional towels or blankets, please call me."

Angel sucked in a breath as she entered the small, old-fashioned room. Her gaze was drawn to the double bed. She fingered the exquisite handmade wedding-ring quilt. "It's beautiful."

"Some of the women made it as a wedding gift for you and Matthew. Many of them were friends of Abigail's."

But Eleanor hadn't contributed, that much was clear. There was a bitter edge to her voice when she mentioned Matthew's mother. Angel wondered whether Eleanor had opposed Jonathon's marriage to his brother's wife.

It didn't matter, Angel supposed, because even Jonathon's first wife would have had very little say when he chose another bride. She was expected to suffer in silence.

"I imagine you two are tired from traveling and would like to settle into your room. I will lead the Bible reading tonight in Jonathon's absence. However, it would be understandable if you would like to have your own reading in your room."

Holy cow. How was she supposed to handle Bible readings when her memory of the book was so sketchy? She'd avoided religion of any kind since her marriage to Kent. Because she had a hard time believing in a God who'd left her to fend for herself.

"I'll lead Angel in prayer and our reading tonight, Aunt Eleanor. Thank you."

"Good night."

Ruth stood in the hallway outside their door, her eyes bright with curiosity. Angel got the distinct impression she was gauging the marital temperature.

"Good night, Eleanor, Ruth." Angel tucked her hand in Matt's, smiling up at him. "My husband and I would like to be alone. We're very…tired." There, let the little Stepford wannabe process that.

Ruth let out a small squeak of surprise and fled.

Matthew cupped her chin with his hand, rubbing his thumb along her jaw. "Yes, very tired."

She thought his gesture was for the benefit of their audience, but then she realized the hallway was empty. Eleanor had retreated after Ruth.

He closed the door and hefted their suitcases onto the bed. "Watch yourself around Eleanor," he murmured. "She's Uncle Jonathon's eyes and ears. And sometimes his cojones, though she'd never be foolish enough to let him realize it."

Angel watched Matthew closely, wondering if his swift change in demeanor was intended to throw her off balance. The tenderness of a few moments ago was gone, replaced with determined movement.

"Jonathon didn't seem to need any help in the cojones area. The term *brass* came to mind."

Matthew smirked. "Probably apt. You're smart not to allow the veneer of civility fool you. He's a dangerous man."

"Duly noted. I'd like to unpack and hit the hay early. I want to keep on top of my game. How do you propose we work out sleeping arrangements?" Angel eyed the full-size bed. She was accustomed to having a queen all to herself.

"I'll take the floor, of course."

Playing the part of the subservient wife would be hard enough when people were around. Angel had no intention of being the helpless little woman in private. "We'll alternate. Flip a coin to see who takes the floor tonight?"

Matthew shrugged. "Suit yourself."

"I will." She removed a quarter from her purse. Flicking it with her thumb, she said, "Call it," as the coin spun in the air.

"Heads."

"You win. You get the bed tonight."

"No." His voice was low, firm. "I get to choose. I choose the floor."

"You're a stubborn man."

"Yes, I am. After you unpack, I'll lead us in Bible study and prayer."

She planted her hands on her hips. "You're not serious, are you?"

"Of course. There are some practices I still observe. Not all their precepts are bad."

"Well, where I come from, we believe in separation of church and state. This is a job and I, for one, don't want to be subjected to your beliefs in private."

"Keep your voice down," Matthew warned. "We don't know who's next door. If we're overheard, it's best I'm fulfilling my role as the spiritual leader of our family."

She eyed the adobe, tempted to tap it with her knuckles to check the density of the walls. Until proven otherwise, it was best to assume anything above a whisper could be heard in the next room. "You're right.

I'll be unpacked in a few minutes. Then I guess I can suffer through a few moments of religious instruction."

"I promise to keep it short and sweet."

"Okay." She lowered her voice. "But one hint of fire and brimstone and we're done. *Comprende?*"

Matthew was intrigued by the bits Angel revealed about herself. "No vengeful, merciless God for you?"

"Uh-uh. I've found people can be vengeful and merciless enough. Who needs a deity like that?" Though her tone was teasing, there was an underlying edge.

"Who, indeed. We may be more alike than you realize, Angelina. My God is just and loving."

"If you think you know me, think again. I'm nothing like the women here who meekly follow orders."

"Wifely submission isn't on your list of approved reading topics, I take it?"

"Not if you want to live to see tomorrow."

"Ah, Angelina, when will you learn I won't be swayed by idle threats?"

"Who said it was idle?"

Matthew smothered a chuckle. Why was he so sure she wouldn't hurt him?

He was anything but a trusting man. Yet he found himself trusting a woman he barely knew. A woman trained to kill a man if she had to.

But there was an integrity in Angel that drew him. Along with well-hidden vulnerability. He'd felt an instant connection with her, as one survivor recognizing another. It was the only way he could explain his hunch that Angel had overcome something horrific. Because his background investigation hadn't turned up anything about her life before she'd entered the University of Houston in 1998. It was as if she hadn't existed before that. Her transcripts had shown transferred community-college credits from Fort Worth, but the college there had no record of her attending.

It was a mystery he was determined to unravel at a later date. But he had more pressing challenges to deal with first.

Angel snapped her fingers in front of his face. "Matt, you gonna stare off into space all night?"

"No, I was just thinking of the perfect reading for our first night as husband and wife under my uncle's roof."

He went to his suitcase and unzipped the side compartment. Withdrawing his Bible, he fingered the hand-tooled leather cover. The cowhide had been made supple with the oil from his hands these many years. Made by Matthew's mother, it had been one of his father's most prized possessions. One Uncle Jonathon had tried to appropriate along with his brother's wife. But Abigail had stood firm in her desire that Matthew would inherit his father's personal things. He only wished she'd stood as firm in her refusal to marry Jonathon.

Angel stepped close. "It's still so important to you after all you've been through?"

"What's important?"

She reached out and tentatively touched the intricately rendered scene on the cover. "Religion."

"No. Religion has no place in my life. God, however, is another story."

"That's a fine distinction."

"No, it's a huge distinction. One that helped me hold on to something precious."

Angel opened her mouth, then clamped it shut.

He could tell she was withdrawing. He longed to grasp her shoulders and convince her. But he knew she had to come to him of her own free will. He kept his voice low and nonthreatening, as if discussing a mundane topic like the weather. "What troubles you about my separating God from religion?"

"It's not that."

"Then what is it?"

Shaking her head, she stepped away. "You're entitled to your beliefs, Matt. Just as I'm entitled to mine. Who am I to say you believe in a fairy tale?"

His heart ached for her. How alone she must feel facing the world every day and thinking there was no one to catch her if she fell. He'd been more fortunate. His mother had never allowed him to doubt God's love. Even in those early days when they'd left the brethren and the world had seemed like a scary, confusing place.

And now, being back among the people with whom he'd once shared meals, a home and practically everything else, the thought of the outside world seemed very far away. God was the only constant.

He touched Angel's shoulder. "Someday you may want to know why I believe. When you're ready, we'll discuss it."

"Don't hold your breath." Her tone was bitter. "I quit believing a long time ago."

No, you didn't.

But he knew better than to voice his thoughts. "Like you said to me, you're entitled to your opinion. Now it'll only take a minute to find the passage I'm looking for."

Matthew watched her peripherally while he thumbed through the tissue-thin pages of his Bible. Her movements were jerky as she pulled her things from the suitcase and placed them in the dresser drawer.

"Here it is. First Corinthians, chapter thirteen. 'Love

is patient, love is kind,'" he paused, seeing Angel's shoulders stiffen. He read more quickly, sensing she might rebel at any moment. The last few verses came out in a rush, "'Love does not delight in evil but rejoices with the truth. It always protects, always trusts, always hopes, always perseveres.'"

Angel turned her back to him.

He'd gone too far. Silently he closed the book.

"Angel?"

"That was some fairy tale, Matt." Her voice radiated resentment.

"It's what I believe."

"Then you're a fool."

Suddenly the room seemed too small. Matthew needed time alone to regroup. Because Angel's barbs were starting to get to him. And if he doubted his faith, he had nothing. No defense against the evil his uncle represented. And no hope of overcoming the broken legacy he'd received.

Matthew tucked his Bible in the nightstand drawer. Retrieving his shaving kit from his suitcase, he said, "I think I'll go shower before bed."

"Whatever."

"Yes, whatever," he said.

Angel released her pent-up breath when the bathroom door clicked shut behind Matthew. She glanced at her shaking hands, trying to summon another dose of anger. Anything to distract her from feeling as if she might jump out of her skin.

Why did she let him get to her like that? He wasn't the first person to try to convince her healing could be found in the arms of a loving God. He probably wouldn't be the last. It was the Bible passage he'd chosen, recited in his rich baritone, the conviction in his voice telling her how much he treasured the words.

But all she could think about was how Kent had twisted love. There had been nothing patient or kind about him, at least not after they'd married. He'd isolated her in a matter of months, and then the abuse had started. Toward the end, she'd turned herself inside out to avoid his wrath, to discover what set him off. But there was rarely any rhyme or reason to it. His coiled tension always returned and could only be released through reducing her to a whimpering mess.

Angel shook her head to rid herself of the memories. The past had to stay firmly in the past. She pulled the cotton nightgown from her suitcase. Quickly she changed, folding her clothes and placing them in the dresser.

Her hand hovered over her toiletry bag. She disliked the thought of going to bed without brushing her teeth or washing her face. But she hated the thought of how awkward it would be when Matthew got out of the shower.

After arranging blankets and a pillow on the floor for Matthew, she slid into bed, turning off the bedside lamp. The light from the bathroom would be enough to show him the way to his makeshift bed.

Angel wanted to be sound asleep by the time he finished his shower. Or at the very least *appear* sound asleep. She slid her hand beneath the pillow and frowned. No weapon. She'd forgotten about shipping her nine-millimeter home on the way to the airport.

Closing her hand over the butt of the weapon was the only part of her nighttime ritual that never changed, even when she was undercover. As a supposed member of whatever gang she was infiltrating, sleeping with a gun under her pillow had never been a problem. At Zion's Gate, however, it couldn't be risked.

Damn.

Angel tried counting sheep. She tried the relaxation techniques she'd learned at the hospital. She even tried humming an old Colombian lullaby under her breath. But her eyes refused to close.

The sound of running water ceased. The room was excruciatingly quiet except for the rustle of movement coming through the bathroom door. It wasn't hard to imagine Matthew toweling dry, the soft terry cloth absorbing droplets of moisture from his body....

Uh-uh. Don't go there.

Angel rolled onto her side, facing away from the bathroom door. She squeezed her eyes shut even though they felt spring-loaded. The last thing she wanted was to share intimate conversation in the dark with Matthew. Habit prodded her to once again tuck her hand under the pillow, where she felt only the cool cotton sheet.

Panic made her pulse pound in the darkness. For a split second, she was back in the home she'd shared with her husband, waiting helplessly for him to come to bed, wondering if tonight would be the night he'd kill her.

Angel heard the bathroom doorknob turn. Opening her eyes, she reassured herself she wasn't back in Fort Worth, waiting for Kent. She rolled to the other side.

"Can't sleep?" Matthew's voice was husky. He was silhouetted in the light from the bathroom.

"Keyed up, I guess."

"Yeah, I know what you mean. I'm tired but wired."

"That's it exactly. Would you mind leaving the bathroom light on and cracking the door?"

"Sure." He complied with her request, making his way to his pallet. "Better get some sleep if you can—you'll need it tomorrow. You'll probably meet the rest of Uncle Jonathon's wives and children. I imagine it can be quite overwhelming to someone not raised in a communal atmosphere. I have to admit, even I'm a little uneasy."

Angel propped her arm under her head so she could see Matt's outline on the floor next to the bed. "Is it weird being back with your uncle Jonathon? Or have you had a chance to process it yet?"

"It's…difficult. I have to keep a rein on my emotions. Distance myself from the past."

Angel was surprised by his admission. Not many men would be that aware. Or if they were, they certainly wouldn't admit it.

"What was it like living with the brethren?"

He hesitated for a moment. "I couldn't have asked for a better childhood. It was a wonderful way to grow up. My father loved all of us. We had plenty of room to roam, but plenty of guidance, too. It gave me a sense of belonging, community, shared ideals. Everyone was happy."

Angel thought it sounded a little too good to be true. "And after your father died?"

"It was very different. Now go to sleep."

Angel bristled at his authoritarian tone. "I can't. I'm wide-awake."

"Strange place?"

"Yes," she lied.

"What do you do when you work undercover? Go home every night?"

"When I work undercover, I have my weapon."

"And you don't here."

"No, I don't."

"I think I understand."

"You don't understand squat, Matt."

He chuckled in the dark. "I stand corrected. How about if I told you a few stories of my youth?"

"That'd be enough to send me off to sleep, I'm sure. All that bucolic stuff."

"I'll tell you about the calf I raised one year. He followed me around like a dog. I wasn't supposed to name him because I'd get attached and he was raised for food."

"But you named him anyway." Angel could almost imagine him as a tow-headed boy leading around a calf. And maybe getting into mischief once in a while.

"His name was Spot. Very original."

"Probably better than Cheeseburger," she murmured, her eyelids fluttering.

Matthew chuckled. He told her stories of Spot and the numerous barnyard cats. Of catching frogs and fire-flies. And of making apple cider.

Contentment stole through Angel. It was surprisingly nice, here in the dark, talking to Matt. She snuggled deeper under the covers. Her eyes closed, her breathing deepened....

CHAPTER FIVE

ELEANOR GESTURED toward an empty space at the oblong dining room table. "You may sit there."

"Thank you," Angel murmured. The wooden chair was hard and unyielding against her rear.

Angel glanced at the two empty picnic-style tables. "When do the children eat?"

"My children are grown. Their bedrooms upstairs were converted to classrooms. The younger children come here every morning for classes. I used to do all the teaching, but Ruth is fulfilling many of the duties."

"I see."

Eleanor pursed her lips. "I hope you slept well."

Angel got the impression she hoped the opposite was true. Sarcasm didn't suit the older woman.

"Yes, we did. Is there anything I can do to help with breakfast?"

"Not now. An extra pair of hands would have been welcome an hour ago, though. Perhaps tomorrow you can get up earlier and help prepare."

Angel bit back a retort at the implied criticism. Calling Eleanor a sanctimonious bitch wouldn't help matters. It would make Angel feel much better, though. Sighing, she exercised self-control and let her annoyance go. "Perhaps. If my husband doesn't have other plans for me."

"I'm sure he could spare you for an hour."

"I'll talk to Matthew. He should be here in just a minute." Angel had fled the bedroom, flustered by the intimacy of sharing the small space with him. Or maybe it had been the intimacy of his stories the night before and how easily she'd fallen asleep. She felt safe with Matt, and that fact in itself terrified her.

Afraid to feel safe. How messed up was that?

"Ruth, help me with the food," Eleanor said, nodding toward the young girl, who had slipped into the room.

"Yes, Sister." Ruth scurried to help, her voice breathy when she asked, "Where is Brother Matthew?"

Angel ignored the quick stab of possessiveness. She was merely feeling territorial because of her tenuous position here at the ranch. She was an outsider and she doubted Eleanor would let her forget it.

"He, um, wanted to have time alone for Bible study."

Eleanor nodded. "We'll wait breakfast for him."

"Thank you."

"What lovely lace." Angel fingered the crocheted runner gracing the center of the table.

"I made it myself."

"Wow. This is really fine work."

"It'll do." Eleanor's words were spare, but her cheeks were pink. Angel wondered if she'd received much praise in her life.

"Aunt Eleanor is a whiz with any kind of needlework." Matthew entered the room.

"Thank you." The older woman pulled out a chair at the foot of the table. "You may sit here, Matthew."

Angel assumed the seat at the head of the table was reserved for Jonathon.

As if reading her mind, Eleanor said, "Jonathon

won't be joining us for breakfast. He called to say he'd like to see you in his study at eight-thirty."

Angel's pulse quickened. Jonathon's study. Probably where he kept important documents. Maybe even something to implicate him in his landlord's drug and weapons running? Or possibly records confirming young girls were being married off to old goats?

"His study's here at the house?" she asked.

"Yes. And he has an office in the main administration building."

Angel filed away that tidbit of knowledge.

Matthew leaned forward. "I'm looking forward to getting reacquainted with my brothers and sisters."

His statement confused Angel for a moment. Hadn't he said he only had one sister left? But then she realized he probably had dozens of half sisters and brothers.

Eleanor passed a basket of biscuits. "I'm sure they're eager to see you, too."

"Will Uncle Jonathon arrange some kind of get-together?"

"You will have to ask him."

Angel noted the older women didn't deny or confirm knowledge of Jonathon's plans. Interesting.

"If you'd like to take a walk later, I could show you around the settlement." Ruth's voice was sweet and shy, but there was a predatory gleam in her eyes. Or was Angel merely jumping to conclusions? She didn't like the girl. Didn't trust her. And she'd learned a long time ago to listen to her gut instinct.

"What a lovely offer, Ruth." Angel forced a smile. "Matthew and I would enjoy having you show us around."

Angel thought she saw an amused smile twitch at

Matthew's lips, but it was gone so quickly she couldn't be sure.

"Yes, Angel and I would appreciate that, Ruth. I'll have to see what my uncle has planned first, though."

"Of course."

Matthew commented, "Our accommodation's quite comfortable. Thank you for giving us a corner room—as newlyweds, we appreciate the privacy. Is anyone in the room next to us?"

"No. It's used for storage right now."

Good. That meant they could talk in low voices in their bedroom and not worry about being overheard.

Matthew ate heartily, Angel noted. Eggs, sausage, hash browns, pancakes. Apparently Eleanor had never heard of a Pop-Tart.

"The meal was delicious, Aunt Eleanor." Matthew wiped his mouth with his napkin.

"Thank you. I always make a hearty breakfast. A man can't work on an empty stomach."

Ruth nodded in agreement. Though the girl kept her eyes mostly downcast, Angel still intercepted a few adoring glances sent in Matthew's direction. She got the distinct impression Ruth would love to cook for Matthew. And attend to a few other wifely duties, too.

Matthew, for his part, seemed oblivious. Glancing at his watch, he said, "Looks like I've got a few minutes till the meeting." He rose, picking up his plate and utensils.

"Ruth will clear," Aunt Eleanor informed him.

"I can take these to the sink. It's no trouble."

"Nonsense. Ruth, take his plate, please."

The girl complied.

Matthew gave a slight shrug, his expression bland.

Apparently, he'd forgotten men in the group were treated like royalty.

He said, "If you'll excuse me, I'll go get a little fresh air before our meeting with Uncle Jonathon."

"I'll come with you." Angel picked up her plate, figuring nobody would rush to take it from her. She was right.

"Angel, dear, you can stay here and help clean up. You ought to be nice and rested since you slept so late."

Angel winced inwardly. The woman had essentially called her lazy and done it in such a way that Angel would seem like a paranoid bitch if she called her on it.

"Of course, Aunt Eleanor." Although she'd meant to sound conciliatory, Angel feared a touch of insincerity had reached her voice.

Eleanor's mouth thinned. Yes, she'd heard the false note, too. Well, good. Put the old battle-ax on notice that Angel wasn't a mindless twit to be ordered about.

Matthew grasped her chin with his hand, kissing her tenderly on the lips. At least it probably looked tender. The firmness of his grasp telegraphed a warning: *Be good. Don't cause any trouble.*

Funny, she'd received the same warning as a child. Until her parents had realized admonishing her did no good. Angel did what she thought best, and to heck with the consequences.

That was one of the reasons her parents hadn't investigated when she'd essentially dropped out of their lives. They'd accepted Kent's excuses when they'd called. And on the few occasions she'd been in the room when Kent told his lies, she'd been too afraid to protest. Too afraid to demand contact with her parents. Because she'd known it would all become twisted into a huge act of disloyalty sure to send Kent into a rage.

"Be good," Kent murmured. Only it wasn't Kent. It was Matthew.

Habit and residual survival instinct prodded Angel to nod, her motion jerky. And then she hated herself for reverting to the easily manipulated girl she'd once been.

The urge to tell Matthew off was almost overwhelming. He'd put her in a position of subservience she'd sworn never to allow again. Anything less than being a full partner was dangerous.

She clenched her fists, her fingernails biting into her palm. This was a job, an assignment. It was merely playacting and had nothing to do with her past.

"Yes, Matthew." She'd tried to achieve an adoring coo but fell short. Grudging acquiescence seemed to be the best she could do.

It seemed to be enough, because Matthew nodded. He grabbed his Windbreaker and went out the front door.

Angel released her breath. Some of the tenseness eased from her shoulders. Funny, Matthew was on her side but seemed like the enemy. She felt much more comfortable with Eleanor and Ruth, who she suspected would like nothing better than to get rid of her.

Angel separated utensils and stacked the plates, her motions automatic.

"At least you're not afraid of a dirty dish," Eleanor commented.

"I bussed tables at a Mexican restaurant in high school. Then waitressed my way through college." She lifted the heavy stack of plates and carried them to the kitchen.

"Ruth, you can go get the children's lessons ready while Angel and I do the dishes."

"Yes, ma'am."

The older woman bustled past Angel, taking the stack of plates from her and placing them in the sink. She ran water, added dish soap and retrieved clean, dry towels from the kitchen drawer. She handed a towel to Angel. "Here, you dry."

Angel resisted the urge to salute. She was beginning to understand why Matthew insisted Eleanor might have nearly as much power as his uncle.

They worked in silence for several minutes.

"Jonathon indicates your marriage to Matthew is a love match. Your parents didn't arrange the marriage? Or church elders?"

"No. We met in Phoenix. My family lives in Houston. I'm not Mormon, but I've promised Matthew I will abide by the teachings of the brethren."

"Many young women find our ways too…strict."

Angel met Eleanor's gaze. "I was looking for a change."

"Hmm. How did you know Matthew was suitable if you didn't know his family?"

"I just looked at Matthew and knew. His eyes were so deep and kind. They never lie." Angel was shocked to realize she believed the hogwash about Matthew's character. At least she hoped it was hogwash. Because if Matthew really was one of the good guys, she was in deep, deep trouble. Being thrown together in close quarters on an assignment was *not* the time to let her guard down with a man.

"He always was a kind boy. Patient with the younger children. Bringing home hurt birds. Caring for the barn cats."

Angel tried to regain her equilibrium, steeling herself against the hint of affection in the older woman's voice. She didn't want to see Eleanor as a person. She didn't want to like Matthew. Yet she had to show wifely interest in her husband's history. "Matthew mentioned he had a pet calf named Spot."

A smile touched briefly at Eleanor's lips, then was gone. "Yes. He was heartbroken after Spot was slaughtered."

"I bet."

"It was a necessary learning experience. We needed the animal for food and Matthew was aware of that. He chose to get attached."

"He was a little boy, for goodness sake. Of course he got attached."

"You're from the city. You wouldn't understand."

Angel bit back a retort. She dried silently until she could get her temper under control. "What was Matthew's mother like then?"

"Abigail was a righteous woman. But she lost sight of our way of life."

"Did you know her when she was younger?"

Eleanor glanced at her sideways. "Of course I knew Abigail. She was my older sister."

Sister?

"Matthew didn't mention you were sisters. You must have missed her when she left."

Eleanor hesitated, her expression softening. "There are days when I still miss her," she murmured. "She was my closest friend growing up."

Angel was surprised at the admission. "I, um, got the impression there was no love lost between you two."

"There is much you don't understand. Things changed after Matthew's father died."

"Because she married Jonathon."

"It's not unusual for a man in our community to marry his brother's widow. It's a way of caring for widows that dates before Joseph Smith, back to biblical times."

"I, um, guess that's one way to take care of it." Angel preferred the idea of a nice fat whole-life insurance policy.

She shuddered to think of marrying into Kent's family if he'd had a brother. It would have been like going from the frying pan into the fire. As it was, she hadn't seen her in-laws since before Kent's death. They'd held the funeral for their only son while she was in the hospital, never contacting her. No get-well card, no flowers, no I'm-sorry-our-son-was-a-monster-and-almost-killed-you phone calls.

"Are you prepared to welcome a sister wife into your home when Matthew thinks it's time?"

The soapy plate slipped from Angel's hand. Years of experience handling dishes came to her rescue and she managed to catch it before it hit the floor.

It was a good diversionary tactic, unintentional though it was. "Whew. Glad I caught that. I'd hate to break one of your dishes my first day here."

Eleanor made an assenting noise low in her throat.

Matthew entered the kitchen and came up behind Angel. He wrapped his arms around her waist and kissed the back of her neck.

For some silly reason, the gesture made her blush.

Maybe it was the wistfulness in Eleanor's eyes.

Or maybe it was because the gesture of affection seemed so natural and reassuring.

"Matthew, don't." She made a token protest.

"Mmm. You smell good." His breath tickled as he kissed the hollow behind her ear.

He was taking the loving-husband bit too far. She elbowed him in the gut. Not hard enough to knock the air out of him but enough to let him know to back off.

"Ow." He rubbed his side. "Someone certainly is grumpy this morning."

"Not grumpy. We don't want to embarrass Aunt Eleanor."

"I imagine she and Uncle Jonathon kissed every once in a while. Didn't you, Aunt Eleanor?"

"It's not seemly to discuss intimate subjects. Some things are best left in privacy. You have forgotten our ways, Matthew."

"No, I've just remembered what I want to remember." His tone was light, but Angel sensed an undercurrent.

"Jonathon will expect more than that. Complete obedience is necessary in our life. There is no place for self-centered desires."

Angel wondered how much self-centered desires figured in with the elders taking multiple young wives.

"I apologize. I didn't mean to make you uncomfortable, Aunt Eleanor," Matthew said. He released Angel and stepped back a pace. Angel was almost sorry to be deprived of his reassuring warmth.

Eleanor nodded, accepting his apology. "Go on ahead for your meeting with Jonathon. You know how he admires punctuality."

"Yes, I remember. Are you ready, Angel?"

Angel nodded, drying her hands on the dish towel.

"Jonathon wanted to see you alone, Matthew." Eleanor's tone was stern.

"Anything he can say to me, he can say in front of Angel."

"He will be displeased. He intends to take you to the

elders' meeting this morning. It is not right for a woman to be involved in men's business."

"Then the elders better save their business for another day. I want Angel to meet them and have a chance to talk to Uncle Jonathon. I want my wife to know my family."

Eleanor sighed. "You always were a headstrong boy. Sweet but headstrong."

"What do you think, Angel, dear? Does that pretty well describe me?"

Angel tilted her head, smiling in spite of herself. She couldn't resist the opportunity to tease him. "Definitely headstrong. I'm not sure I agree with the sweet part."

He stepped closer. "Then I guess I'll have to show you later how sweet I can be." The heat of his gaze left no room for misunderstanding. Either he was a very good actor or he was mentally making love to her.

The thought sent a shock through her. "Um, well, we should probably meet Uncle Jonathon."

"Yes, I believe I saw him arrive a few moments ago." Eleanor gazed out the kitchen window.

Angel hadn't noticed his arrival and she'd been right by the window, too. But then again, she was beginning to believe Eleanor had almost otherworldly powers of observation. The woman didn't seem to miss a thing.

"I'll show you to his study." Eleanor dried her hands on a towel, then patted her hair into place.

Angel thought it was kind of cute that the woman still cared what she looked like when her husband saw her. She also thought it was kind of sad, because Eleanor could never have the security of being Jonathon's one and only love.

They followed her down a hallway. She stopped at a closed door and tapped. "Jonathon, Matthew's here to see you."

She didn't include Angel in her announcement. Smart woman. She was going to let Matthew explain why he'd brought the little woman to a guys-only meeting.

CHAPTER SIX

MATTHEW TOOK A DEEP breath, steeling himself to see his uncle in the light of day. His hand at Angel's elbow, he urged her forward.

Jonathon sat behind a large mahogany desk, a desk Matthew remembered from his childhood. It had been his father's.

He suppressed a flash of anger as he followed Angel to the lone chair opposite the desk. When she glanced inquiringly at him, he nodded toward the chair. He stood behind her, resting a hand on her shoulder.

Forcing a smile, he said, "Good morning, Uncle."

"Matthew." His uncle inclined his head, appearing every inch the regal leader. "I didn't anticipate you would bring your wife. I imagine Angel would be more comfortable chatting with Eleanor and Ruth this morning. You and I will be meeting with the elders later."

Matthew chose to ignore the underlying command in Jonathon's observation. He intended to keep Angel as close as possible until he was sure she was safe. "Angel will stay with me this morning."

"Do you really think that wise?"

"I don't see a problem."

"You've indicated you wanted your wife to be tutored in the ways of our life. God made men and women with different strengths and weaknesses. Women are better suited to tending the home, not interfering in men's business."

Angel's shoulders tensed beneath Matthew's palm. He didn't blame her for being angry. Unfortunately Jonathon's thinly veiled condescension was the least of his crimes. And Matthew intended to prove it.

"Of course I want Angel to learn the proper ways. But we are newlyweds, Uncle, and I want her at my side today."

"I was a young man once myself and remember the passion of youth. However, I've found self-control to be a valuable trait. You will be all the more glad to see your bride this evening. As the old saying goes, 'Absence makes the heart grow fonder.'" Jonathon smiled, but there was a dangerous glint in his eye.

Angel shifted. Matthew knew she had to resent being discussed as if she weren't in the room. He squeezed her shoulder. However appalling he might find his uncle's values—or lack of them—he had a job to do. And to be effective, he had to appear to agree.

"I understand, Uncle." He stepped forward, catching Angel's eye. "It is my heart's desire to spend every waking moment with you. But my uncle is right. You should join the women while the elders meet."

Her eyes flashed a warning. Then she lowered her gaze, her voice barely audible when she said, "Yes, Matthew."

He exhaled in relief. He'd worried she might tell him what he could do with all this crap. He reminded himself she was a professional and very good at her work.

Undercover *gang* assignments. A far cry from posing as a pliable Zion's Gate wife.

He turned toward Jonathon. "It's my fondest desire for Angel to meet my whole family. That is not possible if she secludes herself at Aunt Eleanor's house."

"We will hold a celebration of your homecoming after services on Sunday. There will be ample opportunity for Angel to meet everyone."

"Good. I look forward to introducing her to my sister Rebecca. She will also be there Sunday, will she not? Or could we perhaps visit with her this evening?"

Jonathon frowned, leaning back in his chair and gazing out the small window set high in the wall.

Matthew's heart pounded. He'd pushed too hard, too soon, possibly tipping his hand. *Please, God, please let her still be alive.*

"Rebecca hasn't been feeling well, but possibly she can be persuaded to attend on Sunday."

Matthew released a breath. She was alive and he would see her Sunday. That was all that mattered.

"AMEN," JONATHON intoned. The closing prayer officially completed the meeting of the elders nearly four hours later. Their only break had been for lunch, cold chicken served by two of Jonathon's wives. Matthew didn't know the women, who appeared to be in their early twenties.

Matthew fought the urge to make a run for the door and the fresh, cool air outside. He'd almost forgotten the claustrophobic feeling of never, *ever* being alone.

He managed a leisurely pace as he headed for the door.

Raphael fell in beside him, clapping him on the shoulder. "Good to have you back, Matthew."

"It's good to see you, too, Brother." Half brother, to be precise. Raphael's mother had been Matthew's father's third wife.

"I'll walk you back to Eleanor's house."

"Not necessary. I can find my way."

"I'm sure you can. But Uncle Jonathon has indicated you are not to be wandering around unescorted."

"He doesn't trust me?"

"He doesn't trust anyone. Except maybe Eleanor."

Matthew sighed, longing for his Phoenix condo. Solitude was a luxury with the brethren, a luxury he'd grown to appreciate in his time away.

"Did you marry Theresa? You two were sweethearts as long as I can remember."

Raphael glanced away. "No. Uncle Jonathon received a vision. Theresa is Brother Benjamin's eighth wife."

"Benjamin must be nearly seventy." He couldn't quite keep the outrage from his voice.

"Yes. But it was ordained."

Matthew wanted to grab his brother by the shirt and shake him. God didn't ordain that kind of marriage, man did. One very selfish, evil man.

"It's been over twenty years since Theresa became Benjamin's bride. I have three faithful wives of my own. It was for the best." Raphael's voice held a note of resignation.

"Yes, I suppose so," Matthew muttered, the lie sticking in his throat. He didn't suppose anything of the sort. Truth be told, he ached for his brother's loss.

And wondered, not for the first time, if he himself was any better off for having left the brethren. Yes, he had freedom, wealth and the ability to execute decisions based on what he valued and held true, not simply what Jonathon decreed as truth. But he didn't have a wife or family to show for it. At least not a real wife, he reflected wryly.

Maybe there was a trade-off involved. He'd won his freedom but paid a price.

The thought saddened him. Sure, he'd had relationships, but he seemed to seek out women who weren't interested in the long term. It worked well on many levels. At least most of the time.

"Your wife is beautiful, according to Uncle Jonathon," Raphael commented.

Matthew was disoriented for a second. "Angel. Yes, she's very beautiful. She has a fine spirit, too."

"I look forward to meeting her Sunday."

"She's at Eleanor's. Why don't you come in for a few minutes. We're almost there."

"I'll meet her Sunday. It's what Uncle Jonathon wants."

Matthew shrugged. "Suit yourself. See you later."

"Yes."

Matthew watched Raphael walk quickly to one of the smaller houses and let himself in. He caught a glimpse of a sallow, plain woman before the door closed.

Suddenly he was very eager to see Angel. To revel in the way her dark eyes sparkled at their verbal sparring.

But the Angel who greeted him as he walked through the door bore no resemblance to the Angel he'd left that morning. Her hair was braided tightly and wound around her head. Her expression was pinched.

"Ah, Angelina, you're a sight for sore eyes."

"Welcome home, husband." She clasped her hands together and stared at her feet. "May I get you a cold drink before supper?"

He almost told her he'd love a beer but remembered alcohol was strictly forbidden. Anything with caffeine was out of the question, too. "Uh, ginger ale would be good. Or a lemon-lime soda?"

She nodded and headed for the kitchen. She returned quickly and handed him a glass of ginger ale.

He sipped the drink, the sickly sweet flavor taking him back to his boyhood when he'd loved the stuff. Now it only reminded him of restricted choices and arbitrary rules.

"How was your day with the women?"

"Fine. Please, sit down and make yourself comfortable until supper. I'll bring your Bible if you'd like to spend some time reading."

Matthew shook his head. Her subservience gave him goose bumps. It was as if someone had given her a lobotomy while he'd been gone. "Angel?"

"Yes?"

"Are you okay?"

She glanced over her shoulder to where Ruth stood in the doorway to the kitchen, her eyes bright with interest.

"Yes, Matthew, I'm fine. Eleanor has been instructing me what is expected of a wife at Zion's Gate."

"I can see that."

She raised her face for the first time, her expression bland. "Do my lessons please you? Eleanor said it was important for me to please you in other ways besides the bedroom."

Matthew swallowed hard. "She what?"

Angel nodded. "She said I must show more modesty or I would bring disgrace to your name. That a man values a wife of virtue. One who had many talents like cooking, sewing, keeping a spotless house. Teaching the children the proper ways. Accommodating her husbands procreational activities but not expecting to find fulfillment in them."

Matthew was speechless. He knew he should be

relieved Angel seemed to be assimilating so well into the brethren's way of life. She would be safe if everyone truly believed her to be meek and subservient. But the hair on the back of his neck prickled at the change in her.

"Angelina, I was pleased with the woman I married. I hope your instruction here will merely bring us to a higher level."

"That is my wish, too." She lowered her eyes, once again focusing on the floor.

Damn.

Matthew suspected he would get exceedingly tired of staring at the top of her head where the braids wound like tortuous snakes. He wanted to see her eyes sparkle in challenge. He wanted to hear her put him in his place.

Sighing, he said, "I'm very tired. I would like to retire shortly after dinner." And get her the hell away from Eleanor and Ruth before they did any more damage.

"If that is what you wish."

"Yes. It *is* what I wish."

Eleanor bustled into the room. "Was the meeting of the elders instructional, Matthew?"

"Yes, very." And a reminder of the myriad reasons he wasn't cut out for this life. His uncle's egomania being first and foremost.

"Good. Angel, we still have several chores to complete before we start cooking supper."

"Yes, of course. If you will show me what is necessary."

"Certainly."

He didn't want Angel whisked away again so soon. She was his touchstone with the outside world, a world where sanity prevailed. "I was looking forward to Ruth giving us the tour of the compound. I'm sure Angel would like that, too."

Ruth stepped into the room, her eyes downcast. "I'm sorry, Brother Matthew. I was being forward. It is not my place. Jonathon will show you the grounds when he feels it's necessary."

He tried not to show his surprise. Jonathon had been conducting the meeting all morning. When had he had the opportunity to put the kibosh on the impromptu tour?

Eleanor nodded approvingly. "Jonathon will show you around later."

She'd obviously spoken on her husband's behalf. Matthew had forgotten how in tune she was to Jonathon, seemingly anticipating his every need.

"Will Uncle Jonathon be having supper with us this evening?"

"No. He will be elsewhere."

"At Aunt Belinda's? Aunt Emma's?"

Eleanor's mouth tightened. "It is not for us to ask."

Things had changed then. In the past, Jonathon had kept a day calendar noting where he would spend the night. That way special events like birthdays or anniversaries could be accommodated. It was the only way a man with many wives could keep track of where he should be at the end of the day. And woe be to the man who got his days mixed-up. It was an event sure to cause an undercurrent of hurt feelings and animosity between the sister wives.

"Two of your sister wives served lunch. I didn't know them."

"Yes, God has continued to bless our family with additional wives." Eleanor's tone was bland, as if she were repeating something she'd heard many times. "I don't see them much these days. They are busy with their lives."

"Is Ruth one of Jonathon's wives?"

"No. Ruth is merely staying for a while to help me with the children's schooling."

Matthew frowned. That wasn't the usual chain of events as he remembered them. A girl stayed in the family home until the elders decided she would wed.

"But—"

"Ruth, Angel, come with me. We'll finish chores and allow Matthew time to reflect on the elders' meeting and perhaps seek illumination through reading his Bible." She bustled out of the room. Angel and Ruth followed like two baby ducks.

He rebelled against meditating on Eleanor's schedule. But what else did he have to do? It was pretty clear he wasn't supposed to be exploring the grounds. He was bored, something unheard of in his father's day. The only veterinarian in a rural area, Joshua Stone had always seemed busy, being called out at all hours for emergencies.

Matthew longed for his laptop with an intensity that surprised him. Not only was it a link to the outside world, but it also symbolized his success in business and as a man. Fortunately he had a capable assistant able to handle the lion's share of his investing online while he was gone.

Glancing around, he decided seeking illumination in the solitude of his room might not be such a bad idea. He headed upstairs, suddenly grateful for Eleanor's suggestion.

Matthew breathed a sigh of relief when he closed the bedroom door behind him. Alone at last. No Angel. No houseful of women. No disapproving elders. Just him.

His gaze fell on Angel's suitcase, the corner peeking

out from beneath the bed. He'd bet his bottom dollar Uncle Jonathon's henchman hadn't divested her of all means to contact the outside world. Maybe she had a gadget with remote Internet access?

He was sorely tempted to check her luggage.

Shaking his head, he refused to stoop to a new personal low. Just being in the same vicinity as Uncle Jonathon seemed to bring out the worst in him. Besides, he could always be direct and ask Angel.

Retrieving his Bible from the nightstand, he kicked off his shoes and sat on the bed, leaning back against the headboard. He flipped through the pages, taking comfort in the familiarity of the ritual. Uncle Jonathon and this place couldn't take that away from him. He had a connection with God that had nothing to do with an intermediary.

As he read, his eyelids grew heavy. He had slept very little the night before, knowing he was once again under his uncle's control.

ANGEL TAPPED ON THE bedroom door. When there was no answer, she let herself in.

She saw Matthew prone on the bed, his Bible slipping from his fingers. He had to be as bone-weary as she felt—maintaining the constant facade was exhausting. Feeling her way through a morass of sometimes contradictory rules and traditions even more so.

"Matthew." She touched his shoulder.

His eyes opened. He smiled sweetly, totally unguarded. The smile faded as awareness crept into his expression. "I, um, must've fallen asleep."

"I figured as much. Supper's ready, and Eleanor wants you to stand in as lord and master to say the blessing. I was all for letting you sleep, but she thought it was important."

"Whew. For a while this afternoon I thought she'd managed to totally brainwash you."

"Hardly." She rotated her shoulders, willing away the knots of tension. "You have no idea how difficult it is to constantly bite my tongue. Worse yet, I have to make sure none of it shows in my expression."

"Oh, I think I have some idea."

"I figure that's why the women look at the ground so much and don't make eye contact. They're afraid somebody will see a huge 'screw you' in their expression."

He chuckled. "You could be right. As a teen, I had to constantly censor my thoughts. Once I reached an age where I might attract female attention, I knew I had to keep a low profile. I'd seen too many boys compete with the elders for girls and end up out on their rears."

"Yet you eventually did leave."

"Let's just say I finally couldn't control that 'screw you' expression anymore. Someday maybe I'll tell you the whole story."

Angel was intrigued. None of this had appeared in Matthew's dossier. Maybe it would help her understand the contradictions in the man. "Tell me tonight, after supper? I imagine Eleanor's about ready to send out a search party. She likes to keep everything regimented."

"Yeah, you're right. Probably because she has so little control over the other things in her life."

"Like who she has to share her husband with?"

"No, as his first wife, she has veto power over the new wives. But I have yet to see her stand up to Uncle Jonathon and win. Otherwise my mother never would have married him."

"I'm sorry, Matt. Even as a guy, it sounds like you had it rough growing up in this group."

Matthew rose from the bed and shrugged. "It wasn't what I would have chosen." Then he offered her his arm in a courtly gesture. "Mrs. Stone."

Angel laughed. "Around here, you could be addressing the majority of the female population." She didn't call him on redirecting the conversation.

"True. But you're the one and only Mrs. Matthew Stone."

"Be sure you keep it that way, Matt." She grinned. "I don't like to share."

"Duly noted." He kissed her on the nose and led her out the door.

CHAPTER SEVEN

ANGEL BOWED HER head while Matthew said grace, a long, complicated giving of thanks. Her stomach growled loudly in protest.

Finally Matthew intoned, "Amen."

Eleanor stood, retrieved Matthew's plate and started filling it from the steaming dishes in the center of the table. No one else moved a muscle.

Eleanor took great care in selecting only the plumpest pieces of fried chicken and the fluffiest biscuits. Then came heaping servings of green beans, mashed potatoes with gravy and corn on the cob.

Angel met Matthew's gaze as Eleanor set the heaping plate in front of him. She raised an eyebrow. He remained expressionless.

Eleanor retrieved her own plate and made a similar though slightly smaller selection for herself. Then she sat down and inclined her head. "Angel, Ruth, go ahead."

Angel's mouth watered as she selected two golden pieces of chicken. "Frying chicken was a lot harder than I expected," she commented as she passed the platter to Ruth. "And I have the burns to prove it."

"Burns?" Matthew frowned. "Are you okay?"

"Yes. Badges of honor, I suppose. Eleanor doctored them with aloe and they feel much better."

"The chicken is excellent, ladies." Matthew wiped his mouth with his napkin. "I'm just sorry injuries were incurred."

"And I snapped green beans." Angel warmed to her subject, amazed that simple chores could be so rewarding. "I've never done that before."

"Angel," Eleanor warned. "A quiet wife is a gentle wife."

Angel managed to refrain from rolling her eyes. She'd forgotten enthusiasm was considered sinful. She lowered her gaze and brought her voice down a couple of notches. "Yes, Eleanor."

After that, she concentrated on eating while listening to Eleanor grill Matthew about the meeting. Eleanor had an indirect interrogation method that would have made a hostage negotiator bow at her feet.

"Was the meeting of the elders much as you remembered?"

"There are fewer elders now. All of them are close friends of Uncle Jonathon's."

"Yes, Jonathon values loyalty." Eleanor waited expectantly, one eyebrow raised a millimeter.

"They did what they could to explain the sect's goals to me. And, of course, Uncle Jonathon led us in study."

"Goals?"

"Increasing self-sufficiency in all areas. Proper reserves of food, water and financial resources."

"Tithing has fallen short of his expectations." Eleanor sipped her water. "It disturbs him."

"Yes, apparently he has received prophecies of increased hardship in the land."

"Are the elders still resistant to increasing tithes?"

Matthew hesitated. "A few. Now I've told you about

my day, I want to hear what my beautiful bride learned today."

Angel opened her mouth, but Eleanor took the lead. "We started with needlecraft, but it will take time to develop her skills. I gave Angel practice swatches for this evening."

"I've never sewn before, either. I'll get it tonight, though." *If it kills me.* She would tackle it like any other new challenge, subduing the darn needle, thread and fabric into submission.

She glanced up to see Matthew smile. "I'm sure you will. You do anything you set your mind to."

"Her education has been lacking." Eleanor's voice held a note of censure. "What are these young women taught in the world today?"

Angel wondered what Eleanor's reaction would be if she knew the truth about Angel's studies. Strength training and martial arts. Investigative skills. How to subdue a suspect.

Eleanor would probably be horrified.

Angel smothered a smile. Maybe she couldn't thread a needle, but she could incapacitate a man twice her size.

The meal continued and Angel was lulled by the quiet conversation.

"I tried to teach Angel how to make biscuits," Ruth said, shaking her head sadly. "They were hard as rocks."

Angel's face grew warm. She wanted to feel empathy for the girl who'd been raised in such a restrictive environment, but something about her rubbed Angel the wrong way. It was one thing for Eleanor to pronounce her a domestic failure, but Ruth had no right to ridicule her.

Her reply was tart. "Fortunately there are some wifely skills my husband values more than baking."

But her barb seemed to go right over Ruth's head. The girl's pretty brows knit together in a frown.

Eleanor's expression was bland. The woman would have made an excellent poker player.

It was Matthew who came to her rescue. "Angelina, you are a bride among brides. I'm always pleased with your wit and loyalty."

"And you, Matthew, are my heart and soul." Her voice came out softer, dreamier than she'd intended.

Matthew's expression warmed, his eyes darkened. She must've laid it on thick, because it looked as if he believed her.

Shaking her head, Angel hoped he was simply a better actor than she'd originally thought.

A few minutes later Matthew leaned back in his chair. "Aunt Eleanor, that was a wonderful meal. Ruth, Angel, thank you, too."

Eleanor nodded, smiling briefly. "You are most welcome. Ruth, would you please sort the children's laundry Grace brought over today? Angel, you can help me with the dishes."

Fatigue seeped through her. But she figured leaving dirty dishes soaking till morning was unacceptable to Eleanor. Sighing, she said, "Yes, Eleanor."

Matthew stood, reaching for his plate.

"Matthew." Eleanor's tone was sharp. "We will attend to clearing."

His mouth tightened. He shrugged. "I'll go on the front porch and get some air."

"As long as you're inside by dark. There's a curfew."

He nodded. "I'll abide by the rules."

Angel was surprised at his easy compliance. Why did these people blindly obey rules that seemed arbitrary? After only a short time the restrictions were weighing heavily on her. Earlier she'd found humor in the silly ways in which the women ingratiated themselves with the men. Then she'd gotten angry. Now, tired and out of her element, the rules made her sad.

Matthew paused, his hand on the doorknob. "Angel, I'll be ready to have my bath drawn when I come inside."

"What?"

"You heard me."

Right, like that was going to happen. She'd clear and wash dishes, then drag her exhausted body up the stairs to run *him* a bath.

Angel braced her hands on her hips. "Your arms don't look broken."

Eleanor stepped forward. "It is our way. A small show of concern for your husband's well-being."

A wave of homesickness hit Angel hard. She longed for her own bed and people who genuinely cared about her. "What about me?" she whispered. "What about my well-being?"

Eleanor touched her shoulder, her eyes warm with concern. "What is good for the family is ultimately good for you."

Angel wiped moisture from her cheek, amazed that she'd teared up. "Is it really, Eleanor? Or is it merely a way to persuade me to give up my rights as a human being?"

She didn't wait for a response. She brushed past Matthew and ran upstairs to their room.

MATTHEW STOOD ON the front porch, leaning against the house. There were no rockers or chairs as there would have been in his father's day, when it was considered good for folks to gather in fellowship. On the contrary, Eleanor had given the impression Jonathon didn't like folks to congregate on their own. *Why?* he wondered.

He was torn between defying the curfew to see what happened and going upstairs to make sure Angel was all right. Her fragility after dinner scared him. He wondered if, despite her brave front, Zion's Gate might be too much for her. But they had an important purpose for being here; he only hoped she could fulfill her duties.

Glancing around, he noted the layout of the lane. On closer inspection he realized that what appeared to be typical Mexican adobe homes were in reality small fortresses. Thick adobe walls, small high windows protected by decorative wrought-iron bars. Stout front doors—apparently only one way in and one way out. Except for Eleanor's house, where there was a separate entrance to Jonathon's study.

Shadows lengthened and an eerie quiet fell.

The door opened behind him. He looked over his shoulder. "Eleanor."

"It's almost dark."

"I'll be in shortly."

She stepped beside him. "Are you sure coming here was a good idea? Our way can be difficult for someone not born to it."

"I *know* it was the right thing to do." How else would he find out whether Rebecca was alive and well? And find out how his father really died so many years ago. "Angel will adjust."

"I hope so."

He watched a sliver of a moon rise over Raphael's

house. A mournful howl nearby made his scalp prickle. "Coyotes?"

"Probably. Or one of our neighbor's dogs. He keeps many."

"Does he breed dogs?"

"No. They patrol his compound."

"Sounds kind of sinister."

"This is a different world than what you were used to in Arizona. There are…dangers."

"What kind of dangers?"

"You will have to ask your uncle. Please, come inside. He'll hold me responsible if you're seen out after dark."

His aunt knew him well. He might have rebelled against the edict just to see what happened. But not if it meant making life hard for her.

"I'll come inside. Suddenly I'm very tired." And he was. Deep down in his soul.

MATTHEW STOOD AT the bathroom door listening to the soft lap-lap of water whenever Angel shifted in the bathtub. At least that was the only explanation he could devise for the sounds. An occasional trickle or splash were the only interruptions.

He smiled, amused by Angel's quiet rebellion. It reassured him after her tears. Wandering into the sleeping area, he wished for a TV. But televisions had not been allowed, even in his father's day. It was seen as a waste of time and sometimes downright evil. There were occasions when he had to agree. Now wasn't one of them.

Matthew retrieved his Bible from the nightstand and read for a few minutes. Then he realized he hadn't heard a sound from the bathroom recently.

He went to the bathroom door. "Angel?"

When he didn't receive an answer, he called again. Still no reply.

Uneasiness prickled the back of his neck as he contemplated several scenarios. None of the possibilities were good. She had seemed upset earlier, but she was a fighter, a survivor at heart. But people slipped in the tub all the time. What if she'd sunk below the water and was drowning at this very moment?

"Angel?" Twisting the knob, he was relieved to find the door unlocked. He hesitated. Before he could have second thoughts, Matthew opened the door and stepped into the small bathroom.

Angel reclined in the tub, eyes closed, her hair piled on top of her head. A few stray wisps clung wetly to her neck, next to the earphone cord. Somehow she'd managed to smuggle in an MP3 player.

Matthew exhaled in relief.

Then he saw that she was naked, really, truly naked. His gaze traveled over her bare breasts, down the curve of her hip visible through the water. She had to be the most perfectly formed woman he had ever seen.

Heat pooled in his groin.

Shaking his head, Matthew called himself every kind of fool. What kind of man spied on a woman in the bath?

He turned to leave, hoping she would never know what he'd done.

"In or out, Matt. You're letting in a breeze."

He froze.

Damn.

Slowly he closed the door and rested his forehead against it. This had to look bad. "I'd hoped to get out of here without you knowing I'd been here."

"Peeping doesn't suit you, Matt. Very undignified. And desperate. You don't impress me as a desperate man."

If only she knew.

But his intentions had initially been good. How would she react if he admitted being afraid she'd hurt herself? It would bother her that he might suspect she wasn't as self-reliant as she'd like everyone to believe. "I came in here to remind you of your place. Is this how you interpret 'running my bath'?"

"Nobody said I couldn't use it first."

"Correct, as usual, Angelina." He chuckled, pushing away from the door. He turned but kept his gaze fixed on her face. "You followed the letter of the law, if not the intent."

"Sorry, Matt, the devil made me do it."

His gaze was drawn to her chest in spite of himself. He focused on her MP3 player on the floor. "Do you have any other electronic gadgets you got past the inspection?"

She shrugged, an action that drew his gaze like heat-seeking radar and nearly raised her bare breasts above water level.

He swallowed hard.

Reaching for a towel, Angel said, "Now, since someone let in all that cold air, I'm going to get out of the bath. I'm not particularly prudish, but I would appreciate some privacy."

"Yes. I'll leave you alone." Matthew stepped out of the bathroom and quickly shut the door behind him, glad to escape the humiliation of being branded a pervert.

Angel's chuckle mocked him through the door.

Then he realized she'd never answered his question.

CHAPTER EIGHT

ANGEL WAS SO BORED she was afraid her eyeballs would roll back in her head. Sunday at Zion's Gate was pure torture. Church lasted *all* day. Matthew had warned her it would be. But she'd thought he was exaggerating.

First, they'd had services with the whole population of Zion's Gate. Jonathon's sermon had been full of fire and brimstone, of how the principle of plural marriage was the only salvation, the only hope of a righteous place in heaven. Glancing around her at Jonathon's wives and children sitting together, she figured he must have a pretty darn good place reserved.

Next, she'd helped Eleanor teach one of the children's classes. After that they'd taken a break long enough for the women to return home to retrieve food they'd prepared the night before. A potluck picnic lunch was planned in honor of Matthew's return. Then there would be more classes and Bible study for the remainder of the day.

Sitting next to Matthew at a long picnic table, she felt like an exhibit at the zoo. People streamed by, welcoming him, congratulating them on their marriage. And glancing frequently at her belly.

Angel longed to jump up on the table and scream, *No, I'm not pregnant! And I don't intend to be. Not now. Maybe not ever. And certainly not by a Stone.*

But she managed to retain her composure, keeping her attention focused on her plate, nodding every once in a while when Matthew referred to her. Nobody seemed to expect her to contribute to the conversation.

Matthew nudged her with his elbow. "Angel, I'd like you to meet my brother, Raphael."

She looked up to see a man with sandy hair and a medium build. Goodness seemed to emanate from him, casting him in a warm glow.

Taking his outstretched hand, she was stunned by the beauty of his smile.

"Pleasure to meet you, Angel," he murmured. "These are my wives, Beatrice, Mary and Grace."

Angel had quit trying to remember Jonathon's wives' names. At least Raphael's were in a manageable number. She nodded to the women and said hello. *Plain* was the adjective she would have chosen to describe all three. And for two of them, it would have been kind.

They moved on, summoned by Raphael's mother, who had already been introduced.

"We were very close until our father died. Then Raphael's mother was sealed to an older elder and my mother was sealed to Uncle Jonathon."

"Raphael seems like a nice guy."

"Yes, he is." Matthew held her gaze. "That surprises you, doesn't it? That there are good men at Zion's Gate?"

She shrugged. "I guess it does."

"The fundamentalist sects have gotten a bad rap in recent years. Many of them deservedly so. But Raphael is a good man and would make an excellent leader for the group."

"But your uncle will never allow it."

"Precisely. That's why Raphael isn't given any real

responsibility. Why he only has three wives. And probably the reason the wife of his heart was given to another man."

"Seriously?"

"Yes. He and Theresa were in love for as long as I can remember. But apparently Uncle Jonathon and the elders learned of their infatuation. Theresa was married off to another elder. In time, Raphael received his wives."

"Women nobody else wanted."

Matthew glanced away. "That I couldn't say. I believe Raphael has been kind to them. And they have gifted him with children."

"So that makes it okay?"

"Yes."

"How sad."

"Yes, it *is* sad. There's much about our life that's sad."

"Matthew?"

"What?"

"That's the only time I've heard you refer to it as 'our' life, present tense." A horrible thought occurred to her. "You're not thinking of staying on, are you?"

He shook his head. "No. There's nothing here for me."

"Yet it draws you all the same."

"It was everything I knew until I was fifteen. The people, the conventions, everything is familiar yet different. It was very hard to leave."

"Yet you think you can leave a second time?"

"I'll have to."

Their conversation was interrupted when another family came up to offer their congratulations.

After they left, Angel rose. "I'm going to walk a little. Then I'll help the women clean up."

Angel strolled around the square, aware that glances followed her every move. She resisted the urge to turn around and make a rude gesture.

Oddly enough, she found comfort in knowing she was a complete outsider and would probably never be accepted here. For the most part, people gave her a wide berth when she wasn't with Matthew. Breathing deeply, she reveled in the feeling of being alone in the midst of all this togetherness. The tension eased from her shoulders.

She admired the intense blue of the sky interspersed with wispy clouds. Peace stole over her. In some ways, the Zion's Gate life was simple. Every thought and action was prescribed. It might be very easy to just go with the flow. If she were a different kind of person, that is.

The first couple of days had been especially difficult. She was accustomed to action, challenge, danger. But now she was becoming used to the repetitive domestic work of cooking, cleaning and washing clothes. Unfortunately Eleanor didn't allow her to participate much in the children's schooling. She probably feared Angel would corrupt their fresh, inquisitive minds.

"Hello, Sister Angel." Ruth fell into step beside her.

"Ruth." She nodded stiffly. It was bad enough she had to tolerate this girl at Eleanor's house.

"Brother Jonathon's sermon was very moving."

"Um, yes, I guess." Only if she referred to her digestive tract.

Ruth glanced at her sideways. "You see the importance of the principle?"

"I think I understand Jonathon's point."

"Then you will welcome more wives for Matthew when the time comes?"

Angel was rendered speechless, something she'd thought nearly impossible. Her smart mouth had never failed her. She took a deep breath, reminding herself that Ruth was a product of her environment. Who could blame her for setting her sights on Matthew? He was young, handsome and possible heir apparent to Jonathon. For a girl with few prospects except marriage to a much older man, Matthew would be the most eligible guy around.

She tempered her instinctive response, trying to sound open to a lifestyle she found abhorrent. "I will always try to make Matthew happy. To be the best wife possible."

"Even if that means sharing him with another wife?"

Angel stopped. "Are you applying for the job?"

Ruth smiled coyly. "I would obey the Lord's will if He chose Brother Matthew as my husband."

"Yes, I'm sure you would." Angel narrowed her eyes. A wave of possessiveness had her fighting to remember this was a cover, nothing more. "But I have the final say, don't I?"

The girl nodded, her smile fading.

"Matthew and I are newlyweds. It's much too soon to consider a sister wife. But it looks like Brother Raphael could use some beauty in his life. Maybe you should see if he's ready to add another wife."

Ruth's eyes widened.

"Now, if you'll excuse me, I need to help the rest of the women clean up the lunch mess. And spend some time with my husband."

Returning to the picnic tables, Angel busied herself with cleanup. The repetitive work helped her clear her mind and regain perspective.

She felt much calmer when she returned to Matthew's side. But he seemed distracted, constantly scanning the crowd.

"Still haven't seen your sister?"

He shook his head. "Jonathon promised she'd be here today. I'm not sure I'd recognize her after all these years."

"Women change pretty quickly in appearance when they pop out a baby every year."

A half smile twitched at his mouth. "Yes, I guess so."

"You're worried about her."

"Yes." He lowered his voice. "There are people who used to report on Rebecca's welfare to my mother. But since the group moved to Texas, the reports stopped. The authorities indicate they weren't able to locate her on any of the satellite surveillance photos, either."

"The women don't get out too much."

"No, they don't. But most work at least a few hours a week in the vegetable garden. Not Rebecca, as far as I can tell."

"You're shut in with the elders most of the day and we haven't been given an opportunity to explore. We haven't met anyone but Jonathon's immediate family up till now. But I can see why you're concerned."

"You don't know the half of it."

She touched his arm. "Why don't you enlighten me?"

"Not here, not now." Matthew glanced over his shoulder, as if recalling Jonathon had eyes and ears everywhere.

As if by magic, Eleanor approached. "Angel, it's time to rejoin the women for afternoon studies."

"Yes, Eleanor. I'll be along."

The older woman nodded and headed toward the meeting room designated for the women.

"Is that why you came, Matthew? To help Rebecca?" she asked. Their official reason for being at Zion's Gate was to determine how heavily armed the enclave was and assess the danger of another Waco. If they found evidence of other illegal activity, all the better. And Angel's pet project was helping the women and children of Zion's Gate. Now it appeared Matthew had a pet project of his own.

"One of several reasons I can't discuss here. Too much chance of being overheard. It's important I find Rebecca, though."

"I'll keep an eye out for her. I think I recall a photo of your sister in your file."

He held her gaze. "Thank you, Angel. It means a lot."

"Hey, family is important. It can't be easy for you to be back, and I imagine you have a pretty good reason for being here. Above and beyond whatever carrot was dangled."

She waited for him to protest, but he didn't. His silence confirmed her suspicion that the government had offered him something to bring her here and provide a cover. Something they didn't necessarily want her privy to.

One thing was certain—Matthew's concern for his sister was genuine. "If nothing else, maybe we can go to her," she said.

"I've tried, but Jonathon was evasive about her location."

"Let me see what I can find out. I better go."

Angel hurried to the women's meeting hall, scanning the women's faces. Occasionally she'd come to a female who vaguely resembled the photo of Rebecca. But there was a basic family resemblance to many of the Zion's Gate residents. It seemed all were fair-skinned and light-eyed.

Finally she gave up finding Rebecca. Instead she tried to focus on the endless testimonies, readings and sermonettes. Funny, the women professed to be as avid in their dedication to the principle as the men, maybe even more so, but Angel found their words hollow.

Toward the end of one particularly long lecture, the hair on the back of Angel's neck prickled. She could feel someone watching her. And it wasn't the same as the curious stares she'd endured all day. It was more personal. Or so the sixth sense she'd developed while married to Kent told her.

Glancing around, she mostly encountered the vacant stares of women trying to appear interested when in fact they'd zoned out.

Across the meeting hall, her gaze locked with that of a young woman who quickly turned away. But not before the shock of recognition passed through Angel.

Rebecca.

Angel started to rise, but Eleanor grasped her arm.

She tried to shake off Eleanor's hand. The woman's grip was firm.

Angel glanced back toward Rebecca. She was gone.

MATTHEW PACED THEIR small room. Frustration and lack of physical activity made him feel as if he might jump out of his skin. "You're sure it was Rebecca?"

Angel sat cross-legged on the bed, her cotton night-gown hiked up around her knees. "I can't say for sure. I only saw her for a minute. This woman was older than the girl in the picture."

"Which would stand to reason."

"Yes."

"Did she look well? Happy?"

Angel sighed. "Matt, none of the women around here dance with unbridled joy. I wasn't able to assess her mental state."

"You're trained to observe detail. Surely you can remember something?"

Angel closed her eyes. "She was fair, like in the picture. Pretty. Laugh lines around her mouth. That would suggest she's happy at least part of the time. But also deep frown lines. And her complexion is different."

"The picture is probably old."

Nodding, Angel opened her eyes, and what he saw there made his stomach drop. Compassion. Or pity.

"What did you remember?"

"Her skin had a grayish pallor. Like someone who's sick. And she was very thin."

He swallowed hard. "Jonathon said she'd been ill. But I thought it was an excuse to keep me from seeing her."

"Why would he do that?"

"Until he's sure of me, he's probably afraid I might convince her to leave Zion's Gate. I bet that's why she's not in this area with the rest of his wives."

"Excuse me?"

"I told you there were elders interested in marrying my sisters. Rebecca married Jonathon shortly after we left." The words were bitter on his tongue. "We…were forced to go without her."

"But that's obscene. She's his niece."

"That wouldn't stop my uncle. He feels he's above the rules. He takes what he wants."

"Did Rebecca want to stay?"

"That's what I'm here to find out." And correct the wrong he'd allowed to happen so many years ago.

"Matthew?" Her voice was soft.

"Yes?"

"I'm sorry you were dealt such a crappy hand. Why does your God allow bad things to happen to good people?"

He sighed. "You don't know how many times I've struggled with that myself."

"Did you ever find an answer?"

"Not one that satisfied me."

She tilted her head. "Yet you still believe."

"Yes, I do."

"Why?"

"Because if I lose my connection to God, I lose everything."

"Even a God who allows evil to hurt you?"

He frowned, choosing his words carefully. "I think it breaks His heart when His people hurt. But we are given a free will. To do good or evil."

"That really sucks, Matt. There were times when I cried out to Him and He didn't help, didn't answer." Her voice trembled. "I realized I was on my own."

He went to her, cradled her head with his hand. "Oh, Angel, He was there. Caring for you, protecting you, even when you thought He wasn't."

She wrenched away from him, scooting off the bed to stand on the other side. "You know nothing of what I went through. No god who loved me could have stood by and watched. So don't offer me your platitudes."

Angel turned and stalked to the bathroom. The door slammed shut behind her.

Matthew paced the length of the room, wrestling

with the knowledge that it was vital for her to open up to him. His mission was too important, too dangerous, to risk being blindsided.

Nodding, he came to a decision. He waited five minutes then knocked on the door. "Angel? We need to talk."

"I'll be out shortly."

"I'll give you five and then I'm coming in after you."

"Yeah, you and what army?"

He had to smile at her bravado. "I don't need an army. I can get Aunt Eleanor."

"No, don't do that." He thought he detected a note of panic in her voice. Apparently Eleanor had managed to earn her grudging respect. Or fear.

"Five minutes."

"Okay."

He went back and sat on the bed, glancing at his watch. He heard the bathroom door open in just over four minutes.

Angel brought over the straight-backed chair, perching on the edge. "What is it?"

"We're both here to do a job. I can't do mine unless I know what's bugging you. If you have issues, it could well endanger me, too."

She leaned back, crossing her arms over her chest. "I don't have issues."

"We all have issues."

"Speak for yourself, buddy. I'm the picture of emotional health."

"I didn't say you weren't. There's something in your past that's a hot button and I need to know what it is. If we're going to continue working together so closely, you've got to trust me."

"No, I don't. I merely have to tolerate you."

"Look, I'm probably more sensitive to personal freedom than most. I wouldn't normally press. But this could be vital to our success here. Maybe even vital to our survival."

Angel raised her chin. "I went through a battery of psychological tests to become a DPS officer. My superiors are satisfied that I'm capable of doing the job. Why can't you back off?"

"Because I have a personal stake in this mission." Urgency vibrated in his voice. This mission meant keeping promises to the people he loved, promises to himself.

"I don't owe you a thing."

"No, you don't. But I confided in you about Rebecca. Now you need to be forthcoming with me. It's the only way we can be an effective team." Matthew waited, holding his breath.

Angel sighed. "Fair enough. I'll share, but then you get off my case."

He nodded.

Taking a deep breath, she said, "I was a lot different ten years ago. My father said I'd never met a stranger. I was friendly and outgoing and trusted everyone." She hesitated, plucking at a loose thread on her nightgown.

"Someone destroyed that trust?"

"Yes. I met Kent in college. He was wonderful—everything I ever wanted in a man. Handsome, intelligent, attentive. I fell head over heels for him. Six months later we married."

Matthew absorbed her admission. It fit with some of the things her father had said at their wedding.

"Almost immediately Kent decided he didn't want to finish school. Said he could make more money working construction. Someday he hoped to have his own company. It sounded logical to me." She smiled wryly. "He could make anything sound logical. When he got a job offer in Fort Worth, we both quit school. I intended to start again in the fall, but it didn't happen."

"Why not?"

"Kent started to change. He couldn't seem to hold a job. We needed my cashier job for the income and benefits. And, truth be told, I don't think he wanted me to finish school."

"How did your folks feel about you moving from Houston?" Matthew recalled their protectiveness.

"They said they would miss me, but understood I needed to make a life for myself. I missed them horribly. It didn't take Kent long to cut me off from my family, my friends, everyone. They had no idea what he was really like. Soon I did medical transcription from home because my other job caused too much friction. Kent was convinced I was having an affair with every guy who came through my line."

Matthew's stomach knotted. Isolation. Jealousy. Control. It all fit a pattern. "Did he hit you, Angelina?" his voice was calm and, he hoped, nonthreatening.

"Yes. And punched and kicked and…all sorts of awful things." The stark sadness in her eyes told him it was worse than he could imagine. "He was evil, Matthew. Absolutely evil. And he'd told me he loved me, couldn't live without me. He was only trying to keep me safe. But the person I needed protection from was him."

She stood and wandered over to the cross-stitch sampler hanging on the wall. Trailing a finger across the glass, she said, "I begged and pleaded with God to protect me. And when he didn't, I begged Him to release me from hell on earth. And one day it seemed I would get my wish. Kent had told me he didn't want his jeans pressed with a crease anymore. I worked and worked and worked, trying to get rid of the crease. But it was permanent. When he put on his jeans, he went ballistic. Called me all sorts of names, threw me against the wall. Choked me."

Matthew could have gladly killed Kent. How could anyone treat another human being like that?

"I fought back. I knew it only made things worse, but this time I fought back. He grabbed a kitchen knife and stabbed me. I thought I was dying. He obviously thought I was dying, too, because he left me there." Her voice was monotone as she relayed the rest of the story.

Matthew suppressed a flash of rage. But Angel didn't need his anger, she needed his understanding. Stepping behind her, Matthew touched her shoulder.

She walked into his open arms. "Angelina, I'm so sorry." He kissed the top of her head, wishing he'd been there to protect her. Wishing God had protected her. No wonder she had turned her back on the idea of a savior. When she'd needed one most, hers had seemed to desert her.

She wrapped her arms around his waist, burying her face in his chest. But there was no weeping. He suspected she'd cried for the young Angel long ago.

"What happened to Kent?" he asked.

"He died instantly."

"That's too bad."

Angel leaned back and met his gaze, a question in her eyes.

"It was too easy a death for someone like him. He should have suffered the way you suffered."

"What about turning the other cheek?" She touched his face.

"Most times I try to live that part of the scriptures."

"And others?"

"I believe in an eye for an eye." Especially where monsters like Angel's husband were concerned. And that included his uncle Jonathon.

CHAPTER NINE

"THERE, NOW YOU KNOW." Angel put plenty of space between herself and Matthew. "You know my deep, dark secret—my hot button, as you put it. I assure you it won't get in the way of doing my job. I dealt with it a long time ago."

Doubt slithered through the back of her mind. Was she sure?

Angel raised her chin, willing confidence to radiate from every pore. What was it the counselor had told her? Fake it until you make it? It saddened her to realize she was back to faking it when she'd thought for so long she'd really made it.

"You're a professional and I understand you're very good at what you do." Matthew's tone was matter-of-fact, as if he sensed her need to get back on professional footing. "I don't think you'd intentionally allow your feelings to interfere. But it's necessary for me to know your history."

"My *history,* as you put it, is nobody's business but my own. And I'm getting tired of waiting for Jonathon to give us the official okeydoke to move about freely." She pulled the extra blankets from the bed and grabbed her pillow. "This place is messing with my mind. There are times when I wonder who I really am anymore."

"We have to be patient. Jonathon's suspicious already, we don't want to give him added ammunition. But you might want to be careful. Losing your identity is the first step in mind control."

Angel stopped midstride, her expression incredulous. "You think I'm falling under Jonathon's spell?"

"No. I think you're human and so am I. It will be a challenge for both of us not to be drawn into Jonathon's skewed version of reality. Doubly so because we must give the impression of having been won over to his way of thinking."

"All this analytical crap has given me a headache. I'm going to bed." She arranged her blankets on the floor. Glaring at Matthew, she waited for him to argue as usual about taking the bed. He insisted on being gallant. She insisted on being equal partners, alternating nights on the floor.

Tonight he didn't argue. "Good night, Angelina."

She'd won. So why did it feel as if she'd given away a piece of her soul?

ANGEL EYED MATTHEW as he ate his scrambled eggs. His manner was composed, his appetite impressive. He hadn't given any indication this morning that their conversation last night had ever occurred. Good. That was the way she wanted to keep it. It embarrassed her that he knew about that time in her life. And in a more cynical moment, she worried that he might use the knowledge against her. She didn't like people knowing her Achilles' heel.

He slid his empty plate away and leaned back in his chair. "Aunt Eleanor, I'll be coming home for lunch today. I'd like you to help Angel arrange her schedule so she can spend time with me."

Great. Just great. She shouldn't have told Matthew about Kent. Now he was going to treat her like something breakable. Or, worse, something damaged.

"I'm really very busy, Matthew. It's important to me to contribute to the household and make a comfortable home for you," Angel said. "Besides, Jonathon's other wives might stop by."

He grasped her hand. "I appreciate your efforts, my bride. But I'm sure you can be spared for an hour. I'd like you to take your lunch with me, then walk about the compound a bit."

Her interest sparked. An opportunity to scope out the place at last. How in the world had he arranged it with Jonathon?

"Angel's right, Matthew. She's needed here. It's not seemly for her to be gallivanting during the middle of the day."

"I'm her husband, Aunt, how could it not be seemly?"

"People will talk about…unnatural appetites." Eleanor's cheeks grew pink.

"Eleanor, my only appetite is to share lunch and a walk with my wife. I don't think that's too much to ask."

"If Jonathon approves—"

"Jonathon *will* approve. I intend to speak to him this morning." There was a dangerous glint in Matthew's eye.

Angel got a kick out of seeing him stand up to Eleanor—and, in essence, Jonathon. She only hoped he knew what he was doing. From bits and pieces she'd read, people who openly opposed Jonathon in matters great or small ended up leaving Zion's Gate.

"I'll look forward to it." Angel gently disengaged her hand. "Now you don't want to be late for the elders' meeting. You know how your uncle values punctuality."

"Yes, I do." Matthew stood, reaching for his plate. "I'll get that. Go to your meeting."

He shrugged and left, whistling a tune as he went.

Angel suspected it had been very difficult for him to acquiesce to his uncle up till now. He was a born leader.

Tilting her head, she wondered if Matthew realized his innate leadership abilities made him a much better choice to take Jonathon's place than Raphael.

"Quit your daydreaming." Eleanor's tone was tart, but there was a twinkle in her eyes.

"I wasn't, um…I mean…" Angel's cheeks grew warm. Had she been daydreaming about Matthew? A disturbing thought. Almost as disturbing as blushing for the first time in over ten years. She would have to be very, very careful where Matthew Stone was concerned. Because she was vulnerable now that he knew about her past. And she certainly couldn't afford to make another disastrous error in judgment.

Ruth sidled into the room, interrupting Angel's thoughts. "Eleanor, several of the children seem to have had a stomach ailment. Perhaps Sister Angel can help laundering the bed linens."

"No, Ruth, I'll need Angel's help with the baking this morning. I'm confident you can handle it."

Ruth glared at Angel from beneath her lashes. In Eleanorland, Angel's status had just risen a notch. And Ruth's had fallen.

The rest of the morning was spent cleaning breakfast dishes and baking loaves of bread. Humming under her breath, Angel was surprised to find she'd overcome her earlier biscuit disaster and enjoyed baking. She enjoyed Eleanor's company, too. Who'd have thought?

Someone stepped up behind her. Angel instinctively

started to jab with her elbow, prepared to fight off the unexpected attack.

A subtle, familiar male scent signaled her brain to stop the blow before it landed in Matthew's ribs.

He wrapped his arms around her waist and nuzzled her neck. "Mmm. Smells delicious in here."

His breath tickled the fine hairs at her nape. She couldn't help but giggle.

Oh, Lord, she'd blushed *and* giggled all in the same morning. Hell must be freezing over.

Angel turned and swatted at Matthew. "I'm trying to work."

Eleanor bustled over and placed a towel over the dough Angel had pummeled into submission. "I'll take care of this after it rises. The weather's perfect. You go and have a picnic lunch with Matthew. Take a few of those sandwiches and some fruit."

Matthew went over and hugged Eleanor, then turned her loose. "You're the best. I'll grab sodas from the fridge."

Angel wrapped the sandwiches in wax paper, selected two ripe red apples and tucked them in a canvas tote. Her anticipation rose as she joined Matthew at the door. Funny how such a simple outing could elicit excitement. Her perspective had changed in the ten days she'd been at Zion's Gate. An opportunity to explore outside and simply relax with Matthew was to be treasured.

As she turned to close the door behind her, Angel was surprised to see Ruth standing in the kitchen, watching, her eyes flashing with anger.

She ignored the girl's pique and resolved to soak up the fresh air and sunshine. It was a treat she'd sorely missed.

Matthew commented, "There's a grassy area between this group of houses and the next. We'll spread a blanket under the tree."

"Sounds lovely."

Matthew grasped her hand, swinging his arm as they walked. "Yes, it does."

"I'm not sure if this is a good idea." She glanced down at their clasped hands.

"We're married. No harm, no foul."

"I haven't seen a couple hold hands or kiss since we've been here."

He shrugged. "I have only one wife. I can show affection without worrying about how it will affect my other wives."

"I never thought of it that way. I bet they have some hellacious catfights. Poor women, it can't be easy living so closely with rivals."

"Every once in a while there's a tiff. From what I remember, it's all on the sly. Heavy undercurrents of competition. And a lot of crying behind closed doors."

"I can imagine."

They walked along in companionable silence. The day was mild, the air heavy with the scent of desert blossoms.

"It's beautiful here, in a stark way," she observed.

"Yes, imagine what it would be like if water were plentiful. As it is, Jonathon is concerned about running low. This patch of grass will be dead soon. No lawns, no ornamental planting allowed. Only vegetable gardens and fruit trees."

"I'd like to see the gardens." Angel raised her face to the sun for a moment. The warmth lifted her spirits. "Maybe even work there. But Eleanor says not until I'm fully acclimated, whatever that means. It gets boring being shut in Eleanor's house all day."

"It means they don't totally trust you yet. Me, either. I figured we should get this little ritual started to stave off boredom and see a little of the layout. The fresh air's good for us and it will give us an opportunity to share information without the fear of being overheard. Besides, it probably makes your superiors less nervous if you're regularly observed alive and well."

"Good point. It's so desolate out here they wouldn't get close to the compound. Satellite photos are the best they can do most of the time." She tried not to think about how vulnerable she and Matthew were, with no backup if things went wrong. At least with undercover gang work, Angel knew help wasn't far away.

Matthew nodded toward the lone spindly tree. They walked across the gravel path and spread a blanket beneath the tree. "Let's hope the satellite passes over at lunchtime. I'd hate for the authorities to think they have to come in and rescue us."

Angel smothered a disbelieving chuckle. "They made it pretty clear I'm on my own. If things go wrong, they'll deny knowledge of me. Fortunately Jonathon's men didn't find the pocket PC I tucked away with a supply of feminine products. I'll need wireless access, though."

Matthew allowed his mind to skip right past her rather ingenious way of hiding the pocket PC. "I was hoping you had some way to communicate with the outside world. I meant to ask the other night but got sidetracked." By the sight of her naked body in the bathtub.

He swallowed hard. No need to go there.

Angel didn't seem to notice his preoccupation. She

eyed the cluster of homes near the small park. "I'd love to walk the perimeter. Get an overview of the layout."

"Me, too. But we better start out small so we don't arouse suspicion. Besides, you might get a chance to explore when the elders go into town."

"They don't do that often, do they?"

"No. But Uncle Jonathon announced this morning they'll be making a trip into town soon to sell some of our extra produce at the farmer's market. I'm hoping they'll include me. Maybe I can slip away and send an e-mail for you."

Angel nodded. "Interesting that they sell produce. With the heavy emphasis on preparing for hard times, you'd think they'd can or preserve most of the fruits and vegetables. I wonder if maybe it's a cover for something else?"

"I get the impression Jonathon thinks cold, hard cash is just as important in preparing for hard times. Only one way to find out if something's going on. I'll help unload the produce if possible, see if there's more involved." Matthew sat on the blanket cross-legged, gesturing for her to join him. "Will you let me take your PC with me?"

Angel sat next to him, removing the food from the canvas bag as a way to stall. He was asking her to trust him with her only contact to the outside world.

She handed Matthew a sandwich. His gaze was steady. He seemed to have *trustworthy* written all over him. Maybe a little too good to be true.

Angel shook off her doubt. She'd learned a lot about detecting character in the past nine years. Wasn't it time she listened to her instincts? "I guess that's okay. I'll make sure to charge it tonight."

He smiled, warm, sincere, as if he understood how great an honor she'd bestowed. "I'll take good care of it."

"I expect you to." *Please, please don't disappoint me, Matt.* "If you break it, I'll have to break body parts."

"I'll guard it with my life."

Uneasiness skittered along her nerve endings. In her line of work, statements like that were best avoided.

Angel changed the subject. "I'm curious—what do you guys talk about in the elders' meetings?"

"Finances, opportunities to make more money for the group. Reports of persecution, the latest on Warren Jeffs and his sect, speculation on whether the threat might spread to Zion's Gate."

"Are you getting any indication of gun or drug trafficking?"

Shaking his head, Matthew said, "I've barely scratched the surface. My uncle is a very cautious man. I'm sure he doesn't trust me yet. The elders pretty much parrot back the party line, but I sense undercurrents. Not all of them are happy with the way Jonathon's running things."

"I feel like I should be doing something besides baking bread and cleaning house." She bit into her sandwich, thinking while she chewed. Swallowing, she said, "I'm not sure if waiting till the elders go to town is necessary. I could slip out at night and do a little scouting. Maybe when we're supposed to be deep in Bible study."

"I'm getting restless, too, but I don't want Jonathon to have reason to mistrust us. We're better off biding our time."

"I don't do well with that biding-time stuff."

Matthew smiled. "That doesn't surprise me. But I

know you don't want to endanger the mission. It's very important we find out if they have substantial weapons on hand. The trip to town could be the key."

"What's the mood of those meetings like?"

"Jonathon keeps everybody on their toes. He's prophesying a lot about the end-times, and that worries me. He may have crossed the line into paranoia."

Angel sipped her soda. "But then again, he allowed us here. Maybe he's not so paranoid after all."

"Or maybe it's a self-fulfilling prophecy, no pun intended."

"How so?"

Matthew leaned close, his voice low. "He imagines the government is out to get him. So he fortifies the place and anticipates the worst. The authorities see a situation with volatile possibilities and decide to keep an eye on him. He senses he's gained government attention and gets more paranoid. And the cycle gets more intense."

"To be honest, if Jonathon has done the things our informants say he's done, I won't feel bad if he gets caught in a crossfire." Angel reduced her voice to a tense whisper though there was no one in sight. "Our sources say Jonathon has been offering underage girls to his cronies and saying it's okay because they're 'married.' And turning a blind eye to emotional, physical and sexual abuse. If a few of Jonathon's buddies go down along with him, all the better. But what about the women? They're innocent in this as far as we know. And the children never asked to be born into a rigid patriarchal cult."

Matthew rubbed her hand where she had a white-knuckle grip on her paper napkin. "Well said," he murmured.

She glanced away. "I guess I got carried away."

"No need to apologize. I agree with you, by the way." His gaze was direct.

"Is it hard to hear me talk about your relatives that way?"

"There are some I'll never forgive for what they did to my family. But I try hard not to paint everyone with the same brush. You seem to try to stay objective, too. You remind me of my sister. I think you'll like Rebecca."

"It's hard to be objective about family." Hadn't her parents convinced themselves she was having a wonderful new life in Fort Worth with Kent, when she'd actually been held captive? Was that what Matthew feared was happening with Rebecca? If the thought hadn't occurred to him, she didn't want to be the one to suggest it. Instead she asked an open-ended question. "Did you ask Jonathon about her?"

"Yes. He said she wasn't feeling well enough to attend church. I didn't tell him you thought she was there."

"What kind of illness is she supposed to have?"

"Female problems."

Angel snorted. "An ambiguous answer certain to make most men immediately back off."

"Yes, that's what I thought. I did back off, but not because I was embarrassed. Because I don't want Jonathon to know how much I want to see her."

"You have more patience than I do, Matt. Of course, my performance reviews always mention my impulsiveness. Apparently the powers that be think it's a liability in an officer."

"No comment."

"You think I'm impulsive?"

"Sometimes. It's kind of cute."

She sputtered and coughed. "Cute? I've worked hard for nine years to erase any trace of cuteness, and here you're telling me I've failed miserably."

"No, I wouldn't call you a failure. I'd call you a survivor. And that trumps cuteness any day."

She might have thought he was teasing her, except his eyes were dark and unreadable. She shook her head, trying not to take pleasure in his assessment of her. She couldn't get drawn into caring what he thought of her.

"Eat your sandwich, Matt, and keep your observations to yourself. It doesn't matter whether I'm cute or a survivor. It matters that I do my job and do it well."

"Of course." Matthew's solemn reply did nothing to allay her misgivings. The man would do whatever he pleased and she knew it.

At least they had that much in common.

CHAPTER TEN

A FEW EVENINGS LATER, Jonathon leaned back in his chair at the supper table and sighed. "Exceptional meal, Eleanor."

Eleanor nodded in acknowledgment. Though her expression remained impassive, Angel detected a spark of pleasure in the woman's eye. "I've made your favorite lemon pie, too."

"How delightful."

After seeing the man only occasionally over the past two weeks, Angel still wished Jonathon would quit with the beatific-saint act. It didn't suit him. And was about as believable as Angel pretending to be a debutante, though her parents did belong to a country club.

"I made the biscuits, Brother Jonathon." Ruth glanced up at him from beneath her lashes, her mouth curved in a sweet smile.

Angel wondered if Ruth was angling to become a permanent fixture at Eleanor's house—as a new sister wife for the woman. Maybe Matthew was the girl's second choice? After all, a woman's rank at Zion's Gate depended heavily on her husband's rank. And beneath Ruth's simpering, Angel detected a calculating mind.

Jonathon's smile was benevolent. "Yes, Ruth, you'll be a jewel in some lucky man's heavenly crown some day."

"If the Lord wishes it." The girl's voice could have melted butter.

"Ruth, why don't you come with me and help serve pie." Eleanor's tone was terse. It wasn't a question. "Angel, we'll need your assistance, too."

Angel followed them into the kitchen. Eleanor slammed the refrigerator door after removing the pies. She retrieved dessert plates from the kitchen hutch and shoved them at Ruth. "Take these and distribute them."

The younger woman had no choice but to accept. Her pretty little mouth turned down at the corners.

The temperature in the kitchen was decidedly cool. And dropping by the second.

"Go," Eleanor commanded.

Ruth raised her chin, apparently thinking of rebelling.

Angel hoped she did. The ensuing verbal thrashing would be worth witnessing.

Ruth seemed to have ideas along the same line, because she lowered her chin and murmured, "Yes, Eleanor."

Darn. Angel had been ready to witness a catfight.

After Ruth left the room, she said, "You could have taken her, Eleanor. With one hand tied behind your back."

"I don't know what you mean."

"Sure you do. And she would have had it coming. I don't know why it doesn't happen more often."

Eleanor held her head high. "There are challenges to living the principle at times. Our goal is to live in harmony. I didn't do well with that tonight."

"So you'll accept Ruth as a sister wife if Jonathon suggests it?"

"You ask too many questions, Angel. It is not seemly." She glanced meaningfully toward the kitchen door. "Mind your manners."

The boss was home. Everyone on their best behavior. The rest of the time, Eleanor was boss. Angel wondered if it was hard for the older woman to adjust to having her husband home.

Her question was answered after pie when Jonathon checked his day calendar and announced his intention of spending the night. "Happy Birthday, Eleanor."

Eleanor's smile was beautiful, her joy at having Jonathon remember her birthday unmistakable.

The display made Angel want to gag. "Brother," she muttered under her breath.

"Did you say something, Sister Angel?" Ruth asked, her eyes round and innocent.

"I started to say, Brother Jonathon, what a lovely sentiment. I wasn't aware it was Eleanor's birthday."

Jonathon beamed at his wife. "Her special day."

Angel got a mental vision of Jonathon presenting himself buck naked to Eleanor, a big red bow tied around his—

"Are you all right, Angelina?" Matthew touched her shoulder. "You look a bit pale."

"I'm, um, fine." As long as she could get that vision out of her mind. "I'd like to retire early tonight. The walk and fresh air today made me tired."

"Certainly."

"A few of the elders noted your absence at lunch these past days." Jonathon's smile faded. "Many have matters to discuss with you. Perhaps it would be best if you curtailed your visits home during the lunch hour."

Angel felt Matthew stiffen. This had apparently been a bone of contention between the two.

Personally she would be disappointed if their picnic lunches and midday walks were discontinued. Not only did she enjoy the time outdoors, but she also enjoyed Matthew's company and the opportunity to talk to him without the threat of being overheard.

"Uncle Jonathon, the elders will have to find another time to approach me." Matthew sipped his water. "I can stay late after the meeting if necessary."

"They have commitments themselves, families of their own to return to. Sometimes a man must surrender his own will for the good of the brethren."

And how often did Jonathon surrender his will for the good of anyone? Not very often, she'd bet. Oh, how Angel longed to fling the accusation in his smug face. But she couldn't. As a good celestial wife-in-training, she lowered her gaze to the floor, pretending she had no opinion.

"I am a newlywed, Uncle. My place is at my bride's side as much as possible. By sharing my lunchtime with her, I'm able to ease her transition to our way of life."

"There's no need to coddle her. She must learn her rightful place from the start. She is a strong woman. She'll adjust. And make you a fine wife, as Eleanor has made a fine wife for me."

"But—"

"You'll lead us in the evening Bible reading and prayer, won't you, Jonathon?" Eleanor tucked her hand under Jonathon's arm, her attempt at changing the subject obvious.

Angel held her breath, doubting the ploy would work.

Strangely enough, she thought she saw a glint of relief in Jonathon's eyes as he accepted Eleanor's offer. "Yes, I'll lead. Matthew, you and Angel will join the family this evening."

Matthew nodded curtly. "Of course."

In his way, Jonathon had allowed Matthew to stand firm in his conviction but made it seem as if Jonathon had won. All facilitated by Eleanor, who smiled innocently.

MATTHEW CLOSED THE bedroom door behind them. He'd never been so glad to plead fatigue in his life. And it had absolutely nothing to do with his lovely bride, as Jonathon's knowing wink had seemed to suggest. Rather, staying under the same roof with his uncle had brought emotions to the surface he would have rather left buried.

Angel sat on the bed. "I thought his prayer would go on forever. And all that end-days apocalypse stuff is creepy."

"It seems to be his focus."

"He sure is passionate about it." She stared at him. "You okay, Matt?"

"Yes. Fine."

"You look flushed."

"It *is* warm in here, don't you think?"

"I guess so."

"This room could use some ventilation. Too bad there's no window. I'd give my left arm for even one of those small windows with the bars over it."

"It's not that bad, just a bit stuffy. I hope you're not getting sick." Angel pressed the back of her hand to his forehead. "Nope. No fever."

"I'm just feeling kind of closed in."

"Yeah, I imagine Jonathon has that effect on a lot of people. Seems to suck the air right out of a room."

The accuracy of her statement struck him. That was exactly how he felt. But he didn't dare allow Angel know he was affected so intensely. "I can handle Jonathon. No big deal."

"Still, this must be like old home week for you. Probably takes you back to those 'Stepdaddy dearest' days."

Matthew swallowed hard. Memories were clamoring for attention. Memories he didn't want to revisit. *Ever.*

"Like I said, I can handle it." His tone was harsh, impatient. "Look, I'm sorry. I'm just on edge."

Angel shrugged. "No big deal."

"It's not like I'm a fifteen-year-old kid anymore. I'm strong. I'm smart. I escaped and built a new life. He has no power over me."

"Not as long as you stayed away, he didn't."

"He has no power over me now." He wiped sweat from his brow. His sport shirt clung to his back. But the moisture gave him no relief from the searing heat.

"Only if you hand it to him on a silver platter. Only if you let what happened before get all mixed up with what's going on now. If you do that, he'll win. Like you pointed out to me, he's an expert at mind control."

Matthew wished he could escape. Run out the door, past the guard shack and the iron gates and simply run till he couldn't go any farther.

Somehow he managed to present a calm facade long enough to make his pallet on the floor, get ready for bed and slide between the blankets.

But then the heat enveloped him again. He kicked off the covers but was still bathed in sweat. He tossed and turned for what seemed like hours.

Then someone was shaking his shoulders. "Matthew, wake up. You're having a nightmare."

He sat up, his heart pounding. He glanced around wildly, panicked and not knowing why.

"You're okay, Matthew," Angel crooned. Kneeling

beside him on the floor, she smoothed the damp hair from his brow. Her hand was cool and reassuring. He leaned his face into it for a moment while he regained his equilibrium.

His breathing became less labored and his heart stopped thudding against his ribs.

"Good. That's better." Her voice was soft. Funny, he'd never expected Angel to have a maternal side. It suited her.

"I'm okay."

"Yes. You're fine." But she didn't move away.

"You can go back to bed."

"I will in a minute."

"It was just a nightmare. I can't even remember what it was about." That much was true. He rarely remembered the dream. His only impression was of hot flames melting his flesh and Satan's laughter ringing through the pain.

"I don't believe you. But unlike some people, I'll allow you to keep your issues private."

"I don't have iss—" He caught himself in time. "We're more alike than we think, huh?"

"Could be. I distinctly remember telling you *I* didn't have issues." She grinned. "And what was your response?"

"We all have issues."

"It would appear so."

"You're enjoying this." If he were really lucky, maybe he could distract her from further prying.

"Am I enjoying turning the tables on calm, cool, collected Matthew Stone? You bet. Do I take pleasure in your pain? No. I've had too many of those nights myself, buddy." She patted his arm and rose. "If you ever want to talk about it, I'm all ears."

Her sudden departure left him wishing she'd pressed for details. Maybe it *was* time he talked to someone about it.

A few minutes later her voice came from the direction of the bed. He could visualize her leaning on her elbow in the dark, her brown hair spilling over her shoulder. "When did these dreams start?"

"I thought you weren't going to pry."

"I'm asking a very general question. That's not prying."

"You're walking a fine line."

"So humor me. When did they start?"

"When I was sixteen."

"And you were how old when you left Jonathon's Arizona compound?"

"Fifteen."

"Hmm."

"What?"

"If your dreams were connected with your life at the settlement, I would have thought they'd have started immediately after you left. But there's a gap."

"So it's probably not connected." He was testing her. Why?

To see how perceptive she really was. And how hard he'd have to work to keep her from discovering the truth.

"If you told me your whole story, I bet we'd find a connection there somewhere."

"But we agreed I'm not going to tell you my whole story."

"I agreed not to press. There's a difference."

He smiled in the dark. "Yes, a world of difference."

Which meant Angel would go through the back door to get the information she wanted. But her usual information sources wouldn't be any help, even if she could contact them. The root wasn't on record anywhere as far as he knew. He doubted there was even an official death certificate.

Matthew clamped down on his mental wanderings. Nothing good would come from speculation. He needed to know straight from the source what had happened the night his father died. His mother had only discussed it once, leaving more questions than answers. He'd have to confront Uncle Jonathon. What were the chances he'd tell the truth?

Slim to none.

Unless, of course, he was given the right incentive.

A familiar sense of purpose stole through Matthew's exhausted body and troubled mind. And along with it came the power he'd temporarily relinquished to his uncle. Things would be different this time. Very, very different.

ANGEL STUDIED JONATHON across the breakfast table the next morning. He was downright ebullient.

Eleanor hummed under her breath as she set a plate of pancakes in the center of the kitchen table. She'd been absolutely glowing throughout the meal preparations. The birthday sex must have been hot stuff.

"Smells wonderful." Jonathon inhaled deeply. "You've outdone yourself, ladies."

"It's nothing." Eleanor's smile dimmed a bit. Probably from having to share his praises with Ruth and Angel.

Angel didn't blame her. Eleanor had to share too much as it was without her birthday afterglow being up for grabs, too.

"Aunt Eleanor's a fabulous cook," Matthew added.

"She's the only one besides my mom who can make pancakes as fluffy as these."

Eleanor blanched.

Jonathon flushed.

Oops. Major faux pas, Matthew. His heart was in the right place, but the guy's sense of timing was atrocious.

Angel rose from her seat. "Eleanor, I almost forgot those lovely peaches you wanted me to set out. Where are they again?"

"In the root cellar. Do you remember where it is?"

"Yes, I do. I'll be back in a sec."

Eleanor nodded, the color returning to her face.

When Angel returned with the preserved peaches, everything seemed much as usual. Which meant Eleanor was back to her micromanaging self.

"Here, I've got bowls and spoons. Angel, you dish those out and Ruth can see that the children have some later for a snack."

"Yes, Eleanor," Angel and Ruth murmured in unison.

When Ruth and Angel were seated at the table again, Jonathon said the blessing. It wasn't nearly as long-winded as his dinner blessing. Maybe he wanted to get breakfast over with so he could leave. One evening under Eleanor's roof would last him for weeks—or so she'd heard.

"At church, someone mentioned a baby had been born last week. That's wonderful news." Angel hoped they'd talk about some of the other residents of the compound. As it was, she rarely saw anyone outside Jonathon's immediate family—sixty strong or so as it was—unless it was at church. Eleanor's sister wives seemed to avoid her. And Angel and Matthew rarely saw folks out and about when they took their afternoon walks.

"Yes, Leah blessed Brother Jamison with a good, healthy boy," Jonathon said. "She has stayed true to the principle and set an example for other young women to follow."

"I remember Brother Jamison from when I was a child. He seemed old as Methuselah then," Matthew commented.

"Matthew," Eleanor admonished. "Great wisdom is bestowed on our elders."

Great wisdom and a pinch of horny dust. Angel kept her eyes lowered demurely. She hid her smile behind her napkin.

Jonathon ate quickly, cutting his food in precise bites before shoveling them into his mouth. At last, he pushed his plate away. Eleanor jumped up to clear it from the table.

Angel opened her mouth to protest but shut it again. Eleanor should have finished her own meal while it was hot. But it was none of Angel's business.

When Eleanor returned, Jonathon cleared his throat, sitting straighter.

"I received a vision last night." He paused for effect. His voice took on a booming, godlike quality. "It is time for Matthew to take a second wife."

CHAPTER ELEVEN

ANGEL'S BLOOD WENT cold. She tried to catch Matthew's eye, but his attention was focused on Jonathon.

"I just married, Uncle. I want to spend time with Angel before we bring in another wife. And don't you think I should have my own home first?"

"Eleanor has room here. The bedroom next to yours is vacant, as a matter of fact. That will do until we can find housing for you."

"No, Uncle, absolutely not."

Jonathon's eyes narrowed. "Are you telling me you don't believe in the principle of plurality?"

"I didn't say that."

"Perhaps it was a mistake to bring you here, Matthew. You don't seem to be embracing our way of life. First you defy the elders and leave our fellowship at lunch. Now this."

"I need time to adjust."

"You've had time to adjust. I'm the spiritual leader. I've never been questioned when I received a prophecy."

"I'm not questioning your prophecy. I just need more time."

Angel shifted in her chair, wanting to help. As it was, she had to simply sit by and watch.

"There is no time." He leaned forward, his eyes

flashing. "The marriage will take place tomorrow morning in my study or you will leave Zion's Gate."

Matthew sighed. "May I ask who's been chosen as my bride?"

"Ruth will make an excellent addition to your household."

Angel gaped. Jonathon discussed adding a wife as if she were nothing more substantial than a new sofa. "Don't I have a say in this?"

"We'll discuss this later," Matthew warned.

"Of course you have a say in the choice of a sister wife." Jonathon's smile was tight. "However, a woman sets aside her own desires for the family's best interest. It is the husband who knows how the growth of the family will meld with the growth of the community."

I'm royally screwed. She glanced helplessly at Matthew.

Later, he mouthed.

"WHY DO YOU REFUSE to talk about it?" Angel demanded, peeling an orange.

"I'm not refusing to discuss it. I simply suggested we wait till after we've eaten."

"You're stalling."

"No, I'm not. I had enough tension with Jonathon at supper and breakfast. I'd like to have one meal where I can relax while I eat."

"Looks like you're done to me."

Matthew eyed the apple core and crumpled wax-paper wrapper on the blanket before him. Not a morsel left. He reached into the canvas bag and withdrew an orange. "See, I'm still eating."

Coward. She didn't say it. She didn't have to.

"Maybe I *am* stalling. But don't you think you can give me this one reprieve? I promise we'll talk before we go back."

"I guess so. Besides, there's nothing left to eat once you're done with the orange."

He peeled slowly.

"Here, let me do that." With her oval nails she removed the fibrous skin in a matter of seconds.

"Um, thank you."

"I live to make your life easier." Her grin was wicked.

"Sure you do."

Matthew picked up the wrappers from their lunch and put them in the bag. Then the orange peels. "Have you noticed we've started to sound like a married couple? You prodding me to talk, me retreating. Pretty cliché."

"Yeah, except most couples don't argue about bringing another wife into the family. What are we going to do, Matthew? Besides being morally reprehensible, it's illegal and beyond the scope of our cover. The government tends to frown on that kind of stuff."

"I'll think of something. It's really a pretty smart tactic on Jonathon's part. Tie us to the group and test my sincerity. And, of course, I'd be breaking the law, too."

"Possibly several laws—I doubt Ruth's over sixteen. Yes, Jonathon's intelligent and dangerous. Do you think he actually has visions?"

Shrugging, Matthew said, "From what I understand, Jonathon's visions usually further his agenda. That includes taking any woman he fancies."

"Like your mother?"

He nodded. "And Rebecca. He didn't care what effect his actions had on any of us. He wanted my mother because she and my father were deeply in love and he couldn't stand it. He wanted Rebecca because she looked so much like my mother when she was younger. Jonathon doesn't believe rules apply to him."

"You're describing a sociopath."

Hesitating, he said, "Yes, I guess I am."

"And yet you agreed to come back?"

"There are things you don't know about. I didn't have a choice."

"So tell me about those things."

"Not now."

"You always have a choice, Matt."

Wanting to deflect her curiosity, he turned the tables. "Did you? When Kent treated you so horribly, did you have a choice to leave or stay?"

Matthew had seen how devastating mind control could be and doubted she'd seen an alternative at the time.

Angel's eyes widened. "That's not fair."

"You made an absolute statement, no shades of gray. There isn't always a decent choice. Admit it."

"I had a choice." She avoided his gaze, intent on twisting her paper napkin into a corkscrew shape. "I wish I had done things differently. Maybe if I'd left him, Kent would have gotten help."

When she looked up, the intensity of her pain almost bowled him over. He had to get through to her. "You don't really believe that, do you?"

Angel met his gaze. "No, not really. Kent didn't think he needed help. He always said it was my fault. There was just something inside him lacking…. I guess he thought if he could control me, I'd keep thinking it was my fault and wouldn't discover that lack. But the controlling quickly became physical."

"You were fighting for your survival. No matter what

he told you, it wasn't your fault. It would have ended in someone's death no matter what you'd done."

Nodding, Angel said, "If I'd left, he would have hunted me down and killed me. Then he would have found another woman to love like he loved me. And the whole nightmare would have happened to someone else."

"You did the absolute best you could at the time, Angel. Kent manipulated reality until it seemed you had no choice." He grasped her hand. "I'll think of something. Some way to get out of this and still stay at Zion's Gate. Because if we leave now, the past weeks have been for nothing."

"We'll *have* to find another way. If you go along too much, it will destroy your soul. I've seen it happen undercover…and I lived it with Kent."

ANGEL PEELED OFF the dreadful gown and stepped into the shower. It had seemed like playing dress-up the first week. Now she longed for her own clothes. To express her individuality, maybe to reassure herself she was unique and had more to offer than the men at Zion's Gate allowed. Maybe to erase the outward appearance of a woman controlled by others.

Angel wished she'd brought a tight pair of jeans and a T-shirt with a male-bashing slogan written across the chest. Just to wear in the privacy of their room. Just long enough to maintain her own identity.

But she was too much of a professional to pack clothes that could be discovered. She might have been able to explain them away as coming from her previous life. But it simply wasn't worth the risk. Except in moments like these.

She washed her hair, daydreaming of her own

cherry-almond shampoo. And a high-end conditioner, not this crud from the dollar store that left her hair dry and brittle.

After a nice long shower, Angel knew she'd be in for a lecture from Eleanor, who carefully monitored hot-water usage.

She made a face in the mirror as she pulled the putrid pink nightgown over her head. Back to being a meek Zion's Gate wife.

The room was dim when she emerged from the bathroom. Matthew's form was discernible on the floor. He'd been unusually quiet all evening. But who could blame him, with the specter of wife number two on the horizon and wife number one harping on him like crazy. Maybe polygamy wasn't all it was cracked up to be.

Finding her way to the bed, she scooted beneath the covers.

"I had a vision." His voice was low.

"Say what?"

"I had a vision. My own prophecy."

"Do tell." He wasn't serious, was he?

"I'm supposed to get you pregnant before I take a second wife."

"Don't even think about it, Matt."

"Not for real. It's a pretty good stall, though, you have to admit."

"It might just work. Isn't plurality supposed to promote lots and lots of children?"

"Yes. So it's my duty as a husband to make sure you're expecting a bundle of redemption before I go on to, um, pollinate other flowers."

"Matthew, you are such a geek." Relief flooded through her.

"At times. I've been told it's an endearing quality."

"Who told you that? Your mother?"

"As a matter of fact, she did."

Angel laughed. "I knew it."

"It *was* confirmed by a few of my girlfriends."

RUTH WAS CONSPICUOUSLY absent the next morning during breakfast preparations. Getting ready for the nuptials, Angel supposed. Boy, would she be disappointed.

Angel couldn't help being uneasy about the up-coming confrontation between Matthew and Jon-athon. But if she was unusually quiet, Eleanor didn't appear to notice, probably chalking it up to first-wife pique. She chatted more than usual to make up for Angel's silence.

According to Eleanor, yesterday had been Jona-thon's anniversary with wife number five, so he'd spent the night at her house.

Angel pondered the intricate dance of the polygamist marriage. No wonder Jonathon needed a day planner to tell him where he would spend the night. She figured between anniversaries and birthdays for twelve-plus wives, the man kept a tight conjugal schedule. One more wife and the whole house of cards might fall.

Matthew entered the kitchen, kissing Eleanor on the cheek. "Morning, Aunt."

She glanced sideways at him. "Nervous?"

"A little."

"Good. It's a solemn vow you're taking. Whether it's your first wife or thirtieth."

Angel shuddered at the number.

Matthew held his tongue. He was obviously smart enough to tell Jonathon first. The element of surprise was good. Besides, it wouldn't do to publicly challenge Jonathon's authority.

Breakfast was a quiet affair, with a hum of expectation barely contained by eating. Eleanor seemed especially intent on presenting a happy face. "Things will be much the same around here. Except the men will move Ruth's things into the room next to yours."

"And my husband will be sleeping with another woman." Angel meant the remark to be offhand. Instead her voice was infused with pain.

Eleanor tut-tutted, her eyes warm with concern.

It was a good thing she and Matthew had decided Angel should appear troubled by the upcoming ceremony. As someone new to Zion's Gate, she would understandably have a hard time accepting another wife so soon.

Angel folded her napkin and set it beside her plate. "Excuse me. I seem to have lost my appetite. Please notify me when Jonathon arrives."

She rose and started to leave the kitchen.

Eleanor rose. "Angel—"

"Let her be. She'll be fine," Matthew murmured.

Angel climbed the stairs to their room, suddenly very, very tired.

CHAPTER TWELVE

JONATHON ARRIVED, followed by Ruth and a dour-looking older man and an even more dour-looking woman, who appeared to be a good fifteen years his junior.

"Matthew, have you met Ruth's parents, George and Alma Hearst? They joined us several years ago."

"No, I don't believe I have." Matthew shook hands with the man, nodded to the woman.

"Where's Angel?" Jonathon asked.

"She was…upset."

"I'll go get her," Aunt Eleanor offered.

"No, that's not necessary. Uncle Jonathon, I'd like to speak with you in private please."

"We're in a hurry, Matthew. Can't this wait?"

"No, it can't."

His uncle frowned. "Then come with me."

He turned to Eleanor. "I imagine the Hearsts would enjoy a cup of herbal tea and some of that pie, if you have any left."

"Yes, I do," murmured Eleanor. "George, Alma, please have a seat at the table. I'll brew more tea and get the pie."

Matthew followed Jonathon down the hall toward the study, his steps heavy.

Jonathon gestured to a chair as he lowered himself into a padded leather chair. "Sit. This better be important."

Matthew did as instructed. He felt like a fifteen-year-old again, screwing up the courage to confront a man who was the epitome of authority. "It is important. Uncle…I received a vision last night."

"Oh?" He steepled his hands.

"Very similar to the one I had telling me Angel was meant to be my bride."

Jonathon's face relaxed. He nodded. "Confirming your union to Ruth."

"Not exactly. An angel appeared, holding an infant. *My* son. He said Angel is destined to give me many sons, but I must make her content as a wife first. Only then will she conceive. And I must not take another wife until that occurs."

"Your vision is rather…coincidental."

Like yours? Matthew longed to grab the man by the neck and shake him till his teeth rattled and he admitted what a selfish, evil piece of crap he was.

He took a deep breath and controlled his anger. He couldn't afford to be impulsive in this conversation. Shrugging, he said, "I can't control when I receive a vision. Possibly it was a warning before I entered into a union with Ruth. A warning I intend to heed."

"We have a problem then." Jonathon leaned back in his chair. "Because your vision contradicts mine. Surely you don't believe you have been chosen above me as prophet."

"I would prefer to think my vision merely clarifies the timing of yours. The angel didn't forbid my marriage to Ruth but simply indicated Angel needed to conceive our son first."

"And if I choose not to heed your prophecy? If I insist you go through with the marriage to Ruth today?"

Matthew met Jonathon's gaze without flinching.

His resolve was strong. "Then Angel and I will leave immediately."

Jonathon closed his eyes as if in pain. Or deep thought.

The minutes stretched on. Matthew remained still, suspecting his uncle wanted to intimidate him through silence.

Finally Jonathon opened his eyes. "I have meditated on your vision. You will have the opportunity to father an heir with Angel. Once Angel conceives, Ruth will become your wife."

Matthew exhaled slowly. "Yes, sir."

"I will break the news to Ruth and her parents. It would be best if you and Angel retire to your room for the remainder of the day. I'll tell Eleanor to bring you a tray at mealtime."

In other words, stay out of Ruth's way and get busy on impregnating Angel.

"Yes, sir."

"Please ask George and Alma to come in when you leave."

Matthew nodded. He rose and went to the kitchen, where Ruth's parents were finishing their pie.

"George, Alma, Jonathon would like to speak to you."

Eleanor frowned, a question in her eyes.

He shook his head slightly. "I'll be upstairs."

When he closed the bedroom door behind him, he felt ten years older.

Angel sat up in bed, rubbing her eyes. Her face was tear-stained. "Is Jonathon here?"

"Yes, he's here. I've already spoken to him."

"You were supposed to come get me."

"I thought it best if I talked to him alone. These things are handled by men."

"That's a load of bull."

"Yes, it is. But did you really expect anything different?"

She sighed. "No. I'd hoped the reports of a strict patriarchy were exaggerated. How did it go?"

"It was difficult. I don't know if he bought the whole prophecy thing. He did mention it was rather coincidental."

"And his wasn't?"

He nodded. "I thought the same thing. He was pretty ticked because he thought my vision trumped his. But I pointed out mine merely clarified the timing of his prophecy."

"And that was okay?"

"He still wasn't thrilled. But after five minutes of intense meditation, he agreed to humor me."

"That's a relief."

"Yes, it is. Because I told him otherwise we would have to leave immediately."

Angel's eyes widened. "That was a huge gamble."

"One I was prepared to follow through on. You were right. There's a limit to how much I can pretend to agree with before I lose my integrity. I worked too hard to become a man of principle."

"I'm impressed. I know it wasn't easy taking a stand against your uncle. And though it was my mission you were gambling with, too, I have to respect you for it."

He stepped closer and touched her cheek. "Your respect means a lot, Angelina."

She met his gaze. Her lips parted.

There was a knock at the door.

Matthew rubbed her jaw with his thumb, then regretfully walked to the door.

"Yes?" he opened the door.

Eleanor stood on the other side, her expression unreadable. "Jonathon said you and Angel were not to be disturbed today except for lunch at eleven-thirty and supper at six. George and Ruth's brothers will be moving her things in next door. I just wanted to warn you there might be noise."

"Um, yes, thank you for letting me know."

She hesitated. "Is Angel well?"

"She'll be fine."

Eleanor nodded. "Angel is not like us, but she's a good girl. Take care of her."

A lump formed in his throat. "Thank you."

She nodded and went back down the stairs.

He closed the door quietly behind him, smiling in bemusement.

"Was that Eleanor?"

"Yes. She wanted to let us know there might be some noise next door. George and Ruth's brothers are bringing Ruth's things."

"Still? I wouldn't think they'd want a single woman in such close proximity with a man of reproductive age."

"We're betrothed now. If anything sexual happens, they'll have me marry her in a heartbeat."

"It sounds as if they're hoping something happens. Dangling a young girl in front of your face."

"You could be right. It may be Uncle Jonathon's underhanded plan to get his own way. Or it might be a way to get someone to spy on us. Don't ever underestimate his influence."

"We'll be careful. And you better make sure you're never alone with Ruth. One accusation from her and you're a bigamist."

"Of course." He hadn't really viewed Ruth as a sexual being until now. The thought was discomfiting.

"Have we been sent to our room as punishment, like naughty children?"

"Jonathon's a smart old SOB. He's keeping us from crossing paths with Ruth until the sting of delayed nuptials wears off. And giving me the green light to get you pregnant right away."

"Matthew!"

He chuckled. "And here I thought you were a tough-as-nails woman of the world. You sound downright scandalized."

"It's just knowing they think we're up here going at it like rabbits." She pressed her hands to her cheeks.

"You're blushing."

"I *don't* blush."

"Sure you do. And you're doing it now."

She glared at him. "Say it again and I'll have to hurt you, Matt."

He held up his hands. "I'll stop. You might as well get comfortable. We'll be here a while."

"This is about as comfortable as it gets." She gestured to her dress. "I don't have any jeans or sweat-pants. And my nightgown isn't much better than this glorified gunnysack."

Matthew's neck itched at the thought of the high collar she wore. He went to the closet and flipped through his sport shirts. He chose a shirt and tossed it to her. "Here."

She grasped the soft cotton as if it were cashmere. "I can wear it? Really?"

"You can *have* it. My mother bought it during one of her more misguided shopping trips."

"Yeah, I wouldn't have you pegged as a lavender-and-teal kind of guy."

"You'd be doing me a favor to take it off my hands."

"Gladly." Her eyes sparkled with excitement as she scooted off the bed. "I'll go change."

When Angel returned a few minutes later, his breath caught in his chest. She'd unbuttoned the top two buttons, exposing the hollow at her throat. The hem hit her midthigh. After only two weeks at Zion's Gate, it was the equivalent of parading in front of him in pasties and a thong.

"You look much better in it than I do." His voice came out slightly strangled.

She tugged the hem lower. "Don't suppose you have a pair of sweatpants I could borrow, too?"

"No, but I've got a pair of basketball shorts." He removed the shorts from a dresser drawer and handed them to her.

"You're sure you don't mind?"

"Positive." Otherwise he'd be taking a lot of cold showers in the days to come. Especially if Jonathon kept them sequestered.

ANGEL AWOKE SLIGHTLY disoriented. She glanced around, noting Matthew slouched in the straight-backed chair, reading his Bible.

Glancing at her watch, she was dismayed to see it was only two o'clock.

She smothered a yawn, saying, "You don't look very comfortable."

"I'm not."

"You can sit on the bed as long as you promise to behave."

He raised an eyebrow. "Haven't I been the perfect gentleman?"

"I suppose so. With the exception of watching me sleep when we were in the hotel. That was creepy."

"I explained." He grinned. "Not well, but I explained."

She sat up, propping the pillow behind her. "Yeah, you've gotten better at thinking on your feet. You want to play more Scrabble?"

"No way. I'll only win again, and you don't accept defeat well."

"So I'm a little competitive. Sue me."

"Didn't you bring any reading material?"

"*Guns & Ammo* or *Law Enforcement Digest* might have been a dead giveaway. I've already read the one home-decorating magazine I brought about fifty times."

"I wouldn't have figured you for the decorating kind."

"Hey, I can paint and craft with the best of them. It's a hobby of mine. Relieves stress. I did this really cool mosaic one weekend."

"I'm impressed. That took a lot of patience, and you don't impress me as the patient kind."

"I can be plenty patient. What'd you bring? Maybe I can read some of your stuff."

"I've got a few investment magazines."

She made a face. "Sounds dry."

"Not to me. It's how I make my living."

He went to his suitcase and unzipped the outer compartment. He withdrew two magazines. Padding barefoot, he came over to the bed, tossing them down beside her. "Give them a try. It's that or my Bible."

"I'll read the investment stuff, thank you very much."

"Suit yourself." He shrugged, retrieving his Bible and returning to the bed. He wedged the second pillow against the headboard and leaned back with a sigh. "Yes, this is much better."

Angel chose the first magazine. Articles on multi-stream investment income and mutual funds practically made her eyes cross with boredom. The second magazine was even drier than the first. She set it aside, longing for her Martha Stewart collection. Glancing around at the spare furnishings, she figured Eleanor could use a subscription. Maybe she'd send her one for Christmas. But that was probably verboten, too. Jonathon probably wouldn't want her to have anything frivolous.

"It's hard to concentrate with you huffing and sighing over there." Matthew's tone held a touch of annoyance.

"Your reading selection sucks."

"So sue me."

"It didn't take them long to move in Ruth's stuff next door. Of course, around here, a woman probably isn't allowed much."

"As long as it's functional."

"Why does everything have to be functional? Why can't a woman have something because it's beautiful or makes her smile?"

"I don't know. You'd have to ask Jonathon. My mom could have used a twelve-step program for all her knickknack collecting after we left the group. I never thought about it much, but I bet that's the reason."

"And she shops a lot, too, doesn't she?"

"Yes. Buys some of the most useless stuff."

"*Exactly.* She has choices."

He shrugged. "Probably."

"You don't care?"

"Not really. Her shopping is a quirk. I love her, quirks and all."

"But you don't care about the underlying psychological reason for her obsession with shopping and collecting?" Did the man not have an inquisitive bone in his body?

"No, I don't. I've delved into the past about as much as I'm comfortable. Now I'd like to concentrate here." He gave her a pointed glare.

"Sure. Go ahead. Read your book. While I sit here and die of boredom. I'm not used to inactivity, you know. I should be out jogging or on the shooting range. Not sitting here with only investment magazines to entertain me."

"You're not going to shut up, are you?"

She crossed her arms over her chest. "No, I'm not. Misery loves company."

He carefully closed his Bible and handed it to her. "Here, try this. It's got every story known to man in it. Lust, murder, romance, redemption—it's all there."

She picked up the book. "Really? I never got much past the begetting part."

"Start with the New Testament. Matthew, for instance. It might spark your interest more. Or look up subjects in the back."

Angel was intrigued in spite of herself. She opened the book and starting flipping through until a header caught her attention. "King David was one flawed guy," she commented.

"He was human. But a great leader, too."

"So what makes him different than someone like Jonathon?"

"David lost his way for a while, but he ultimately turned to God for guidance. Jonathon believes he *is* God."

Another header caught her attention. Matthew was right—there were some intense stories. "Hmm. Why don't you look at that finance magazine. I'm trying to read."

His chuckle barely registered.

A few minutes later she checked the index for the reference on love. She wanted to find the passage Matthew had read to her their first night at Zion's Gate. Something about love being patient and kind…

A knock at their door drew her out of her reading. Surely it couldn't be suppertime already?

Matthew answered the door and returned with a tray. His eyes glinted with amusement, but fortunately he didn't say I told you so. Otherwise she would have to kill him.

"Okay, so there're some interesting stories. No big deal. Just don't think you've converted me."

"I would never think I've made an impact on you."

"Good. What's for supper? I'm starving."

He peeled back the foil keeping their plates warm. "Mmm. Pot roast. Mashed potatoes and gravy. Baby carrots. A green salad. Eleanor's outdone herself. And shorthanded in the kitchen, too."

"I feel bad leaving her with all that work while I'm lounging around up here doing nothing. Ruth's hardly any help in the kitchen."

"Can't be avoided. You've gotta pick your battles, and I'd say this is a pretty decent alternative to a second wife." He brightened. "Hey, if Ruth's no help in the kitchen, it's a good thing I have a wife who can cook."

Angel swung a pillow at him, missing his head by inches, just as she'd intended.

They ate supper in companionable silence. Angel stacked the dishes and utensils on the tray and placed it outside the door.

Angel paced the room, wondering if she could jog

in place and not appear odd. Probably not. Besides, she was feeling a bit exposed in Matthew's basketball shorts, even though they reached her calves.

Sighing, she didn't feel like reading anymore. And she wasn't tired, so another nap was out of the question. "You're sure they confiscated the pack of cards?"

"Positive. I'd forgotten they were forbidden. Might encourage gambling."

"I could go for a game of Solitaire right now. Or poker."

"Gambling."

"I see their point. Are you any good at charades?"

"Nope. And I have no intention of trying." He sat down on the bed and pulled out a pad of paper. His movements were sure as he used the pen to bisect the paper into columns.

"What're you doing?"

"Graphing some ideas I have for a long-term business plan. I'm about due for an update. But without my laptop, I'm useless."

"You're sure this assistant of yours has everything under control?"

"Yes, Marlene's as capable as they come. I streamlined my holdings before I left, so she could handle it."

"I bet it was hard letting go and allowing someone else to have complete control over your business, your livelihood."

"I hedged my bets as best I could. And I have confidence in Marlene. But, yes, it was extremely difficult."

"Then why'd you do it?"

"I have a duty to find Rebecca and make sure she's all right. And let her know our mother is gravely ill."

Angel got the impression he wasn't telling her the whole reason. "Did anyone pressure you?"

"Besides my mother and my conscience? One federal agent implied they'd be looking closely at my mother's finances if I didn't cooperate. She's been offered immunity from any welfare fraud Jonathon may have committed."

"Your mom's not sitting on a pile of money. Or at least that's what I, um, understand."

"I know you were provided with a profile on me and my family. I'm not offended. I would have done the same thing. As a matter of fact, I *did* the same thing."

"You investigated me?" The thought didn't sit well. Not only was she unaccustomed to being on the receiving end of a background investigation, it made her nervous to know someone had been nosing through her personal information.

"Yes, standard business practice. It's only prudent."

"Did you, um, uncover anything about my marriage to Kent?"

He shook his head. "No. Didn't go that deep, though I did wonder why Fort Worth College had no record of you under the name Angel or Angelina Harrison."

Angel breathed a sigh of relief. "I just don't want people to know about that time unless I choose to tell them. And when I started with DPS, I didn't want to be treated differently because of what I'd been through. My superiors knew, but nobody else."

"I can understand that. I don't tell many people where I came from. They'd think I was a freak. Besides, I was taught not to talk to outsiders. Silence is a hard habit to break."

"It *is* hard, isn't it? Getting to know people. Trying to decide when to tell them about your past. Wondering if they'll accept you or blow you off."

"Yes. I have a few close friends. I date women who don't expect a lot of shared confidences. It's a comfortable life, I'm not complaining."

Yet his voice contained a trace of wistfulness. As if he'd resigned himself to being on the outside looking in. Or was she merely projecting her own feelings, as her counselor had once told her?

Shaking her head, she refused to be drawn into a discussion of a time that was better left forgotten. Or, if not forgotten, buried so deep it was difficult to uncover.

Angel picked up the Bible. "I'm gonna read some more while you do your business plan or whatever it is."

Matthew nodded. His voice was tinged with relief when he said, "Yes, my business plan." He didn't seem eager to take a trip down memory lane, either.

Angel opened the book, but none of the print registered. Instead her mind traveled down the "what if" paths that drove her crazy. What if she hadn't met Kent? Hadn't married him? Had left him the first time he'd raised his hand to her?

She heard movement on the other side of the wall. At first she thought it was a mouse. Then she remembered Ruth.

"Sounds like our neighbor is retiring early. We'll have to be sure we're careful about not being overheard."

Matthew glanced up from the paper. "Yes. Unless, of course, we want to be."

"What do you mean?"

He grinned. "Here, I'll show you."

He leaned forward, removed the pillow from behind his back and rocked back into the headboard. His shoulder made a dull thud.

Angel raised her eyebrow.

Matthew pulled himself to a kneeling position, facing the wall. He leaned forward experimentally. The headboard tapped lightly against the wall. He motioned for her to join him.

Angel's cheeks grew warm when she realized what he was doing. To their next-door neighbor it would sound as if the newlyweds were making love.

She raised up on her knees next to Matthew and rocked forward experimentally. Her rhythm was off, countering his movement and making it less effective. Concentrating, she matched her motion with his.

Angel grinned when the headboard made a satisfying thump against the wall. The playacting would show Ruth that Matthew loved his wife passionately.

Matthew increased the tempo.

"Not much staying power?" she whispered, matching his rhythm.

"I can keep this pace all night long."

Angel thought of how ridiculous they probably looked and stifled a giggle. The banging of the headboard masked her voice when she said. "Yeah, maybe in the land of make-believe, Matt."

"Angelina, that sounds like a challenge." Interest flashed in his eyes. "Perhaps I'll take you up on that challenge someday."

"Not on your life, Romeo."

He shrugged. "Suit yourself."

"I will."

CHAPTER THIRTEEN

BREAKFAST THE NEXT morning was uncomfortable at best. Freakish at worst.

Angel was grateful to keep her gaze focused on her plate. Staring at scrambled eggs was preferable to having to face Matthew's knowing glances.

They shared a new intimacy that unnerved her. Almost as if they'd spent the whole night making love, not just simulating the sounds for inquiring minds.

And meeting Eleanor's gaze was even more disconcerting. The twinkle in her eye told Angel she figured there would be one more pregnant woman in the settlement soon. What's more, her warmth toward Angel and Matthew said she'd be tickled to hold their child and treat it as her own grandchild.

Angel swallowed hard, telling herself there was absolutely nothing appealing in that tableau. The whole wife/mother thing wasn't meant for her. And the close cocoon of family she felt with Matthew and Eleanor was a stress-induced hallucination. Stockholm syndrome multiplied by latent maternal instincts.

"Did you sleep well, Sister Angel?" Ruth asked.

"Yes, quite well, thank you."

"Good. I'm hoping for a June wedding."

Obviously they'd convinced the girl they were serious about making a baby. June was two months away.

Matthew sputtered, coughing violently. His face turned red.

"Matthew, sweetheart, are you all right?" Angel asked.

"Um, yes, went down the wrong pipe."

"Perhaps your tea is too hot. Would you like me to get an ice cube?" The solicitousness in her voice might have fooled another man.

Matthew's eyes narrowed. "No, Angelina, the tea is fine."

She turned to Ruth, her voice syrupy-sweet. "Did you sleep well last night?"

"I was a bit…restless."

I'll bet you were.

"I hope Matthew and I didn't wake you."

Ruth flushed. "No. Not at all."

"Good. I was afraid we might have been…enthusiastic."

Eleanor frowned. Private things were kept private, a cardinal rule at Zion's Gate. Apparently double entendres included.

"Enthusiastic with our prayers of course," Angel amended.

Matthew had another coughing attack. Baiting Ruth and watching Matthew's reaction could be fun. If Eleanor didn't take a switch to her behind. And judging by the woman's glare, it was a distinct possibility.

"I, um, better get going. Don't want to be late for the elders' meeting."

"I'll count the minutes while you're gone."

"Um, yes, me, too." Matthew rose and took his plate

to the kitchen. He'd scraped his plate and was out the door before Eleanor could protest.

Eleanor chuckled. "Matthew seems a bit...distracted this morning."

"Uh-huh." Angel sipped her juice, trying to assume a dreamy expression.

Ruth made a strangled sound and jumped up. "I have lessons to go over before I teach the children this morning."

Angel smiled and waved two fingers. "Ta-ta."

"You will reap what you sow." Eleanor's mouth was a straight line of disapproval.

"I beg your pardon?"

"You'll be living with that woman. If you are unkind to her now, it will come back to haunt you later. You will need the support and cooperation of your sister wife."

"To take my husband off my hands when I'm too tired to make love? I think not."

"What about when your children are sick with the flu and you're bone-tired. Who will pitch in to help?"

"Their father, that's who."

Eleanor grasped her hand. "You must forget those kind of fairy tales, Angel. They'll only break your heart. Your sister wives can make all the difference in your peace and security."

"What about my husband?"

Eleanor shrugged. "It may seem like Matthew is the center of your world. But as time goes on you will see him less and less. After children arrive, you will be busy with other things. Soon his visits will be no more than a pleasant diversion."

"Or a pain in the ass."

Eleanor grinned but quickly recovered her stern face.

"Your language is most unseemly. And you may not believe me, but there will be times you will be glad your husband has many wives."

"Wait a minute, we were talking one more wife. Now you're expanding to *many* wives?"

"You need to face facts, Angel. Matthew is destined for a leadership role. Leaders have many wives, many children, securing their place in heaven."

Angel bit back a curse. Taking a couple deep breaths, she managed to control her temper. "So I better be nice to Ruth because she'll be more of a companion than my husband?"

Eleanor shrugged. "Possibly."

The door opened and Sister Beatrice marched through, followed by a line of children. Quiet, serious children. They didn't push or shove or chatter.

"Go on up, Beatrice. Ruth is waiting for you."

The plain woman nodded, leading the children up the stairs.

When the echo of their footsteps receded, Angel picked up the thread of their conversation. "What if I don't want my marriage to be the way you've described?"

"Then you must search your heart and decide whether a life devoted to the principle is what you want."

"And if I don't?"

"Leave and never look back. Matthew has his destiny. You can either help him achieve that through the principle or you can leave him now before either of you gets too attached."

"I'm already attached." Angel swallowed hard. The words resonated in the air between them.

"Then you have no choice, dear. You will stay and make the best home possible for your husband."

Angel felt as if the walls were closing in on her. The kitchen had suddenly become stifling. She wanted nothing more than to don Matthew's basketball shorts, knot his T-shirt at her waist and jog for several miles. But that wouldn't be *seemly*.

"Let's be quick cleaning up breakfast." Eleanor was a bit too cheerful. "Then I'll tell Ruth we'll be in the garden."

"The garden?" Angel's spirits rose.

"Yes. I convinced Jonathon you are deserving of increased responsibilities. There's weeding that needs to be done. And we can pick greens for a salad this evening."

Angel hugged the older woman. "You're a life saver."

"So I've been told." Her voice was dry, but her smile was kind.

Eleanor was so different from Angel's mother, yet in some ways very similar. Angel hadn't thought to find a strong woman here at Zion's Gate. Only weak, pathetic women. The thought made her pause. Maybe she'd overgeneralized? It was something to consider while she gardened.

Angel hummed while she washed dishes in record time. Eleanor dried. When the last utensil was in the drawer, Eleanor removed her apron. "I'll tell Ruth, then we'll be on our way."

She was back in a jiff, carrying two large brimmed hats. Contemporary sun hats, by the looks of them.

She accepted the hat, commenting, "I would have expected bonnets."

"Oh, no." Eleanor placed hers on her head. "We haven't worn bonnets in at least five years."

"Really?" Angel squeaked.

"Of course." Eleanor's smile was wide, her eyes glinting with mischief.

"You're teasing me."

"Yes, I guess I am."

Angel chuckled as she followed the older woman out the door. Today certainly seemed a whole lot brighter than yesterday. What a difference twenty-four hours could make.

Eleanor set a brisk pace as they hiked through the compound. Angel figured there were at least two groupings of houses she hadn't yet seen.

Though the homes were generic Mexican structures, she studied the details as they went by, imagining the families who lived there. Wondering if the women were happy, if they were well treated.

Perspiration trickled down her sides. Her face was warm due to the now-unaccustomed cardio work. Yet Eleanor seemed unfazed.

"I'd swear you were a distance runner, Eleanor. Do you have a StairMaster hidden away somewhere."

"StairMaster?"

"Exercise machine."

The woman chuckled. "No. I walk every morning before breakfast. I used to walk in the evenings before it was prohibited by curfew."

"You should be able to walk when you want."

"Curfew encourages the young people to stay in with their families instead of out getting into trouble."

"As if they *could* find trouble here."

Eleanor glanced sideways at her. "You'd be surprised. High-spirited youth can find trouble in the most unlikely places."

"Were you high-spirited in your youth?"

Her smile was wistful. "At times. I fancied myself in love with a neighbor boy."

"This neighbor boy wasn't Jonathon, I take it?"

"No. My love for the boy was childish and never meant to be. I accepted it when my father chose Jonathon."

"Did you know Jonathon well?"

"Well enough to know my parents were right. We would suit."

"What happened to the neighbor boy?"

Eleanor frowned. "He left our group shortly after I married. It was difficult for him to see me with Jonathon."

"What about you? Was it difficult seeing him? Did you want something you couldn't have?"

"I made peace with my destiny."

"That's a pretty cryptic statement."

"Yes, it is. We're almost there."

Angel glanced up. "That's the biggest garden I've ever seen." There was a blanket of green bordered by the tan of the desert.

"We grow the majority of our own produce. We also plant additional to sell at market."

"Yes, Matthew mentioned he might be going in to town for the farmer's market. This is going to sound like a nosy question, but what else do you do for income?"

"Our needs are simple. Many of the younger women transcribe medical records. The men pick up the tapes when they're in town. And some of the men have jobs."

"What about government assistance?" Angel had heard tales of widespread abuse among some of the polygamist families.

Eleanor's mouth tightened. "A few of the needier families receive government aid."

"You don't approve, though?"

"No. We should care for our own. Taking anything from the government is dangerous. I told Jonathon it would come back to haunt us someday."

"Not if it's legitimate."

"Our people have been persecuted for centuries. If the outside world wants to harm us, they will use any means at their disposal."

Angel swallowed hard. What would Eleanor think if she knew Angel was with the government? She had the sinking feeling her friendship with Eleanor would be short-lived.

"Here we go."

Angel inhaled deeply, reveling in the sweet aroma of soil and sun. "It seems cooler."

"The plants and the moisture in the soil reduce the temperature. It's my favorite place to be in the hotter months, when it's difficult to be outside otherwise."

"I can see why. It's peaceful."

"Yes. And when there are many of us here with the children, it's festive. Much laughter, much sharing."

Angel felt a stab of envy. The company of a group of women wasn't something she'd ever enjoyed. She'd had one or two close friends but never felt the solidarity of a group. And as an only child, she'd missed the companionship of brothers and sisters.

Eleanor walked the rows, eyeing the plants carefully. "It looks like the tomato plants could use attention. We'll pinch off the suckers and look for hornworms."

"Suckers? Hornworms?" Angel hated to sound ignorant, but she didn't have a clue what the woman was talking about.

"Here, I'll show you what the suckers are." Eleanor

knelt down next to a bushy plant containing loads of green tomatoes. "See, here, where the stem makes a V?"

Angel nodded.

"This shoot emerging is called a sucker. You just pinch it like this." She demonstrated, with the poor little shoot euthanized in seconds.

"Isn't the whole point to grow plants that are big and strong?"

"Yes. But if we allow the plant to keep producing unlimited stems, then it will use valuable energy that should be directed toward bearing tomatoes."

"Ah. Conserving energy."

"Yes, in a way. You go ahead and start at that end and we'll meet in the middle. If you see any green caterpillars, pull them off the plant and step on them."

Angel shuddered. "And I thought gardening was a peaceful pastime."

"It's like anything else—you take the good with the bad. Go ahead and start, we don't have all day."

Trudging to the end of the row, she hoped the caterpillars were heading out of town. Funny, she could kill a man if she had to, but the thought of crushing a worm made her slightly nauseous.

Fortunately she didn't run into any. Angel hummed as she found suckers and pinched them off. There was something surprisingly satisfying in the action. As if she was really nurturing the plant, coaxing it to grow in a healthy manner.

The repetitive motion combined with the warmth of the sun on her back lulled her into an almost hypnotic state.

So much so that Eleanor's voice startled her when she asked, "How did you meet Matthew?"

Angel was so relaxed she found it hard to remember

the scripted story. "I was in Phoenix on business. We literally ran into each other at a deli near his condo. My soda spilled, he tried to help. We ended up eating lunch together, and the rest is history."

"Matthew saw a vision telling him you were to be his wife?"

"Yes. At first, I didn't buy it. But Matthew can be persuasive."

Eleanor smiled. "Yes, he can."

"It was a whirlwind courtship, but I feel like I've known him for years." Either the lie rolled off her tongue way too easily or it was the truth.

"He was a special boy. Now he's an extraordinary man."

"Yes, he is."

"Matthew has a soft heart that he tries to hide. I'm glad you decided to stay and devote yourself to creating a home under the guidance of the principle. I'm afraid his heart would have been broken if you'd left."

Matt must've been laying it on thick with his aunt. "I would never intentionally hurt Matthew."

"But if you stay, you must know there's no going back for Matthew. You must be totally committed."

"I know what I'm getting into."

"I hope so. For your sake. And for Matthew's."

"When did Ruth move into your house? Isn't that unusual?"

"A few months ago. I've always been responsible for schooling Jonathon's children, but it had gotten to be too much for me. Jonathon felt it would be helpful if Ruth lived in my home, having easier access to the children and allowing them to bond with her. He felt she could help with chores."

"None of your sister wives share your home?"

"No. When Jonathon brought us to Zion's Gate, he had housing built so each of us could have our own home."

"Darn nice of him."

"It's better than some. I enjoy having my own home."

"Except when you have to share it with Ruth, Matt and me."

Eleanor shrugged. "Now that my seven boys are gone, it's rather quiet. I don't mind having you and Matthew stay—Matthew was always one of my favorites. And you keep me on my toes."

Angel laughed. "My mom says the same thing."

"She doesn't mind you coming to live here?"

"She'd rather I didn't, but she understands the need for me to live my own life. Are all your children here at Zion's Gate?" Angel vaguely remembered meeting a few of the sons.

"All but Austin, my youngest. He's in Salt Lake City." The wistfulness in her voice touched Angel.

She cleared her throat. "I didn't know. That must be hard."

"Very. He was asked to leave."

"Jonathon's son was asked to leave? I didn't think that happened."

"Austin is a very handsome young man. And full of himself, as boys his age often are."

"So what did he do that was so bad?"

"Defied curfew. Sneaked out to meet a girl."

Angel chose her words carefully. "I can understand Jonathon being ticked off about the teenage-rebellion stuff. But casting him out? Isn't that a little harsh?"

Eleanor nodded, swiping the back of her hand across her eyes. "I begged Jonathon to give him another chance. But he was adamant. Austin made the mistake of sneaking out to meet a girl one of the elders intended to take to wife."

"I see. I never thought Jonathon would allow that to happen to his own son."

"Neither did I. But the elders demanded he leave. And since Austin had been caught defying the curfew, there was no defense for him. Jonathon is very strict about honoring the curfew. For good reason."

"You didn't have the curfew in Arizona?"

"It was more reasonable. Nine o'clock instead of dark."

"I wonder what changed?"

"Jonathon says it's because we're on the border. There are all sorts of unsavory characters who prey on the unsuspecting."

"That's probably the truth. *Coyotes* smuggling Mexican citizens into the U.S. to work. Drug dealers protecting their turf…"

Eleanor's eyes narrowed. "You are very well informed on the happenings along the border."

"It's in the papers almost every day. Unfortunately a lot of crime spills over into the U.S."

"Yes, I suppose so."

"Do you ever talk to Austin?"

"At first, he called. Jonathon has limited his calls to special occasions like Mother's Day. Once in a while I'll get a letter he's managed to pass through another member."

"He can't mail it to you through the post office?"

"No, it's better this way."

Angel touched the other woman's shoulder. "Is Jonathon keeping him from writing to you?"

"I don't know." Eleanor's fingers were nimble as she plucked suckers from the plant. "I never received any letters through the mail from him, though Austin swears he wrote."

Fury welled up in Angel. She remembered the helplessness of being cut off from loved ones. "You can't allow him to do that, Eleanor. You have to take a stand or Jonathon will continue to control every aspect of your life. Soon you won't have anyone but Jonathon."

"That's silly, Angel. I have my other children. And my sister wives' children. That's enough."

"What about that hole in your heart where Austin should be?"

"Sometimes a woman has to sacrifice her individual needs for the good of the family. The good of the group."

Bullshit.

Angel took a deep breath and remembered her purpose. Her cover was of primary importance. She would sacrifice her personal need to help Eleanor in order to fulfill her mission for the good of the whole. Was she really any more evolved? Or simply serving a different master?

Closing her eyes, Angel wished she'd never agreed to this mission. Because she was becoming emotionally involved. Not only could it be disastrous for the mission, she suspected it could end up tearing her heart out. Or getting them killed. Angel pushed away the disturbing thoughts. She raised her face to the sun, absorbing the rays through her closed eyelids. Breathing deeply, she tried to remember what was right with the world. Some days it was very hard.

CHAPTER FOURTEEN

ANGEL WAS RAVENOUS at lunch. Good thing Eleanor had suggested she pack two sandwiches for each of them. The fresh air and manual labor had been good for her.

She stretched and sighed, reclining on the blanket. "That was good. Now I could use a nap."

"You didn't get enough rest yesterday? Or did I wear you out?" Matthew grinned.

"It was working in the garden this morning. Very therapeutic. Although I flunked Caterpillar Squishing 101."

"Oh?"

"Yeah. We tended the tomato plants this morning. Pinched back the suckers, disposed of the hornworms...."

"I'm impressed. We'll make a country girl out of you yet."

"Not so fast. I could *not* step on those poor caterpillars. Eleanor had to squish the ones I found."

He laughed. "You, the woman with nerves of steel, couldn't put a poor invertebrate out of its misery?"

"No." She hung her head in shame. "I was a wuss."

"Not everyone's cut out for the gory stuff. It's not a sign of weakness. Just an overdeveloped case of compassion, if I don't miss my guess."

"It's starting to worry me, Matt. I'm getting too emotionally involved. My objectivity is slipping."

"I don't think hornworms care about objectivity. They just want to eat as much as they can."

She swatted him on the shoulder. "No, I mean with Eleanor."

"Oh, I see. Just Eleanor?"

"Yes. Isn't that enough?" There was no way she'd admit to caring about him, even a tiny bit.

Disappointment flashed in his eyes and was gone. "You don't ever care about your subjects?"

"Sometimes it's hard to stay detached. But I can still do it. With Eleanor I'm not so sure. It breaks my heart when I hear her talk about how much she misses Austin."

"The town?"

"No. Her youngest son, goofball."

"He must've been born after I left. It's hard to keep track of all the kids. What's the deal with Austin?"

Angel recounted the story, getting a lump in her throat as she thought about Eleanor's fatalistic acceptance. "How can I help her, Matt?"

He took her hand in his, caressing her palm with his thumb. "You can't. It's not within your power. And, as you pointed out, it's not good for you to lose your objectivity. I would imagine that's one of the cardinal rules of undercover work."

"Yes, it is. But I'm human, damn it. How can I not be affected? She's starting to seem like a second mother to me. I'd rather die than allow someone to hurt my mother the way Jonathon is hurting Eleanor."

"You've forgotten one thing, Angelina. Eleanor has a free will, too. She's apparently decided to abide by the elders' decision."

"How can she do that?"

He cupped his hand under her chin. "You of all

people shouldn't need to ask. There's a fine line between allowing someone to influence you and someone blocking the choices until you can no longer think for yourself."

"Do you think Jonathon's…physically abusing her?"

"My guess is no. He's more into mental manipulation—and he's a master at it."

"She's your aunt. She loves you. How can you be so unmoved by this?"

He sighed. "I'm not unmoved. I've simply learned I can't save someone who doesn't want to be saved. Eleanor hasn't reached the point where it's more painful to stay than to go. Maybe she never will."

"What if her life was in danger?"

"Then I might feel I needed to intercede on her behalf until she could think clearly. It's a dangerous position. And who are we to say her lifestyle is unacceptable? It's all she's ever known."

"I need to do something proactive. I'm not used to passively waiting for a situation to develop. I want to explore the compound tonight." And get this mission moving. Because if she didn't, she'd become a danger to herself and everyone else.

"We need to bide our time."

"I can't, Matt. I'll go by myself so if anything happens you won't be involved. But I have to do *something*."

He hesitated. "All right. We'll make a short scouting trip tonight after everyone's asleep. Maybe we can get a fix on the patrol habits of the guards."

THEY WAITED TILL almost midnight, well after their nightly bed-rocking routine. Fortunately the erotic overtones had faded and it had become downright monotonous. But the purpose was to convince Ruth they were trying to make a baby, and that's what counted.

Matthew peered at Angel in the gloom. They'd turned off the lights so no one would suspect they were still awake.

"What about Jonathon's study? Don't you think we should start there?" Matthew whispered.

"My first priority is having an escape route plotted and a plan if things go bad. The study will have to wait till tomorrow night or when the elders go to town."

Her whispered discussion of leaving reminded him time was short and he had objectives of his own. He wasn't leaving until he found his sister and knew what had really happened the night his father died. "I want to get in to see that computer. Hopefully he keeps the majority of his records there. I suppose a word-processing file containing his memoirs is too much to expect?"

"Even if he kept something like that, you know it would just be self-aggrandizing BS."

"No doubt. Too much to hope for incriminating self-aggrandizing BS?"

Angel grinned. "Maybe, but Jonathon likes to hear himself talk—that's a good thing. If he gets caught up in hearing himself touted through a memoir, he'll let down his guard. Maybe you can suggest it to him as a hobby?"

"That's not such a bad idea. My ancestors were big on keeping written records."

"Let's hope Jonathon has carried on the tradition." Angel's voice was low. "I think we can go now. This is an early-to-bed, early-to-rise bunch."

"Especially with the curfew. No Letterman to keep them awake, either."

"Come on. Follow my lead." She turned the doorknob and looked into the hallway.

"You're not exactly dressed for recon," he commented. "Didn't you have anything darker?"

"Nope." She made a face. "Pastels are it."

"Get behind me if a patrol passes."

She glanced down at her pale pink cotton dress. "Purely for practical reasons. Don't get any ideas of protecting me because I'm a woman. I can defend myself in ways that'd give you nightmares. And I'm very effective on the offensive, too."

Matthew forced a grin. No way would he allow her to know she intimidated him at times. She'd never let him hear the end of it. "Yeah, you're effective on the offensive as long as the patrol isn't made up of hornworms."

He yelped as she elbowed him. Rubbing his ribs, he said, "Hey, I'm glad you're on my side."

They stole into the hallway, a small night-light glowing a few feet away. Angel led the way down the stairs. She'd already discovered which boards were likely to squeak if stepped on and avoided them.

When they got to the front door, Matthew pushed forward and twisted the dead bolt. If there was danger on the other side, he wanted to take the brunt of it, Angel's training notwithstanding. It was an instinctive need to protect, and he didn't intend to stop and analyze it.

The fact that the door was locked at all made him pause for a second. They'd never had locks on the doors in Arizona. Was this another indication of Jonathon's growing paranoia?

They stepped outside and waited. The compound was eerily silent. He listened but didn't hear the sound of approaching footsteps or voices.

Angel stood completely still, watching, waiting.

She took the lead and signaled him to follow.

He modeled her behavior, keeping to the balls of his feet, moving quietly, head swiveling, allowing him to visually search their path.

They moved quickly over the open ground, then went past Raphael's homes, hugging close to the walls. He thought of his half brother sleeping in one of the buildings. Which of the wives was he with? Did he dream of Theresa or was he as resigned to his fate as he indicated?

Matthew relaxed a bit as they moved on. Maybe the rumor of patrols was merely a lie Jonathon circulated to keep the rebellious in line.

As they approached the meeting hall, Angel stopped. She grabbed his arm and pulled him around the side of the building, flattening herself against the wall. He did the same.

Male voices floated softly through the night. Matthew couldn't discern their conversation, though the two men passed within yards of them.

He strained to get a good look at their faces in the dark but didn't recognize them. Were they men he knew well or some of the new faces he'd noticed at church? Matthew was more inclined to think they were borrowed muscle from the landlord.

The clouds parted, revealing a half-moon. Silvery light silhouetted the men, allowing him to see each was armed with an assault rifle.

If they were members of Zion's Gate, they were heavily armed, something unheard-of in the past. Matthew's father had abhorred guns and had only allowed a few rifles for hunting. And when not in use, those had been locked in a cabinet in the meeting hall.

Angel looked at her watch, then nodded, motioning for him to follow. They made their way to the front gate, the only legitimate way in and out of the compound.

Light shone from the guard shack several yards from the gate.

Angel crooked her finger. He bent down so she could whisper, "There's nowhere to hide near the gate. It's too exposed for me to check in these clothes." She gestured at her dress reflecting the moonlight, almost glowing white.

He pressed his lips to the curve of her ear. "What do you need to know?"

"A make and model of the locking mechanism. Is there a keypad for numbers? Letters, too?"

He nodded and waited until the clouds covered the moon again. Then he hugged the wall as far as he could before sprinting to the gate.

Damn. He couldn't see a make. And he could merely guess at the model number. But he memorized what he saw. The keypad appeared numerical only.

The rumble of an engine cut through his concentration. Matthew looked up but didn't see a vehicle. Until it was a few hundred yards away.

He slipped away from the gate, taking cover when he got back to the building. Cupping his hand by Angel's ear, he murmured, "Vehicle coming. No lights."

Angel frowned. They wedged themselves into a space between the building and a trash bin.

The black Humvee stopped at the gate. The window on the driver's side lowered. A male, barely discernable with the moon playing hide-and-seek, keyed in a series of numbers on the pad. The well-oiled gate quietly rolled open. The Humvee pulled through and the gates closed.

The guard stepped out of his shack and waved to the occupants of the vehicle. Then he stepped back inside.

The Humvee moved forward, headlights still dark.

"Come on." Angel crouched low, following the back of the building to emerge on the other side, out of the guard's line of vision.

And just in time to see the Humvee back to the rear of the meeting hall. Six men got out of the SUV. One opened the rear hatch.

The sound of approaching footsteps made Matthew's blood run cold. He pulled Angel back around the corner. The two guards they'd seen earlier joined the six men, conferring quietly. Finally the guards nodded and headed for the back of the meeting hall. The other men followed.

Four of the men were huge and sauntered with a gorillalike stride that probably warned most folks to look the other way.

"Come on. Let's get closer," Angel said, her voice low.

"No, we need to get back to Eleanor's house. This looks dangerous."

"I have a job to do, Matt. Let me do it," she protested.

"You have no gun, no backup."

Shrugging, Angel trotted toward the back of the building.

He had no choice but to follow and hope to hell they both didn't end up dead.

Angel slowed as she approached the corner of the building. Then she stopped and listened. So did he.

She peeked around the corner, the lines of her body tense, almost quivering with excitement. She was in her element.

And he felt like a damn fool.

The low murmur of male voices reached his ears. He caught a word here, a word there, all in English. Something about a shipment. Payment. Family.

Then…*vato*. The Spanish slang for friend.

A two-way radio crackled.

Angel turned. "Go. Run."

He didn't stop to ask why. He merely turned and followed her instructions.

She sprinted beside him, pointing toward the nearest of Raphael's homes.

His lungs burned and his blood pumped as he stretched to keep up with her. Though her legs were considerably shorter than his, she was fast and strong.

When they reached the house, she bumped him with her shoulder, sending him sprawling around the corner.

Angel came flying after.

She caught her breath, then murmured, "The guard at the gate thought he saw something. The men are going to fan out on their way to the gate to see if they stir anything up."

A stitch in his side doubled him over. "Need…to…catch my breath."

"No time. Come on."

She grasped his hand and hauled him along the path they'd used less than a half hour earlier.

She didn't seem to worry about staying to the shadows. Just the most direct, quickest route to safety. Probably because Raphael's house blocked them from view.

When they reached Eleanor's place, Matthew turned the knob and pushed. His efforts were met with solid resistance. Panic rose up. They had to get inside before they were discovered.

He turned to Angel, spreading his hands helplessly. "Try again. Maybe it's stuck."

"It was locked."

"Do you want me to do it?" The determined set to Angel's jaw told him she'd kick the door in if she had to. And wouldn't they have a fine time explaining *that* to Eleanor.

Taking a deep breath, he twisted the knob and shoved with his shoulder at the same time.

And fell into the entryway.

Straight into Aunt Eleanor, who stood, arms crossed, with the most forbidding frown he'd ever seen.

CHAPTER FIFTEEN

ANGEL STUMBLED IN behind Matthew, grateful she hadn't been forced to damage Eleanor's door to gain entry. Grateful, that is, until she saw the women herself standing in the entryway, anger written in every stern line on her face.

Angel swallowed hard, trying to think of an explanation for their late-night outing. She would have almost rather faced several armed gang members hopped up on methamphetamines than Eleanor's disapproval. And her razor-sharp perception.

Matthew straightened, raising his chin. "Aunt Eleanor, I'm sorry we disturbed you."

"So am I." Her reply was tart.

Angel tried to think of a logical explanation. "We were, um—"

Matthew interrupted her. "We were eager for an evening stroll."

Angel suppressed a groan. Only an idiot would buy that explanation. She stepped forward. "Eleanor, it's my fault. I wanted some time alone with Matthew—I mean really alone. With no one next door, no one down the hall."

"A lack of privacy can be difficult for newlyweds. But you must learn to accept sharing space with others."

"It started out innocently enough. A midnight stroll.

So romantic. But, um, we sat under the tree at the park and kissed. One thing led to another and—"

Eleanor raised her hand, palm outward. "Enough. You took a risk, even after I explained the consequences of defying curfew?"

Matthew put his arm around Angel's shoulders. "We weren't thinking of consequences. I'm sorry we worried you. It won't happen again."

Rubbing her temple, Eleanor relented. "Just see that it doesn't. I…would hate to lose you, too."

Angel's chest constricted at Eleanor's admission. She hated causing the woman more pain.

Matthew touched his aunt's arm. "You won't tell Uncle Jonathon, will you?"

Eleanor hesitated. "No, God help me, I won't tell your uncle. But don't put me in this position again. If I'm forced to choose between my husband and you, I will choose Jonathon."

The sad acceptance in her voice reminded Angel of another woman at another time who hadn't wanted to choose between her husband and loved ones.

"We understand," Angel murmured.

"Go upstairs, you two. I'll lock up."

Halfway up the stairs, Angel looked over her shoulder and wished she hadn't.

Eleanor leaned against the doorjamb, her shoulders slumped, shaking with silent tears.

A lump in her throat, Angel followed her husband to their room. The woman deserved so much better than to be hurt by the ones she loved.

But, Angel realized, Eleanor would inevitably be hurt when she found out Angel's profession and the real reason she was here.

When she closed the door behind her, Angel released a breath, her knees shaking. "That was close."

"Too close." Matthew's voice was so low she had to move closer to hear. She doubted Ruth was awake, but Matthew's caution was prudent. Especially since their exploration had gone so wrong.

"What did you see before you told me to run?" he asked.

"The big guys from the Humvee were loading boxes in the back. The boxes were closed, nothing to identify the contents."

"What size?"

"Maybe twelve inches by two feet. Like the boxes reams of copy paper come in."

"How many boxes?"

Angel frowned. It had happened so quickly, she hadn't counted. But she did now. Good thing she was trained to recall details. "Four pushed toward the back. Two more in front of those. And the guys carried two more. Eight total."

"The boxes you described aren't large enough for firearms, unless it's pistols or something that could be disassembled."

"That'd be a huge drug shipment, unless it's marijuana."

"Too bad we couldn't get close enough to peek inside."

"No way. Those guys weren't going to let the shipment out of their sight. The men who came out of the meeting hall weren't going to, either."

"Were you able to distinguish features on any of the men?"

Angel closed her eyes, trying to recall everything she'd seen. "No... Except two of the three who weren't from the Humvee spoke fluent Spanish. Mexican, not South American or Puerto Rican dialects."

"The rest spoke English?"

"Yes." Angel tried to recall the bits and pieces she'd heard. Nothing she could put together for a cogent phrase. She opened her eyes. "English as a first language, except one guy spoke English with a Mexican accent. In this area, that doesn't narrow it down."

"No, I don't suppose it does. Did any have Texas accents?"

"I don't remember…. That's weird. I totally didn't get an impression." Her voice trembled with frustration.

"Don't be too hard on yourself. It was only a few seconds. I'm impressed you got as much as you did."

"But I'm trained to observe more."

"Maybe you'll remember after a good night's sleep. I'd suggest you take a nice, soothing bath, but I'm afraid Ruth might wake up and wonder what's going on."

The line between who she was pretending to be and reality was beginning to blur. She could barely comprehend the ramifications of what she'd seen, yet she needed to make the leap to a woman in love. "We *are* newlyweds, aren't we?"

Matthew hesitated. "Yes, we are. And that matters at the moment because…?"

"What, you've never made love in the bathtub?" It was meant to be a teasing remark but came out a challenge.

He stepped closer. Dipping his head, he kissed her on the mouth, then drew back. His gaze was intense. "Oh, yes, Angelina, I have. But never with you."

His breath caressed her face. She leaned into him just for a moment, closing her eyes. The thought of being held by Matthew was surprisingly erotic. She could envision his hard, naked body, making love while the sensual water lapped at their bodies. Maybe she'd been wrong. Maybe the line between reality and playacting was already indistinguishable.

"Angelina." Her name was half caress, half curse. "You have no idea what you do to me." He threaded his hands through her hair and drew her head back.

She opened her eyes, panicking at the restraint. Until her gaze locked with Matthew's and recognition flooded her. He wasn't Kent. He would never hurt her.

"Matthew," she breathed.

He lowered his face, his mouth hot and searching.

For a moment she froze. Then she returned his kiss with a passion she hadn't experienced for a long, long time.

Groaning, he wrapped his arms around her, pulling her snug against his body. Rational thought fled as Angel lost herself in the sensation of learning Matthew.

It was a fully clothed exploratory encounter, without overt possession. Only kisses and promises. Caresses and honest connection.

It was an experience so new, so intense, Angel wanted to cry. Kissing Kent had never been this way.

Matthew pulled away, his voice full of frustration. "What are we doing, Angelina?"

She touched her lips, in awe of her response to him. She'd feared Kent had robbed her of the ability to respond to a man with complete trust. Nine intervening years and a few sexual encounters had seemed to confirm it. Until now.

Resisting the impulse to draw Matthew to her, she stepped back a pace while she tried to regain her equilibrium. "I'm here on assignment. I shouldn't be getting involved." The reminder was as much for herself as Matt. Maybe even more.

He ran his hand through his hair, leaving it ruffled and boyish. "I'm sorry. I shouldn't have put you in that position. It was totally unforgivable."

"No, Matthew, it was…nice." God, that was the understatement of the century. *Beautiful. Mystical. The touching of souls.* He would laugh if he knew he had the ability to make her wax poetic about his embrace.

How could he know her love life had never matured past first love? Because sex with Kent had become a power play, twisting what they'd initially shared into something degrading and shameful. And in the process, the tender, innocent part of her had almost died.

Angel smiled a secret little smile. Matthew had given her the hope that tenderness and passion could coexist, untarnished, in a world abounding with evil.

MATTHEW LAY AWAKE for what seemed like hours. The bed was more uncomfortable than the floor had ever been.

Or maybe it was his conscience that made it intolerable. He shouldn't have acted on his urge to kiss Angel. He'd never been impulsive, so why now? Probably because it hadn't been as spur-of-the-moment as he would like to believe. The thought had been in the back of his mind pretty much since the first time he'd seen Angel.

And after their close call, his adrenaline had been pumping full force. Sexual excitement was an understandable response to danger. That he could accept. But his interlude with Angel had been more than wanting to fulfill purely physical need with hot, uninhibited sex. Matthew wanted to make love with Angelina. Reassure her, treasure her, *love* her. And that scared him.

He rolled onto his side, propping his head on his arm so he could see the covers outlining Angel. She breathed slowly, evenly, apparently unaffected by what they'd shared. Unfazed by what they *might* have shared.

His body ached to complete what they'd started. His mind told him to avoid it at all costs. There was no room in their mission for emotion. The only rational course of action would be to step up his efforts to locate the information they needed. The sooner they had that, the sooner they could leave. And he could return to his well-ordered life.

But suddenly his old life didn't seem very appealing.

ANGEL AWOKE EARLY, glancing at the clock. It wasn't light out yet. She flipped and flopped for nearly half an hour before deciding to get an early start on the day.

She took a shower, dressed and was downstairs just as the sun was beginning to rise.

Approaching the kitchen, she heard the low murmur of voices. Surely Eleanor wasn't awake this early? Angel had hoped to have breakfast well under way before the older woman came downstairs. A peace offering for the trouble they'd caused last night.

Angel entered the kitchen and was startled to see Jonathon deep in discussion with Ruth. They were close, their murmured sentences too low for Angel to hear.

Frowning, Angel wondered what he was doing here at this hour and what Ruth was doing up. Jonathon hadn't been at supper the night before and hadn't been there at prayer time. And she hoped to hell he hadn't been upstairs when she and Matthew came in from their late-night mission.

"Good morning," Angel said.

Jonathon stepped back. "I was counseling Sister Ruth."

His excuse came so easily she knew he'd used it many times before.

"I can see that," Angel commented.

Ruth's shining blond hair cascaded over her shoulders. Her eyes glowed in the low light of the kitchen. She looked every bit like a woman seeing off her secret lover.

Yikes!

"I must meditate on several problems before the meeting today. Ruth, we can discuss this later."

"Yes, Brother Jonathon." Ruth lowered her gaze.

His gaze locked with Angel's. He didn't speak for a moment, as if waiting for her reaction. Or waiting for her to blurt out a secret. Like the fact that she'd seen a Humvee full of men visit the compound in the middle of the night.

He nodded, apparently satisfied. "Please tell Matthew to be early to the meeting today. We have much to discuss."

"I will."

"Goodbye, ladies."

"Goodbye," they replied in unison.

Once Jonathon was gone, Angel said, "Good, I'm glad you're up early. You can help me prepare breakfast."

"I'd love to help, Sister Angel, but I have lesson plans to prepare for the children." She hurried out of the kitchen, her footsteps light on the stairs.

Yeah, sure she'd love to help. When hell froze over. Angel had noticed Ruth managed to have other duties anytime cooking or cleaning was involved. As a sister wife, she would be next to useless. Thank goodness it wasn't meant to be.

When Eleanor came downstairs an hour later, Angel had platters of pancakes and scrambled eggs warming in the oven. The table was set.

"What's all this?"

"The bacon should be done in a few minutes," Angel said. "My way of saying I'm sorry for the trouble we caused."

"Don't mention it. We'll pretend it never happened." A very un-Eleanor-like attitude of avoidance.

"I appreciate that. Please sit down. I'll go check to make sure Matthew didn't oversleep." She turned the heat under the frying pan to low and hurried upstairs.

Entering their room, she was surprised to see Matthew sound asleep. The man never overslept. Good thing she'd been searching for an exit line to get out of Eleanor's way.

Angel stepped close to the bed, reaching out to touch his shoulder, but stopped. Finding him in this unguarded moment gave her the opportunity to study him. He wore a T-shirt to bed, presumably shielding her from the sight of his bare chest, which had been quite nice the few times she'd caught a glimpse. His face was relaxed except for small frown lines between his eyes. She longed to smooth them away with the gentlest of touches. Or maybe a featherlight kiss to his brow.

His eyes opened and she took a step back.

"Kind of creepy watching someone sleep, isn't it?" His voice held a trace of sarcasm.

"I'm starting to understand its merits. Especially with someone as guarded as you."

"Me? Guarded? I'm an open book."

"No, you pretend to be an open book. You're like those proverbial still waters that run deep."

"You're starting to sound like Aunt Eleanor."

"I came up to tell you breakfast is ready. I cooked it myself. An olive branch for Eleanor."

"Very commendable."

"You better get moving. Jonathon wants you at the meeting early. Said you have a lot to discuss. Maybe he'll let something slip about the visitors last night."

Matthew sat up, the covers pooling at his waist. "I doubt it, but we can always hope. Now, a little privacy please?"

Angel shrugged and headed for the door. "Hurry. You don't want your breakfast to get cold. Since I cooked, I've decided we won't wait for one late person, even if he is lord and master of the household."

Closing the door behind her, Angel thought she heard Matthew chuckle. The man had the oddest sense of humor.

"MATTHEW?" ANGEL'S sleepy voice came from the bed the next morning.

"Go back to sleep. It's still early."

"What time is it?"

"Four-thirty."

"The farmer's market—I almost forgot. Do you have my pocket PC?"

"Yes. I'll try to find a wireless connection, but I don't know how closely I'm going to be watched."

Angel reached over and turned on the light. Blinking, she rubbed her eyes. "I remembered something in the night. A partial plate on the Humvee. It was a Texas plate. I wrote it down here somewhere."

She grasped a small pad of paper from the night-stand. Ripping off a sheet, she handed it to him.

"You did this in the dark?"

"One of my many talents."

"I'm sure."

Angel flushed. "I didn't mean it that way. It's too early for double entendres."

"Sorry. I'll remind you of it when you're more awake."

"Please, don't." Her voice was low and serious.

"Do you want to talk about what happened the other night?"

"It was an anomaly. It shouldn't happen again. I was totally unprofessional, and if my peers heard about it, my reputation would be toast. I could kiss goodbye any chance of making it into the Rangers."

"Don't be too hard on yourself. Given the close quarters, it was probably bound to happen. Besides, your secret's safe with me."

"Thanks, Matthew. I appreciate it." She cleared her throat. "I, um, thought it was okay. Another time, another place, maybe things would have been different."

"Yeah, that's the story of my life. Go back to sleep. And if you try getting into Jonathon's study, please be careful."

"Always." She lay down, pulling the covers up under her chin. "You be careful, too."

Matthew found himself humming as he left the room. Because there had been a warmth in Angel's tone that told him she cared whether he lived or died. It was a start, wasn't it?

CHAPTER SIXTEEN

MATTHEW ARRIVED AT the meeting hall just before sunrise. They'd be cutting it close if they were to pick fruits and vegetables and get them to the farmer's market by nine.

He needn't have worried.

Jonathon was directing placement of the last two boxes in the backseat of his Silverado. Two other trucks were loaded with produce.

"Hi, Jonathon. I thought we were going to pick this morning?"

"Morning, Matthew. Our neighbor to the south loaned us some men to pick and package last night. All that was left was loading. You ready to go?"

"Yeah. I was looking forward to getting my hands dirty in the garden this morning, though. I've been getting cabin fever."

Jonathon clapped him on the back and laughed. "You didn't complain too much the other day being cooped up with Angel. Besides, you'll be outside at the market. Why don't you go ahead and ride with Raphael? I bet he can squeeze in one more."

Matthew glanced over to the blue pickup where Raphael sat in the driver's seat.

"Sure. It'll be like old times." He counted the men and figured his uncle exaggerated about squeezing in.

But when they went to get in the vehicles, it was a tight fit. That's when he noticed nobody was riding with Jonathon.

He walked around to the driver's side of the blue truck. "Hey, Raphael, why don't I ride with Uncle Jonathon? I don't know why he didn't suggest it."

"He's going to Just Greens Restaurant first and a few places he delivers to personally. Then he'll meet up with us."

"I'll go offer my help."

"Matthew, stop. If he wanted your help, he would have asked for it. Get in the truck. You can ride shotgun."

Frowning, Matthew did as his half brother requested. It was the first time he could remember Raphael getting short with him.

"Sure. No problem." He settled in the front passenger seat.

The ride to town was quiet. The other men didn't seem inclined to make polite chitchat. They were all new to Zion's Gate and didn't seem to be anxious to get to know him.

That was fine by Matthew. He was content to simply look out the window and watch the sunrise turn the sky a beautiful kaleidoscope of orange and blue.

After the first few miles, the desert view became monotonous, not much different from Arizona in its bleakness. To make matters worse, Jonathon's truck kicked up dust ahead of them, which managed to infiltrate the fresh-air return, making the cab stuffy.

"How often do we go to the farmer's market?"

Raphael shrugged. "It's held on Tuesdays and Thursdays. We go whenever we have an abundance of produce. Usually every other week. Sometimes we go even if we don't have a lot, because Jonathon says we need to generate cash flow."

Matthew wondered if Zion's Gate was really as strapped for cash as Jonathon led everyone to believe. Or if it was simply a ploy to squeeze a few more dollars in tithes.

The hum of the engine and the unending expanse of desert lulled Matthew into an almost hypnotic state. He found himself wondering what Angel was doing back at Zion's Gate. Baking bread? Sparing hornworms in the garden?

The engine growled as the transmission down-shifted. Matthew noticed they were pulling over to the shoulder behind the Silverado.

"Why are we stopping?"

"Sheriff. He's pulling in behind us."

A deputy's vehicle went cruising by on their left, blue and red lights flashing.

"We weren't speeding, were we?"

"No. We never do. But we get pulled over every time we go into town."

"Why?"

"Because we're from Zion's Gate."

"That's illegal." A trace of indignation made its way into his voice. He'd almost forgotten he was part of a similar law-enforcement crusade. But that was different.

Raphael shrugged. "You'll get used to it." He lowered his window, waiting patiently.

A few minutes later the sheriff approached. "Morning, fellas. I'll need to see some ID."

"For what reason?" The question was out before Matthew could stop.

The sheriff squinted at him as if he were trying to

place his face from a book of mug shots. "We've had a report of *coyotes* transporting illegal aliens along this road. Several pickup trucks traveling in a convoy."

Very stupid *coyotes* to travel in a high-profile convoy during broad daylight. But Matthew managed not to voice his disbelief.

"ID, gentlemen," the sheriff prodded.

Matthew reached for his wallet, removing his driver's license. The other men did the same.

The sheriff made notes on his pad with each ID he checked. When he came to Matthew's, he looked up. "Arizona, huh?"

"Yes, sir."

"Why're you here?"

"I'm visiting my uncle, Jonathon Stone."

"I hear Warren Jeffs hails from Arizona. You know him?"

"No, sir, I don't."

"He's a polygamist. Rumor has it he built a big old compound near Eldorado."

"Oh."

The sheriff handed back the driver's licenses. "You have a good day."

"You, too, Sheriff," Raphael said.

"This happens every time you go to town?"

"Yes."

"I read that the Arizona and Utah authorities are looking for Jeffs. Do they think we know him just because he practices the principle?"

"Pretty much. Jonathon hasn't had anything to do with him for years. Jeffs and his bunch were the reason he left Arizona to begin with. Then things get hot in

Arizona and Jeffs hightails it to Texas, too. It's made things hard for all of us."

"I thought maybe Uncle Jonathon was overstating the problem with the local authorities. But I guess not."

"He's got reason to be uneasy."

Raphael waited for the Silverado to pull forward. Then he put on his left-turn signal and fell in behind Jonathon.

Matthew was torn between instinctive family loyalty and the knowledge that the authorities probably had darn good reason to keep an eye on his uncle.

The rest of the trip into town was uneventful. When they reached the outskirts, Jonathon turned off on a side road and Raphael kept going straight.

Delivering produce to a restaurant that specialized in salads seemed reasonable. Matthew wondered about the other customers Uncle Jonathon saw to personally.

When they reached the farmer's market, Raphael backed the truck in near their booth, where customers were already waiting. Matthew was grateful to get out and stretch his legs.

He helped Raphael and the other men unload the produce. The clink of glass on glass in one box piqued his curiosity. His surprise must have shown, because Raphael said, "Honey. Ask Eleanor to show you the hives sometime. We sell it faster than the bees can make it."

Interesting.

There was a similar clank in the next case. "More honey?"

"Preserves."

"Do we sell it faster than the women can make it?"

Raphael grinned. "Just about. Same with the craft items. Folks say the needlework is some of the best they've ever seen."

"Looks like a tidy little operation."

Shrugging, Raphael said, "You'd think Jonathon would be happy. But we never bring in enough to suit him. Sometimes I feel like telling him to man the booth himself and see if he can do better."

This was the Raphael he remembered. Not the careful man who weighed every word he uttered.

"Jonathon's pretty good at supervising, huh? But I bet he finds something else to do when there's heavy lifting involved."

"You know it. His deliveries always take hours. Long enough that most of the work's done when he returns."

Matthew filed the information away. The rest of the morning was a blur as he helped set up the booth, kept the displays replenished, gave Raphael a hand at the till.

He swiped his sleeve across his face. "Whew, it's getting hot."

Raphael pulled water bottles from the ice chest. He tossed one to Matthew. "Here. You don't want to get heatstroke."

"Thanks." He twisted off the cap and swallowed half the bottle. "Do we get a lunch break? I'd like to check out the shops and see if I can find a gift for Angel."

"It slows down about one o'clock. You can do a little shopping then."

"Good. I'll be ready for a break."

"You've gotten soft, Brother."

Matthew smiled. It was almost like old times. "Soft? I bet I can still beat you at arm wrestling any day."

"We'll see, we'll see." Raphael cuffed him on the shoulder, then went to help an older lady select produce.

Raphael had been right. Once the sun was directly

overhead, their business tapered off. Though the booth was in the shade, it was still warm.

"You ready for lunch?" Raphael asked. "There's a great taco stand a few streets over. And some shops that might have something Angel would like. Want to give it a try?"

"Sure. As long as we're not needed here."

"No. The other men have it under control. Let's go."

Matthew fell into place beside Raphael. It seemed like the old days, when Raphael had been his best friend. He was sorry he hadn't kept in touch.

Despite the reminiscing, Matthew scanned business signs, trying to locate wireless access. They appeared to be in an older section of town with mostly small, independent shops. But he didn't spot a single sign advertising wireless access.

Mouthwatering aromas assaulted his senses, making it difficult to think clearly. They turned a corner and found the taco stand Raphael had mentioned. They ordered their meals and found a rickety table shaded by a tree.

Matthew bit into his taco and sighed with bliss. "You were right. They make great tacos. I didn't realize how hungry I was."

"Getting soft just sitting around making your piles of money? Jonathon acts like you're a billionaire."

"Not hardly. Sure, I'm comfortable, but I'm not about to make the cover of *Forbes*."

"Don't tell Jonathon that. He'd be deeply disappointed."

"Is that why he had the sudden interest in mending fences? Because he thought I was wealthy?"

"I'm sure it didn't hurt. I'd be watching my pockets if I were you."

"He's mentioned tithing once or twice but hasn't gotten too pushy."

"Must be lulling you into a false sense of security. I get the impression he's tapped out all his old sources."

"Thanks for the heads-up. Now tell me how many kids you have?"

They talked of Raphael's sixteen children and some of the people they'd grown up with. It made for an enjoyable meal. Matthew was just sorry Angel had missed the experience. Something told him she would have loved the shabby little taco stand and the small shops.

Raphael wiped his mouth with his napkin and stood. "I better get back. Why don't you take a couple minutes and check out the shops?"

"Sure thing. Is there a bookstore nearby?" He prayed there might be a chain bookstore with wireless access. "Angel needs something to read."

"The next street over." Raphael gave him directions. He couldn't think of a way to ask if they had wireless access. As a kid, he would have trusted Raphael with his life. But these days it didn't hurt to be careful.

Matthew followed Raphael's directions, and his hopes rose when he found the bookstore. It wasn't a large place, more of a local hangout trying to look like the big boys. But it had wireless access—or so a sign proclaimed.

Once inside, Matthew glanced around, making sure there was no one from Zion's Gate nearby. Then he brought up Angel's cryptic report and hit Send. It was as simple as that.

He slid the device into his pocket and thought about his cover story. He needed a gift for Angel.

Locating the small Religion section, he was relieved

to find a good selection of Bibles. His hand hovered over a lovely leather-bound student Bible. But he ended up choosing one that came in a metal case, figuring it might seem more familiar to Angel—it looked like something that might contain a weapon.

As he waited in line, Matthew glanced at the magazine rack. There were several movie and pop-culture magazines, along with a famous tabloid in Spanish. But Angel didn't impress him as the type who would care which celebrity marriage was rumored to be on the rocks.

Instead he chose the only other magazine on the rack. The cover contained a peaceful outdoor patio scene, with the table set for a relaxing meal. She liked reading about crafts and decorating, didn't she? Nodding, he hoped Angel didn't roll up the *Martha Stewart Living* and smack him with it.

On his way out the door, he almost collided with Jonathon on his way in.

"Matthew, why aren't you at the farmer's market?"

"Raphael and I had lunch at the taco stand. He returned to the market and I stopped in here to buy Angel a gift. A new Bible."

Jonathon appeared slightly mollified. "Hurry back to the booth, son. I'm sure Raphael needs your help."

His use of the term *son* raised Matthew's hackles. This man had never been a father to him and never would be. But he had a role to play. "Yes, sir. Will you be returning soon?"

Jonathon nodded absently. "Yes," he said and hurried through the doors.

Matthew stood and watched him through the glass. He didn't appear to be meeting anyone.

But Jonathon sat in one of the chairs and plugged in a device that looked similar to Angel's pocket PC, only bigger.

Interesting. Who was Jonathon e-mailing that he couldn't e-mail from home? Matthew wondered if they would find anything useful on the computer in his study.

Starting back to the booth, he tried to forget his uncle for a while and recall his earlier enjoyment of the town.

He noticed a small line at the booth and jogged the last couple of yards. There he pitched in next to Raphael, the two working seamlessly together as if they'd done this all their lives.

By three o'clock, he was grateful when Raphael said it was time to close shop. Only a small selection of their fruits and vegetables remained, which they boxed and dropped off at the food bank on their way out of town.

And, as predicted, Uncle Jonathon showed up as the last table was folded and loaded into Raphael's truck.

"How'd we do, gentlemen?"

Raphael handed him the tallies.

Jonathon frowned. "I'd hoped for more, but as long as you men gave it your best…"

The inference being that if they had given their best, they would have brought in more.

Matthew glanced at Raphael, who shrugged impassively.

Having a hard time being quite so philosophical, Matthew figured it was a good thing he didn't intend to live at Zion's Gate permanently. Because if he did, he would give his uncle a piece of his mind and then get booted out on his rear.

ANGEL PUT THE PEACH cobbler in the oven to bake, glancing at the kitchen clock. Five o'clock. The day had gone by slowly with Matthew gone. She'd sorely missed their picnic lunch.

Truth be told, she felt strangely disconnected, as if she'd been cut off from her very life source. All easily rationalized as relying too heavily on her temporary partner, her only connection with the outside world.

Would Matthew be able to find wireless access? Angel hoped so. After no contact in nearly three weeks, her superiors had to be getting impatient. How could an outsider understand how long it took to earn trust here? Angel felt they were just now making headway.

But their surveillance the other night had been fruitful. *Something* was going on. Why else would there be clandestine transactions at midnight? She only wished they'd gotten close enough to see what they were dealing with. Weapons or drugs?

"Angel?" Matthew's voice came from the living room.

She quickly wiped the flour from her hands and went to meet him. A shock of pleasant recognition ran through her. Her place in this crazy world suddenly seemed right.

"Matthew." She ran to him, throwing her arms around his neck. "You're home."

He wrapped his arms around her and lifted her off the ground. "Yeah, you miss me?"

"I did." She grinned down at him.

He slowly lowered her to the floor. Tipping her chin with his finger, he kissed her, a long, languid kiss full of promise.

Angel surprised herself by returning his kiss wholeheartedly.

A loud cough roused Angel from her absorption with Matthew. She drew back and he released her, regret in his eyes.

"Matthew, you're home." Eleanor stood in the doorway to the kitchen, her eyes alight with amusement. "Apparently Angel missed you."

"Yes, apparently she did. I'll have to go away more often."

"Oh, don't get such a swelled head," Angel huffed. "You were only gone for twelve hours."

He chuckled. "Not that you were counting?"

"Simply an observation."

"Come to the kitchen and have a cold drink." Eleanor led the way. "We made lemonade today."

"I feel like I could drink a pitcher all by myself. You always did make the best lemonade."

The older woman smiled. "It went well?"

"I thought so. We sold out of the honey, preserves and craft items. Just a few fruits and vegetables left over. We dropped those off at the food bank."

"Was Jonathon pleased?"

"He hoped we'd do better."

"He usually does."

Angel thought Matthew seemed different. Relaxed, happy almost. She touched his cheek. "You got sunburned. You should have worn sunscreen."

"A bit. It was great being outside all day, though. Maybe next time I'll wear a hat. It was good spending time with Raphael, too."

"You two always were thick as thieves." Eleanor placed a tall glass on the kitchen table. "Sit, relax."

He did.

Angel pulled out a chair and sat next to him. "I want to hear all about your day."

"First, this." Matthew placed a shopping bag on the table in front of her. "I bought you a present."

"Really? For me?"

"Yes, really."

Angel hesitated, hoping she didn't look as bemused as she felt. Gingerly she picked up the bag and opened it. Inside was a metal box with rounded corners. "What is it?"

Matthew flipped it over. "It's a Bible. Your very own, so you don't need to borrow mine."

But I like reading yours. It was like a treasure hunt, searching through the pages he'd thumbed many times. Reading his handwritten notations in the margins, trying to make sense of them. His Bible was personal. It had character.

She tried to show enthusiasm for the new Bible she removed from the metal box. "How nice, Matthew. Thank you."

"You don't like it?"

"I will treasure it because it came from you."

"There's a magazine in there. I hope it's okay."

She removed the magazine and took one look at the glossy cover and hugged it to her chest. "I love it."

"I didn't know if Martha was quite your cup of tea."

"It looks wonderful." She could barely wait for their evening Bible-reading time. Because after that, she could pore over the latest issue of one of her favorite magazines. Small pleasures had taken on greater significance since she'd come to Zion's Gate. Maybe it was a lesson she could take away with her when she left.

She jumped up and kissed his cheek. "Thank you, Matthew. You're so sweet. I'll take these upstairs."

"See what Matthew bought for me?" She showed her treasures to Eleanor as she danced past the woman.

She patted Angel's cheek, her eyes moist. "Very nice, dear. He's a good boy."

CHAPTER SEVENTEEN

ANGEL TRIED TO ignore Matthew's presence so close to her on the bed.

He rubbed her calf with his foot, his face relaxed as he read his new business magazine. In the past, invasion of her space would have made her angry. Now it was comfortable, though slightly unsettling at the same time.

And she was growing accustomed to Matthew touching her. The stray caress, the kiss hello or goodbye. It seemed natural, almost as if they really were husband and wife. Except for the whole consummation part. And she wouldn't allow her thoughts to stray *that* far.

"You're sure the e-mail went off without a hitch?" she asked.

"Yes. If I'd have known it was that easy, I would have e-mailed my assistant."

"And I would have asked you to e-mail my folks. They start getting anxious, especially when I'm under-cover. They try not to let it show, but they're so relieved to hear from me. Probably because of the time I dropped out of sight with Kent."

"That would be a horrible thing for a parent to live with. Knowing after the fact that their child had been in danger, when they assumed she was simply involved in her new life."

"Well, Kent made sure he set their minds at ease."

"I'm sorry you went through that, Angelina. I'd give anything to be able to erase it." He fingered a lock of her hair, which touched his shoulder. "You deserved someone who would give you the world, not destroy you minute by minute, hour by hour."

Angel swallowed hard. "What a lovely thing to say. Coming from anyone but you, it would sound corny."

He shrugged and grinned. "As the great philosopher Popeye once said, 'I yam what I yam.'"

"You? A Popeye fan? Please tell me you're not one of those guys who watches cartoons all Saturday morning."

"Not *all* Saturday morning. Just an hour or two." His eyes twinkled with humor. She'd always thought that a man who could laugh at himself was sexy.

"Oh, brother, there goes my whole image of you."

"You and my mother are the only ones who know my deep, dark secret. When we left the sect, the outside world was a wonderful, scary place, full of things I hadn't even known existed. Animation was one of them."

"I never thought about how difficult the transition must have been. It was probably like being from another country. No, another planet."

"Exactly. I spoke the same language, but the culture was foreign. I had to learn a lot to blend in. Fortunately my mother found a few people who'd left similar communities and they helped us acclimate."

"Yeah, I bet the kids were real friendly when you used terms like 'acclimate.'"

Matthew shrugged. "I knew I was different, that there were some people who would think I was a freak if they knew my background. So I was very careful who I told."

Angel hesitated. "Did anyone you trusted end up thinking you were a freak?"

"Unfortunately. A girl I dated in college. I thought because she was pretty on the outside, she was pretty on the inside. Not true. A hard lesson."

"What happened?"

"She dumped me in a very public manner. And told people I had, um, certain physical defects because of inbreeding."

Was the woman crazy? Matthew had to be the closest thing to a perfect, green-eyed, blond specimen of manhood she had ever seen. Had she really thought he was bland at one point? How could a man with such heart, such humor, ever be bland? Or defective. "What kind of defects?"

"Let's just say they pertained to my, um, family jewels."

Amusement warred with outrage. Amusement that Matthew hesitated when he referred to genitals, even in a euphemistic way. Outrage that some bitch could be so intentionally cruel.

"That is so unfair." Angel plucked a pen and pad of paper from the nightstand. "Give me her name. I've got a friend in the IRS who would love nothing better than to audit her for, say, decades."

Matthew laughed. "Angelina, you are one scary woman. And you've restored my wounded pride."

"I'm serious, Matt. Give me her name and she'll regret she ever messed with you."

Grasping her hand, he twined his fingers with hers. "She did me a favor. I learned to be more discriminating in the company I keep. And here I am, in bed with you."

Angel's mouth went dry. His words were teasing, but

there was a question in his eyes. He'd be willing to take their fake relationship into the realm of reality. What would it hurt? Nobody would ever have to know. It wasn't as if she didn't find him attractive. And she liked him more than any man she'd met in a long time. She enjoyed spending time with him and missed him when he was gone. Was that a crime?

No, but bedding him would be criminal stupidity.

Angel tried to pretend she hadn't understood his conjecture. "Yes, Matt, here we are. And I've got a job to do. How about we break into Jonathon's study tonight?"

"Not the late-night activity I'd hoped for. But, yes, let's give it a try."

Damn him. He was even gracious about being shot down.

"Eleanor obviously hadn't hit her REM sleep cycle by midnight the other night. You want to try two o'clock? We can set the alarm, catch some sleep between now and then."

"There are other ways I'd rather spend the time."

"Yeah, I kind of got that impression, Matt. But it can't happen. Not only is it unprofessional, it's not fair to start something that would never work in the real world."

"You're very sure we wouldn't be good together in the real world?"

"Positive." It would have been a convincing statement if her voice hadn't been two octaves too high. She cleared her throat. "Positive," she reiterated in a normal speaking voice.

"So you say. I'll set the alarm if you want to use the bathroom first."

Some of the tension eased from Angel's shoulders.

Everything was going to be okay. She'd delineated her boundaries and he had respected them. End of story.

When Angel emerged from the bathroom, she was surprised to see Matthew still ensconced on the bed. The pallet wasn't anywhere to be seen.

She pulled the blankets from the closet and tossed them on the floor. "Your turn on the floor."

He glanced up from his magazine. "Yes, I know."

Propping her hands on her hips, she said, "Get off my bed."

"Of course. But haven't you forgotten something?"

"What?" She bared her teeth in an exaggerated smile. "See, I brushed. Good oral hygiene. I'm ready for sleepy time."

"We're newlyweds. If we don't make love after being separated all day, I'm sure people will talk."

"I'll make a big show of laundering our sheets again tomorrow, okay?"

"But Ruth will assume our lovemaking has slipped into passionless mediocrity. I'm not sure if I want my future wife thinking that." He set his magazine on the bedside table and held out his hand to her. "I'm very tired tonight. It doesn't have to be long."

Angel sighed. "Okay."

She knelt beside him on the bed. He turned to face the wall, raised up on his knees and rocked forward.

Nothing.

"Harder."

"See, I knew you'd come around," he murmured, his eyes sparkling with laughter.

She smacked him on the shoulder. "Keep it clean, Matt."

They rocked again. Silence. The bed didn't seem to be cooperating in its usual manner.

"Get up," Angel ordered, crawling off the bed.

Matthew grinned.

Holding up her hand, she warned, "No more jokes. It's not going to happen, so don't even go there. Now help me push the bed closer to the wall."

"Yes, ma'am." He saluted, pushing the bed up against the wall.

"Try again."

They tried again. The headboard made a slight tapping, but not the resounding *thwack* they were accustomed to.

"You're not trying," she accused.

"Maybe I don't have proper motivation."

"I'm almost afraid to ask."

"Here." He grasped her shoulders, turning her and pinning her on her back in one fluid, near-perfect move. Straddling her thighs, he waited.

"What the hell do you think you're doing?"

"Optimizing physics. Are you comfortable?" he asked.

She tried hard to summon anger, but all she felt was curiosity. And a spark of…excitement. Definitely different from the split second of panic she would have felt had another man pinned her. Of course, it helped knowing she could emasculate him if his little experiment got out of control.

"You know damn well I'm not comfortable. And that's the biggest load of BS I've ever heard."

"Possibly. Let's give my theory a try." He braced his arms on either side of her head.

"Go for it, cowboy."

He settled into a leisurely rocking motion, the headboard responding with an anemic bump against the wall.

"Looks like your theory doesn't hold water."

"I'm just getting started." Matthew held her gaze while he increased the pace and momentum. His eyes darkened.

The friction of his fully clothed body against hers was enough to remind her that lovemaking had once been pleasant. Her breasts tingled and her stomach tightened. She ran her tongue over her dry lips. "Maybe this wasn't such a good—"

"Shh." Matthew dipped his head and kissed her, his tongue teasing her mouth.

Parting with a sigh that couldn't have been her own, Angel's lips betrayed her, inviting his tongue to play. He deepened the kiss, his body moving against hers. Whether by accident or design, his hips fit with hers as if they were making love. Even through two layers of clothing, her body welcomed his erection.

A firestorm of emotion nearly robbed her of the ability to think and breathe. Body and soul, she wanted Matthew to make love with her.

Matthew nibbled her lower lip, then pulled back a fraction, his eyes heavy-lidded, his breathing labored. "See, I told you."

"Told me what?"

Instead of answering, he drew her earlobe into his mouth, sucking gently. The heat and moisture made the rhythmic caress almost torture.

Angel arched upward, sure she'd scream from the pleasure.

"I told you it would work." He placed his finger over her lips, his movements strong. "Listen."

Stifling a whimper of frustration, she forced herself to focus on his words rather than her instinct to beg him to continue.

"What worked?" she asked, her voice sounding hoarse and unnatural. *Everything* he'd done had worked all too well.

He bent close, his body moving the bed in an energetic rhythm. God, she hoped he'd do that earlobe thing again. "The headboard against the wall," he whispered.

The familiar *thwack-thwack* of wood meeting wall filtered through her haze of need. With one last powerful thrust, Matthew rolled off her.

Leaving Angel more frustrated than she'd ever been before in her life.

MATTHEW STARED UP at the ceiling while his breathing slowed.

Angel didn't move, didn't speak.

He didn't know what he'd expected from his ploy, but it definitely wasn't silence.

Should he stay or go?

His body told him to stay and pick up where they'd left off. His brain told him to get the hell out of her bed. And his heart, thudding painfully in his chest, felt bruised and uncertain.

He was falling for Angel, plain and simple. He wanted to take a chance on them. And trying to get her to acknowledge their attraction was only the start. Fool that he was, he wanted her to admit she cared about him. As much as he cared about her.

Angel propped herself up on her elbow. "Why?"

Her question took him by surprise. "Because I've been thinking of it for a long time."

"No. I mean why did you stop?"

"I wanted to force you to look at me in a different way. Pretty twisted, huh? As if one person can ever force another person to feel a particular way." He chuckled low in his throat.

Angel rolled onto her back. She hesitated. "I'm not sure I wanted you to stop. No, I take that back. I'm certain I *didn't* want you to stop."

"That's, um, good to know." He squeezed his eyes shut. Because if he looked into her big brown eyes and saw an invitation, he'd be a goner.

Her hand snuggled into his, there on the mattress between them. Her voice was nonchalant when she asked, "Just out of curiosity, did you bring condoms with you?"

"Believe it or not, yes. Fortunately Jonathon's friends weren't very thorough searching my travel kit. It could have been…awkward."

"So you figured you'd get laid this trip?"

"No. I always keep them in my kit. Like American Express says, don't leave home without them." He chuckled.

"That was a lame joke, Matt."

He smiled. "Very lame."

"You think we should postpone the trip to Jonathon's study?"

"Definitely." Because he felt as if he didn't have a coherent thought left in his head.

"And, Matt?"

"Yes?"

"That's good to know about the condoms. Not that I intend to act on the knowledge."

"No, of course not." They were back on familiar footing. But her barriers were dropping one by one.

His breathing slowed to a normal rate. His heart no longer thudded. He squeezed her hand. Contentment stole over him, wrapping him in warmth and promising sleep.

THE SOUND OF MUSIC intruded on Angel's dream, where she'd been running through the rows of the garden, searching for Matthew.

The alarm. She reached blindly toward the night-stand and managed to turn it off.

Then she remembered Matthew.

She opened her eyes and slowly turned her head. Sure enough, he was there. Sleeping soundly but taking only half the bed, no more, no less. Leave it to Matt not to trespass even in his sleep.

That's why his behavior the night before had surprised her. It wasn't like Matthew to ignore boundaries. And it wasn't like her to invite someone in.

Angel gingerly rolled out of bed, hoping she didn't wake him. She wasn't in the mood for morning-after awkwardness, even if they hadn't made love.

She grabbed a dress and headed to the bathroom, getting ready for the day in record time.

Fortunately all was quiet as she exited the bathroom. Matthew was still asleep, his hair tousled, his cheeks and nose pink from his day out in the sun. All in all, he looked downright irresistible. Good thing he wasn't awake and aware of it or she wouldn't stand a chance.

Eleanor was already in the kitchen when she came downstairs. Surprisingly so was Ruth, who stopped speaking midsentence.

She gave Angel a nasty look and flounced out of the room.

"What's with her? She's up earlier than usual."

"She wanted to speak to me about a problem. Apparently you and Matthew kept her up half the night." Eleanor raised an eyebrow.

Angel's face grew warm. "Oh."

"Perhaps you can make a special effort to contain your...enthusiasm in an effort to be considerate."

"Yes." Angel tried to appear appropriately concerned. "We'll try."

"Good."

The rest of the morning went downhill from there. Angel failed miserably at baking a peach pie. Dropped a plate and it broke. Was all thumbs and couldn't string together a coherent sentence when Matthew came downstairs. And soon he would be home for their picnic lunch. She had to snap out of it.

Her movements were slow and hesitant as she wrapped their pasties—small meat pies she and Eleanor had just baked. Selecting fruit and sodas by rote, she removed her apron and smoothed a strand of hair behind her ear.

"You look fine, dear." Eleanor smiled. "Matthew will think you're beautiful."

Angel wanted to tell her it didn't matter whether Matthew found her attractive. But she couldn't.

Instead she changed the subject. And if she got information in the process, all the better. "Eleanor, do you know what's wrong with Matthew's sister, Rebecca?"

"She has a...delicate constitution."

That was an ambiguous answer if Angel had ever heard one. "Is that what keeps her from seeing him after all these years? I know he would love to see her."

"Rebecca isn't out and about much these days. Her condition keeps her inside much of the time, from what I understand."

"Why isn't her home clustered with the rest of Jonathon's wives?"

Eleanor's mouth thinned. "You'd really have to ask him. Why so many questions?"

"My mother always said I was more curious than a cat. It worries Matthew that he hasn't seen his sister. I want him to be happy."

Eleanor patted Angel's cheek. "I know you do, dear. Now why don't you wait out front? It will lift his heart just to see you there to greet him."

"Yes, I guess it will."

Angel picked up the canvas bag filled with their lunch and headed out the front door. She stood on the porch inhaling the fresh air.

To someone unaware of the nuances at Zion's Gate, a few moments alone outside wouldn't be seen as a treat. But she thought there was more to it than met the eye. Either Eleanor had been trying to get rid of Angel because of her pesky questions or she was starting to trust Angel. Gradually the restrictions on her were lifting.

Raising her face to the sun, she closed her eyes and absorbed the healing warmth. Sunshine never failed to soothe her spirits.

When she opened her eyes, Angel saw Matthew walking across the hard-packed dirt near Raphael's homes. Recognition sizzled her nerves.

"Hey, you ready to go?"

"Yes. Eleanor suggested I wait for you out here. I think my incessant questions were getting on her nerves."

"You? Get on someone's nerves? Never."

"Wait till the newlywed glow fades."

He stepped close and took the bag from her hands. Pressing his lips to hers, his kiss was tender. "Ah, but you're wrong. The glow will deepen with time and never fade."

Angel cleared the lump in her throat. "Yeah, right, Romeo. Let's go get some lunch."

CHAPTER EIGHTEEN

THEIR PICNIC LUNCH seemed long ago at two in the morning when Angel broke into Jonathon's study—something a good Zion's Gate bride would never do.

Her schizoid existence was definitely wearing on her.

"Hurry," Matthew murmured.

"It's not easy in the dark."

"No, I'm sure it's very…hard."

She turned her head and glared, letting him know his juvenile humor was not appreciated. Then returned to working the lock mechanism with her library card. Thank goodness Jonathon didn't seem to feel elaborate security measures were needed. Probably thought Eleanor was the ultimate in home protection.

Angel felt a pang of remorse for thinking of the woman in an unkind way. Sad but true, Jonathon probably didn't value Eleanor any more than he would a well-trained guard dog.

Angel opened the door and stepped quickly inside. Matthew followed.

Once in the room, they were able to utilize the glow from Matthew's watch to see better.

"You're sure we can't turn on the light?" he asked.

"No. The light could be seen under the door." She switched on the computer. "How are you at hacking?"

"I can find my way around a bit."

"Good, because I missed that continuing-education class."

"Then step aside and let me see what I can do."

Angel watched over his shoulder as he worked around the password protection.

"Let's go for financials first," she suggested. "Any spreadsheets?"

"No, not a one. It looks like the only thing he uses this dinosaur for is researching genealogy. As if he's trying to trace the Stones back to the Garden of Eden."

"You're kidding, right?"

"Exaggerating." His fingers flew over the keys.

"Hey, you're pretty good at this."

"Should be. I spend most of my day on the computer."

"Check his cookies. Maybe we'll find something incriminating."

"Define *incriminating*."

"Child pornography, how to build a bomb in your basement, stuff like that."

"Okay."

Several minutes later he shook his head. "Clean as a whistle. A site with daily devotionals, more genealogy, a couple gardening sites."

"Hey, pull up those gardening sites."

The page loaded for the first site and it turned out as Angel had half suspected. "Hydroponics."

"Gardening in water instead of soil. Sounds pretty boring."

"Marijuana grows well in a hydroponic system. He might not have needed to know how to build a bomb in his basement. What're the chances he's growing weed instead?"

"Of any other leader, I'd say no way. But with Jonathon, I wouldn't bet against anything if he thought it would serve his purpose. It'd have to be a pretty big space, wouldn't it?"

"Yes. Can you think of anywhere with large unused areas? A barn, basement or attic?"

"Not offhand. But it's not like they allow me to explore."

"I don't imagine the tunnel would be big enough. Maybe it's time we resumed our evening explorations around the compound."

"Could be."

Angel thought she heard a noise coming from the hallway. "Shh."

Matthew stilled.

Her pulse pounded. She reached for her weapon, only to find she didn't have one. Just her library card and a butt-ugly cotton nightgown.

The seconds ticked by, but neither of them moved.

A metallic sound came from the door. Slowly the knob turned.

Had she remembered to lock the door behind them? The most basic rule in surveillance, and she couldn't remember.

Holding her breath, Angel resisted the urge to pray. God had ignored her during worse scrapes than this, why should he start helping now?

The knob stopped at a quarter turn, where the lock engaged.

Angel released her breath.

They waited fifteen minutes, completely still and silent, before Angel opened the door a crack and peeked into the hallway. Nobody was there.

She signaled Matthew and he shut down the computer.

This time Angel took deliberate note of twisting the lock tab before shutting the door behind them. They stood still, listening.

When Angel didn't hear anything more than ordinary night noises, she crept to the stairs, motioning Matthew to follow. She made a visual inspection and proceeded upstairs, careful to avoid the noisy steps.

Once in their room, Angel leaned against the door and exhaled. Her pulse pounded and adrenaline surged through her system. "I thought we were caught."

Matthew leaned next to her. "You're sure you heard something?"

"No, not positive. But I've learned to trust my gut. There was a noise I couldn't identify. And the knob turned."

"I have to admit all this cloak-and-dagger stuff is pretty exciting. We make a good team."

Angel eyed him. "Are you sure you're not a frustrated police academy candidate in disguise?"

"Nope. Never wanted to be a cop. I did want to be a firefighter for a long time. The idea of rescuing people appealed to me."

"That doesn't surprise me. You seem to have that protector thing going on."

"I don't like to see people hurting. Particularly innocent people who can't help themselves for one reason or another." Matthew shrugged as if he'd revealed too much. And in a way he had.

"Were you ever abused, Matthew?"

He sat on the bed, silent, his expression thoughtful.

"Matthew?" She went to him and knelt at his feet, grasping his hands in hers.

"Not in the way you mean. I wasn't beaten or sexually abused. But you could probably make a case for mental abuse after my mother married Jonathon. He never missed an opportunity to point out how worthless I was. I felt trapped, with nowhere to turn. And leaving was almost worse in some ways. We were really, truly on our own, cast out in a strange land." He shook his head. "Sounds dramatic, I know."

"No, it sounds like the truth." Her heart went out to him. She hadn't really considered how brave he must have been. "How amazing that you went on to have a normal life and make a success of yourself."

"Anything I've done has been because my mom worked two jobs and searched out financial aid so I could get a college degree. And found the right people to help me learn what it meant to be a man in mainstream society."

She smoothed the laugh lines around his mouth with her fingertips. "No, Matthew, you deserve some of the credit, too. You could have felt sorry for yourself and wasted your opportunities. Or fallen into the blame game."

"Oh, I blame all right."

"You've never acted like a victim, though."

"I try not to let my origins determine who I am. But I haven't learned the forgiveness part and that bothers me."

"Some people don't deserve to be forgiven."

"The Bible tells me differently."

Angel sighed. "I can't debate religion, Matt. But I can tell you my husband was a cruel, evil man. And he totally deserved to die." She glanced away. "I do wonder sometimes what would have happened had he lived. Would I have forgiven him and gone back, only to have him kill me in the end? Or would I still have gone into law enforcement and learned how to protect myself and others?"

"He can't hurt you anymore, Angelina." His voice was low, warm and reassuring. Matthew's presence was enough to make it seem as if Kent had never existed. That she'd always been safe and always would be.

Angel leaned into the reassurance he represented. How she longed to let go of being a survivor and simply be a woman again. It was something she hadn't been able to achieve with the few lovers she'd had since Kent. Sex had been a chore, something to be endured, not enjoyed.

Matthew wrapped his arm around her and kissed the top of her head. "I think you would still have chosen a career helping others. Compassion is as much a part of you as breathing. You try to cover with tough talk, but that's all it is—talk. Because you're afraid people will use your kind heart against you. Like Kent did."

Her eyes burned. She blinked back moisture, nodding. "I guess so."

"I know so." He kissed away the stray tear that managed to escape and trickle down her cheek. His touch was tender, right. Making love with him seemed inevitable. How had she ever fooled herself into thinking otherwise?

"Matthew, you know when I asked you about condoms the other night?"

"Yes?"

"It wasn't just idle curiosity."

He hesitated. "I don't know what to say, Angelina. I've waited for you to realize how good we could be together. But the next move has to be yours."

She stood, holding out her hand.

He glanced at her hand, then her eyes.

She hoped he could tell how much this meant to her. How much she wanted it to happen for the right reasons. Even if she wasn't sure where love fit into the equation.

"Talk to me, Angel. Tell me what's going on in your head." His voice was low. "I can't accept your invitation unless I know why you've changed your mind."

Angel made a noise of frustration low in her throat. This was hard enough as it was without Matthew pushing for verbal intimacy, too.

"Tell me, Angelina." This time it was a plea.

"I trust you. I feel close to you. I think maybe I can make love with you the way I made love before I became afraid."

He studied her face, tracing the line of her jaw with his fingers. "But you don't love me? Even a little?"

"I don't know." The words were wrenched from her. She didn't want to hurt him but couldn't give him the reassurance he needed.

Nodding slowly, he placed his hand in hers. "That will have to be enough. But first, I want you to know I'm falling in love with you."

Angel's instinct was to drop his hand and run from the room. But Matthew held her fast. His gaze locked with hers. "It's okay, Angel. I learned long ago life isn't perfect. And sometimes we have to accept the small unexpected gifts along the way."

Gratitude lifted her spirits. It would be okay. Matthew understood and wanted her anyway.

She tugged on his hand.

He hesitated, then stood. "Where're we going?"

Closing the distance between them, Angel kissed him. "To my bed. Where there's no dishonesty or fakery allowed. I refuse to make love with you for the first time in a bed where we've been playacting for weeks."

Angel led him to the pallet on the floor. Dropping his hand, she grasped the hem of her ugly cotton nightgown and drew it over her head. She stood before him, waiting.

His eyes grew dark as his gaze roamed over her body. "Oh, Angelina, you are more beautiful than I dreamed."

"Thank you." What a lame thing to say. But he didn't seem to expect sparkling conversation.

Matthew traced the curve of her hip with his fingertips, until he met the elastic band of her cotton panties. "Mind if I remove these?"

"Um, no. No, I don't mind, I mean."

He slipped her panties to the floor. She hesitated, then stepped out of them.

"Are you sure you want to go through with this? You can change your mind, you know."

"No," she assured him. "I need you, Matt. I trust you more than I've trusted anyone in a long time. Please, do this for me?"

His smile was slow and sexy. "Of course. I'd do anything for you."

It was the kind of sweeping declaration men made when they wanted to get laid. But with Matthew, she never doubted his sincerity.

"Matthew," she murmured.

He pulled her to him, wrapping his arms around her and holding her close. She could feel his heart thudding beneath her palm. Could feel his erection pressed against her belly.

A responding warmth flooded through her.

He kissed her with a bone-melting passion. Sealing her to him as surely as if they'd exchanged vows of undying love. Through the haze Angel wondered how he would have kissed her if she'd told him she loved him. Because it didn't seem possible a kiss could get better than this.

She lost herself to emotion, and fragments of memories flashed through her. Every heartfelt, honest kiss she'd received. And that was the difference between Matthew's kisses and Kent's. Kent's had been window dressing, masking his lies and twisting his intent. Matthew's were as clean and honest and sensual as his soul.

Sighing, she pressed against him, needing to get closer. His clothing was an unnecessary impediment.

Angel pulled back, placing her finger against his lips. "Shh. This will only take a second."

With surety of purpose, she unbuttoned his shirt and tossed it onto the straight-backed chair. Then Matthew got into the spirit of things and removed his pants.

"Condoms?" she asked.

"Suitcase." He pulled his luggage from the closet, unzipping two pockets before he found his travel kit. He withdrew several packets and returned to her side.

Pressing them into her hand, he said, "For you."

"Thanks, Matt. But I think you might benefit from them as much as me."

"Maybe." He shrugged, his expression unreadable. "Creating a child with you would be a blessing."

Angel raised her hand, palm outward. "Please don't complicate this. Let's just enjoy each other without a lot of dreams and promises."

"If that's what you want."

"It is." She knelt on the blankets, extending her hand to him. "Join me?"

"Of course. You don't know how long I've waited."
His voice was hoarse.

He knelt next to her. Gathering her in his arms,
he settled her against the pillows, his body lightly
covering hers. "You're sure this will be comfortable
enough for you?"

"Of course." Laughter bubbled up inside her. "Because I'm going to be on top."

Matthew raised an eyebrow. Then deftly rolled,
bringing her with him so she was on top. He settled her
against his erection. "I told you I'd do anything for you."

"So you did, Matt. So you did."

CHAPTER NINETEEN

A FEW DAYS LATER, the sun warmed Angel through her cotton dress as she checked tomato plants for suckers and hornworms. She supposed she ought to be grateful polyester wasn't the preferred fabric for the well-dressed polygamist woman or she would have boiled in her own perspiration. Definitely *not* the way she wanted to receive her husband when he returned home for lunch. Because they were getting very good at stealing odd moments for hot, quick sex. And then at night making slow, sweet love as they rocked the bed in earnest.

Ruth had run complaining to Eleanor again. But Eleanor had simply handed the girl some foam ear-plugs and told her to read her Bible if she couldn't sleep.

Angel's smile of satisfaction faded as she spied another pest.

"Yuck." She pulled a fat green caterpillar from one of the robust plants.

Glancing around, Angel was disappointed to find that Eleanor was too far away to assist in the execution.

Angel placed the caterpillar on the hard-packed walkway and prepared herself to do what was necessary. She raised her foot, hesitated, then lowered it to the ground. The pest scooted toward the safety of the plants.

She picked it up and again placed it in the middle of the path, giving herself a mental pep talk. *You can do this. You've been trained to kill, swiftly and without mercy.*

The caterpillar made for the other side of the path. This time she let it escape.

"You're too soft," a lyrical voice said from behind her.

Angel turned and shielded her eyes from the sun with her hand. "I'm practicing being merciful."

The tall, thin blonde nodded. "I thought as much." Humor crinkled the corners near her sparkling green eyes, so much like Matthew's. She extended her hand. "I'm Rebecca, Matthew's—"

"Sister." Angel clasped her hand and squeezed. "I'm so glad to meet you. Matthew's told me a lot about you."

"I've been absolutely dying to meet you, too. So Matthew is all grown up and a husband now. You must be quite special."

"I don't know about the special part, but your brother and I, um, see eye to eye on many things."

Rebecca released Angel's hand. "That's good. Consensus is important in a marriage. So is love."

"Um, yes." The conversation was taking an uncomfortable turn. She wasn't prepared to share sisterly confidences.

But, studying Rebecca's expression, Angel thought she detected a trace of wistfulness rather than curiosity. Rebecca covered quickly with a smile. "I can't stay. I just wanted to introduce myself while I was here. I found I had no decent store-bought tomatoes to slice for Jonathon's sandwiches and I thought ours might be ripe by now."

"I'm glad you did. I know Matthew is eager to see you."

Rebecca backed a few paces. "Please tell him I'll meet with him soon and not to worry."

"I will."

Rebecca glanced at her watch. "I must hurry."

"I saw a few ripe tomatoes on those plants over there." Angel nodded in the direction of the prime specimens.

"Thank you." Matthew's sister picked several tomatoes. "I look forward to chatting with you again." Then she hurried away.

"Yes, when you can stay a little longer," Angel murmured under her breath.

A moment later Eleanor's voice startled her. "Jonathon coddles Rebecca because of her delicate health. He's…protective. Keeps a close eye on her to make sure she doesn't overdo it."

Angel turned to face her mentor. "I've known people who have done horrible things in the name of protecting those they love."

Eleanor knelt down and picked several tomatoes. "I don't believe Jonathon would hurt Rebecca. His love for her is real. But I can see how a woman might come to feel resentful of such intense…devotion."

"Some would call it controlling."

"Not in our community. Rebecca has a difficult path. I try to watch out for her."

Angel thought she understood the subtext that was inherent in many of Eleanor's conversations. "You told her I'd be here, didn't you?"

She shrugged. "I thought it might be good for both of you."

"Don't get me wrong, I'm pleased we were able to meet. But it's really Matthew who needs to see her."

"Unfortunately Matthew spends much of his time with

Jonathon and the elders." Eleanor tucked a strand of gray hair behind her ear. "It's impossible for me to arrange a meeting for him. But you—that's another story."

"Eleanor, you are a very complex woman."

"Not as complex as you think. But loyal to those I love—as long as they don't betray me." She bent down and plucked a caterpillar from its leafy hiding place, dispatching it with efficiency. "Perhaps you can harvest something nice for supper?"

"Yes, ma'am," Angel responded quietly. Had Eleanor somehow guessed at Angel's true reason for being at Zion's Gate? Shaking her head, Angel dismissed the thought. Eleanor was still her champion in many ways. No, it seemed there might be someone else who had betrayed the woman and needed to be squashed like a bug.

Angel mulled over the enigma that was Eleanor while she harvested okra and put the odd-looking vegetable in her basket. By arranging the meeting with Rebecca, Eleanor had defied Jonathon's express wishes. Yet she stressed she was loyal to those she loved.

Could Jonathon have betrayed Eleanor in a way more heinous than sleeping with a multitude of other women? Or maybe Eleanor was finally seeing him for the evil tyrant he was.

TIRED OF PACING THE room, Matthew sat on the bed waiting for Angel to get out of the shower. He might have joined her at another time. But not tonight.

Jonathon had made it impossible for Matthew to leave at lunch today, so he'd barely had a chance to talk to Angel other than receiving a whispered message that she'd met Rebecca.

Angel exited the bathroom clad in a robe and toweling her hair. Loose, her hair was a vibrant mass of tangled waves. She was the most beautiful, passionate woman he'd ever met. How he hated seeing her change into the demure Zion's Gate wife, donning shapeless dresses and restraining her glorious hair in braids. Worse yet was watching her pile the braids on top of her head, pinning them so tightly it had to hurt.

But she'd learned to look like a proper Zion's Gate bride. Sometimes she did it so well it was eerie. Then he'd see the mischief lurking in her eyes and know his uncle and the elders would never control her spirit.

Angel walked past him and propped her foot on the chair. Her robe gaped open as she applied lotion to her long golden legs. How was he supposed to concentrate with that temptation in his face? He forced himself to focus.

"Tell me about Rebecca." His voice was husky.

Angel went to the bathroom and retrieved a wide-tooth comb. Drawing it through her hair, she said, "Rebecca looks a lot like you. Same eyes, same smile. I imagine the same dry sense of humor, though I didn't get her to talk long enough to know for sure."

"Is she well? Happy? Will I see her soon?"

Perching on the bed, Angel was unusually solemn. "She impressed me as a woman who is being controlled in an unhealthy manner. She wouldn't stay past a couple minutes and made up an excuse for being in the garden—I imagine in case Jonathon finds out she was there. But she wanted me to deliver a message to you. I was supposed to tell you there's no reason for you to worry and she'll meet with you soon."

"That's it?" His frustration rose. To be so close to

his sister and not be able to contact her was making him edgy.

"That's all." Angel hesitated. "I got the impression she took a risk to come meet me. And that Eleanor took a risk arranging it."

"Why? Was it something she said?"

"No, she didn't say anything out of the ordinary."

"You're holding something back. What is it?"

Angel wished she could simply ignore Matthew's question. He was too damn perceptive. Her heart ached at what she was about to tell him and she would have given almost anything to be able to lie. But their relationship was based on a foundation of trust, fragile though it was. So fragile that she felt she had to uphold the tenet, even if it meant hurting the man she deeply cared about.

Taking a deep breath, she said, "Rebecca reminded me of how I was with Kent. The detailed way she orchestrated the trip. How she kept looking over her shoulder. And kept a close eye on her watch."

"There could be another explanation."

"It's my gut feeling she's been abused. I could be wrong—usually I'm not. The vibes I'm getting are those of a woman afraid for her physical safety. Or afraid for the safety of her children."

The color drained from his face. He sat down. "I was hoping that, despite my doubts about the man, Jonathon had been good to my sister. Because all these years I've been afraid Rebecca sacrificed herself so my mother could be free."

"What do you mean?"

"I was the only one supposed to leave. Like a lot of the guys my age, the plan was just to cut me loose. My mother was expected to resign herself to never seeing me again."

"Like Eleanor."

He nodded and stood, pacing. "But my mother was concerned. She'd heard stories of kids coming to a bad end trying to make it in a world they didn't have the skills to survive in. My mother met with Jonathon. They had a huge argument. I couldn't hear all that was said, only the end. Jonathon raised his voice and told my mother he wouldn't allow her to leave Zion's Gate."

Angel went to Matthew, touched his arm, trying to remind him he no longer had to carry this burden alone. "What happened?"

"I don't know. My mother told him if he didn't let her go with me, she would tell."

"Tell what?"

"I never found out. I've always suspected Jonathon was involved in my father's death and my mother had evidence. Jonathon told her she would never have the opportunity to tell."

Swallowing hard, Angel fought a wave of nausea. Jonathon's words were eerily reminiscent of the words Kent had used with her. The threat was obvious.

"Yet he changed his mind?"

"That's what doesn't make sense. My mother came to me later that night and told me to grab my things, we were leaving. I never saw my sister again. My mother said Rebecca refused to go with us."

"Rebecca married Jonathon?"

"Yes, immediately after we left... I have to find her, Angel. I have to talk to Rebecca." There was a desperation in his voice she'd never heard before.

"I know, Matt. But Rebecca said she would see you soon."

"That's not good enough. For all we know, she was stalling, trying to smooth things over."

That was exactly Angel's impression. "Weren't you the one who said we should be cautious? I'm getting more freedom, you're allowed into town for the farmer's market. We don't want to jeopardize the rapport we've built."

"Rapport, my ass."

Matthew's language confirmed Zion's Gate was taking a heavy toll on him. He was desperate to find his sister. And desperate men often ended up dead men in the world of undercover.

She placed her palms on either side of his face. "Matt, I know you're frustrated. We'll find her. You have my promise. Just don't do something foolish."

"I may not be in law enforcement, but I assure you I'm no fool."

"I didn't mean it that way. All I'm saying is we're in this together. Don't shut me out. If you want to search, we'll search. Together."

He held her gaze. Grasping her hand in his, he kissed her palm, his lips warm and alive. God, it was so very important she keep him alive. Because she couldn't handle losing him.

"Thank you, Angelina," he murmured. "We'll search tonight."

And they did. But it was nearly a repeat of the first time they'd investigated the meeting hall. Same black Humvee with its lights off, same men, same boxes. Only this time Angel and Matthew were better prepared and didn't raise an alarm. They even slipped back into the house without waking Eleanor.

The biggest difference, however, was that they made

love when they returned. Cocooned beneath the wedding-ring quilt, they pretended, for a few hours, that the world they lived in wasn't confusing and dangerous.

"WHAT'S THE HURRY, Matt?" Angel broke into a trot to keep up with his stride.

Matthew tried to slow his pace but couldn't. He felt driven to talk to her immediately. Grasping her hand, he hauled her along toward their tree at the park.

His movements were jerky as he helped her spread the blanket on the ground. Instead of lifting their lunch items one by one from the canvas tote, he simply turned it over and dumped the contents on the blanket.

"Matthew." Angel's tone was shocked.

"We've got to hurry. Things have been getting weird at the meetings. Jonathon's jumpy and he's applying pressure to find new short-term ways to increase income. I wouldn't be surprised to be yanked back to the meeting hall before we finish eating."

"Did anyone say why he's so jumpy?"

"No. Raphael's never seen him this bad. And Jonathon's pressing me to tithe immediately to demonstrate my devotion to God and Zion's Gate. I offered to write him a check for ten thousand dollars just to allay his suspicions. But he's adamant I should give ten percent of my net worth. And make it by wire transfer to an out-of-state account when we're in town tomorrow."

"Farmer's market again?" Angel asked.

"Yes."

"I've noticed the trips to town seem to happen after the Humvee brigade visits. It might be just a coincidence. But, then again, I don't believe in coincidences."

He shook his head. "I used to. But not anymore. If

the exchange of the smuggled goods is made at the meeting hall, then why do we need to go to town? What are we transporting for them?"

"Cash from the transaction is my guess. Jonathon may be laundering money for his landlord. And I bet the evening patrols are the landlord's idea, too, allowing him free access to the meeting hall and surrounding area."

Matthew handed her a sandwich and a soda. He unwrapped a sandwich for himself but had very little appetite. "Sounds possible. But what's Jonathon getting out of this?"

"Money. Protection against U.S. authorities. Protection against the lawless influences in this area. It's a sweetheart deal. Except dealing with drug traffickers gets dangerous no matter what. I know of two brothers who tortured and killed their own mother because she threatened to turn them in."

"That's sick."

"But maybe not that much farther out on the moral spectrum than what Jonathon practices. Once you start bending rules, it gets easier to lose all perspective on right and wrong."

"You'll get no argument from me." Matthew hesitated. He hated to even voice the thoughts swirling in his head. But if he ignored his suspicions, people he loved might get hurt. Might even die. "With all his talk of doom and God's wrath, I'm afraid Jonathon's planning something drastic."

"I don't like the sound of that. Especially since we know there are at least a few semiautomatic weapons. But I don't want to make dire predictions without proof. Can we get inside the meeting hall tonight?"

Matthew shook his head. "Nope. Our landlord has

offered to have his men help pack the produce tonight. They'll be all over the place."

"Damn."

"Angel, I know this is what you're trained to do, but I worry about you getting hurt."

"No need to worry, Matt. I can take care of myself." She hesitated. Her voice was low, tinged with defeat when she said, "It's you I worry about."

He grasped her chin. "Hey, it's okay."

"No, it's not okay. I broke the rules when I got involved with you. What if my lack of objectivity gets someone killed?"

"Aw, Angelina, don't ever beat yourself up over what's happened between us." He cupped her face with his hand. "It was meant to be. I firmly believe that. With the two of us working together, we won't allow *anyone* to get hurt."

CHAPTER TWENTY

THE NEXT MORNING, Matthew wasn't surprised to see the trucks loaded and ready to go when he arrived at the meeting hall before sunrise.

"Matthew," Jonathon said. "I trust you had a thoughtful night."

"Very. I spent a quiet evening praying for God's will."

"And how did He respond?"

"It is right and good for me to tithe, Uncle Jonathon. I'm still unclear how He wants me to do that, though."

Jonathon's eyes narrowed. "The Bible is very clear. Ten percent."

The man must be desperate if he thought Matthew was going to hand over ten percent of his net worth. Though, if it would buy his sister's freedom, he'd do it without hesitation.

"Yes, I agree, Uncle. But not retroactively."

"You're being unreasonable, Matthew. And after all I did for your mother. Taking her in after my brother died, feeding and clothing her children."

Anger burned in Matthew's chest. His mother hadn't wanted Jonathon. Neither had her children, least of all Matthew. They'd still been reeling from the death of Matthew's father when Uncle Jonathon had swooped down and claimed them as his prize of war. Because that's what it had been. A bitter sibling rivalry that went back nearly to the cradle. A rivalry that ended with Matthew's father's death. Coincidence?

Matthew tended to agree with Angel. There were no coincidences.

He reined in his anger. It would serve no purpose now. But someday he would make Jonathon pay.

"And was marrying my sister for my mother's sake, too?"

Jonathon stiffened. "I've been a good, righteous husband to Rebecca."

"Why doesn't she live near the rest of your wives and children?"

"Rebecca is delicate. She can't handle the stress."

"So keeping her in seclusion is for her benefit?"

"I love Rebecca."

Matthew rolled his shoulders. They were getting nowhere. His uncle was as hard to pin down as any politician. So he would get his attention the only way he seemed to understand. "Perhaps worry over my sister is interfering with my prayer life. That could be why I'm so unclear on the whole tithing issue."

"If I arrange for you to meet with Rebecca, will that clear your mind?"

"Yes, I imagine it would help immensely."

"In the meantime, is there any reason why you can't tithe ten percent of your income for this year? I'd counted on your wire transfer today."

"Prorated to reflect the actual portion of the year I've spent in Zion's Gate. And after I speak with my sister, I'm sure my ability to comprehend God's commands will improve."

"Fine." Jonathon flicked the key tab, unlocking the doors of the Silverado. "Get in."

"I'm riding with you? I thought you drove alone."

"I've been remiss, Matthew. I should have spent more time with you once you returned. And I intend to remedy that immediately by spending the day together."

Great. Now his uncle was going to stick to him like glue.

"That's not necessary. I know what a busy man you are." Matthew had no hope of slipping away to send Angel's report if he was with his uncle.

"Yes, I am busy." Jonathon smiled, apparently somewhat mollified. "But we can spend some time together today."

Matthew nodded. A concession at least. And he might acquire new information by accompanying his uncle on his rounds.

Jonathon settled himself in the driver's seat.

Matthew went to the passenger side and opened the door. There was a laptop case on the seat. He picked it up. "Where do you want this?"

"See if you can wedge it in on the floor in the backseat."

Matthew flipped the seat forward and stashed the case on the floor. Pushing the seat back into place, he got in.

The silence grew awkward as they drove toward town. The conversation was even more awkward, if possible.

"How are things going with Angel?"

"Fine. She's a good woman."

"Yes, I'm sure she is."

If Matthew had heard a leer in his uncle's voice, he would have coldcocked him. Fortunately he seemed sincere and not alluding to Angel's attributes. Though *good* didn't begin to describe what they shared.

Matthew loved Angel, pure and simple. Might have loved her since the first day he'd met her at the DPS offices in Brownsville. Smart, lively and strong. Everything he wanted to be.

"Matthew?"

"Hmm?"

"I asked if Angel was with child yet."

"No, we haven't been blessed yet." But they might be soon, if they didn't practice some serious self-control. They'd used the last condom in the night.

"From what I hear, it's not for lack of trying." Jonathon laughed a little too loudly and punched Matthew on the shoulder. He shouldn't try to be one of the guys. He failed miserably.

"We're newlyweds, Uncle. Besides, who told you that?"

Jonathon cleared his throat. "Must've been Eleanor."

Matthew doubted it. Eleanor wasn't one to gossip needlessly, even for Jonathon's benefit.

Then he recalled Angel saying she'd seen Jonathon and Ruth conferring early one morning in the kitchen. And seeming just a tad too chummy for simple pastoral counseling.

But if Jonathon had something going with Ruth, why didn't he simply marry her himself? What was one more wife once you passed the double digits?

Matthew decided to let it go. He had much more pressing things to worry about. Like how he might be able to ditch Uncle Jonathon when they got to town.

The rest of the trip went by in relative silence, a welcome relief. When they approached town, Jonathon turned off on a side road and the other two Zion's Gate trucks kept going.

"We have a few deliveries to make."

"Raphael said there's a restaurant and a couple of small businesses that are good customers."

Jonathon smiled. "Yes. *Very* good customers."

When they pulled behind Just Greens Restaurant, Jonathon said, "You go ahead and make this delivery."

"Sure."

Jonathon got out but left the truck idling. He opened the rear door and hefted a box off the seat. "Here you go."

Matthew accepted it. He found it odd that Jonathon allowed the crates on his pristine upholstery when he had a perfectly good bed liner in the back. And an empty bed.

"This is it? One box?"

"Take that, then I'll have a second one ready for you. When you're done, Antonio will give you an envelope with payment."

Shrugging, Matthew decided not to take his uncle to task for poor time management. Or call him lazy. Two men, two boxes—the math wasn't difficult.

Antonio came out to greet him, eyeing Matthew with curiosity.

"I've got one more box for you."

"*Si.*"

Matthew returned to the truck. Jonathon selected a second crate and handed it to him. He carried it to Antonio and received the payment envelope.

Jonathon put the truck in gear as Matthew swung into the passenger seat.

After the last delivery at a fruit-and-vegetable stand, Matthew handed Jonathon the payment envelope.

Smiling with satisfaction, Jonathon said, "It's good

to have you involved in the family business, Matthew."
His words were layered with meaning.

Matthew got the sick feeling he understood
exactly what his uncle meant. Matthew was now connected with whatever illegal activity Jonathon was
involved in.

ANGEL DRIED THE LAST breakfast dish and sighed.
"Please tell me it's baking day. If it's laundry again, I
don't think I'll make it till lunch."

Eleanor smiled. "Perhaps if you slept more at night,
you wouldn't be so fatigued."

"I sleep like a baby." Which was the absolute truth.
Spooned next to Matthew, she slept better than she
had in years.

"Like a baby. Interesting choice of words."

Angel braced her hands on her hips. "No, I'm not
pregnant. And I'm tired of everyone mentally measuring my waistline."

"Oh, dear, I seem to have touched a nerve. I'm sorry,
Angel." She patted Angel's cheek, her eyes warm with
affection. "Believe me, I only want you to be happy."

Angel's throat got all scratchy. "I know you do. I
guess I'm sensitive because I know everyone is ready
to pounce the moment I conceive so they can marry
Ruth off to Matthew."

Why the thought upset her so, she didn't know.
Because she and Matthew had been careful and she
definitely wasn't pregnant.

"I'm sure everything will work out as it's supposed
to. Now, I have a surprise for you this morning," Eleanor
chirped—and Eleanor was *not* a chirpy kind of woman.

"Surprise?" She was intrigued in spite of herself.

"I'm going to share my passion with you. Follow me to Jonathon's study."

Angel nearly groaned aloud. Please, no more Bible readings or Book of Mormon studies.

"Come on," Eleanor said. "I will show you the world of genealogy."

"That sounds, um, fun." *Not*.

But it would give her a chance to scope out Jonathon's study again. The thought made her hurry after Eleanor.

When they entered the room, Eleanor headed straight for the desk and Jonathon's padded leather chair. A satisfied smile curved her lips as she booted up the computer.

"I wasn't aware you knew anything about computers."

"Yes, dear, Jonathon allowed me to take an online course a few years ago. It opened up a whole new world to me."

"I bet. And you use the Internet to research genealogy?"

"Uh-huh. Among other things."

Hydroponics? But Angel wasn't supposed to know what the computer's hard drive contained.

"Pull up a chair, Angel."

Angel would much rather have wandered around the room to see if there might be a likely hiding place for incriminating documents. Or possibly a safe containing drug money. But she complied with Eleanor's request. The woman seemed so excited to share her hobby.

"I've got it divided into files. The Stone family and the Coopers. Abigail and I were Coopers before we married."

"Ah."

"You'll notice here our maternal great-grandmother was Elena Marquez—I was named for her. Our great-grandfather met her when his parents settled in Mexico when he was a child."

"That's interesting. I would have never guessed you had a drop of Hispanic blood. My mother is Colombian by birth and my father was born in Colombia to Anglo parents from Chicago. They taught English at the university."

"See, we have very much in common. My grandparents took us to Mexico once to visit for the summer." Eleanor's expression grew dreamy. "I recall the brethren there were warm and friendly."

"*Habla Espanol,* Elena?"

"*Si, y tu,* Angelina?"

"*Si.* Matthew doesn't speak Spanish?"

"No. Jonathon and Joshua's parents disapproved of our mixed blood, though it was back several generations. They thought it better if we didn't speak Spanish, particularly around the children."

"That's too bad. I think they would have benefited from exploring the culture."

Eleanor sighed. "I do, too. But some people are not so open-minded."

"I intend to speak Spanish to my children so they can be bilingual."

"What a wonderful idea. Perhaps Matthew will learn at the same time. Or they can teach their papa."

Angelina smiled at the mental picture of Matthew telling bedtime stories in Spanish. The picture was so vivid it made her blink. Then she realized how intertwined her life had become with Matthew's. And how badly she wanted to have children with him. To grow old with him. And share all the other moments in between, happy and sad.

Sighing, Angel couldn't wait for him to return from town. Maybe tonight she would tell him she loved him.

Eleanor grasped Angel's hand. "It's important that you know how much I love you. I was blessed with seven sons, but no daughter. You are like the daughter I never had."

Angel's eyes blurred. "What a wonderful thing to say, Eleanor. And I feel as if you're my second mother. Which makes me truly blessed."

Eleanor glanced at her watch. "Oh, my goodness. How the time has flown. I promised Rebecca I would drop off a jar of honey. Why don't you stay here and investigate your genealogy a bit?"

"I could go with you."

"No, dear, someone might see you and I would have a hard time explaining."

"Well, then, it would be lovely to spend some time at the computer."

"I'll be back in less than an hour."

"Thank you, Eleanor."

A few moments later Angel heard the front door close. She filled in some of her family information and did a quick search on the genealogy site in case Eleanor checked.

Then she explored, starting with the desk drawers. Locked. She'd come back to those later.

Standing, she paced the perimeter of the room. None of the anemic pastoral scenes on the walls yielded anything but solid wall behind their frames. The floor was a weathered Mexican tile with the patina of many footsteps and many years. More than ten? She doubted it.

A brightly colored wool rug covered the center of the room, running beneath the desk. As she pushed back in the chair, the wheels caught on something.

She leaned over and felt along the wheels with her fingers. Probably a pen someone had dropped. But she encountered nothing.

Curious, Angel stood, moving the chair to the side of the desk. Flipping back the rug, she noted the grout around one of the tiles was worn and chipped, probably from the desk chair rolling repeatedly over it during the years.

Angel opened the top desk drawer and found a letter opener. She inserted the point in the cracked grout, wiggling it beneath. The tile popped out with very little pressure.

Her fingers shook as they closed over the flat cotton drawstring bag. Opening it, she found several floppy disks inside.

Inserting the first disk into the drive, she almost laughed aloud when she saw it appeared to be a manuscript written by Jonathon Stone. Maybe Matt hadn't been so far off course when he'd suggested they might find memoirs handing Jonathon to them on a silver platter.

But *Death at Zion's Gate* appeared to be a thriller, full of drug deals gone bad and international espionage. Jonathon definitely had a vivid imagination. Unfortunately his talent as a storyteller was next to nonexistent.

Angel had just inserted the second disk when she heard the front door open. Cursing under her breath, she ejected the disk and put it back into the bag. Did she dare steal the disks? There wasn't time to copy and replace them.

Angel made a quick decision and lifted her skirt. Fortunately she could tuck the packet into the waist-band of her briefs and no one would be the wiser.

Smoothing down her skirt, she replaced the tile and folded the rug back into place. She had just rolled the chair back when she heard her name being called.

"Angel?"

"Yes, Eleanor, I'm still in the office." She maximized the genealogy page.

Eleanor entered the room smiling broadly. She handed Angel a piece of fabric with intricate embroidery. "Rebecca wants you to have this. It will be lovely once it's framed. It's a sampler."

Angel ran her finger over the stitching. "Yes, I know. It's beautiful. I must thank her next time I see her."

"Yes." Eleanor glanced away. "Or I can tell her for you."

"See, I got some of my information input. I'm afraid I'm very slow on the computer."

"A little bit at a time, that's how most things get done. Why don't we go bake a peach cobbler? It's Matthew's favorite and I'm sure he'll be famished when he gets home."

Angel wanted to scream in frustration. She had three disks tucked away beneath her dress and she wanted nothing more than to pore over them. But first and foremost she was supposed to be a good Zion's Gate bride.

They chatted about inconsequential things while they made the peach cobbler.

"You've improved much as a cook since you've been here. You're a very gifted baker when you set your mind to it," Eleanor observed. "Even your biscuits are exceptional now."

Angel warmed with pride. She *was* a good baker, a talent that would have remained buried if she hadn't been assigned to Zion's Gate. And she never would have met Matthew and fallen in love with a genuinely good man.

Contentment mingled with the aroma of baking cobbler. The thought of falling in love was something that had scared her since Kent's death. But with Matthew, it was just a natural extension of their relationship and who he was. Angel couldn't comprehend *not* being in love with him.

And though she enjoyed Eleanor's company at lunch and the antics of the children taking a break from their studies, she missed Matthew terribly.

When he finally walked through the door at almost five that afternoon, she hurried to greet him.

"Matthew," she exclaimed, running to meet him. He drew her into his arms and held her close. "I missed you."

"I missed you, too, Angelina."

"Matthew, I trust the trip went well?" Eleanor asked from behind Angel.

Angel stifled a flash of annoyance. In a community like Zion's Gate, she had to share Matthew, even if they'd been separated all day and she wanted him to herself. What had Eleanor said once? *Sometimes the needs of one must be sacrificed for the good of many.*

Matthew released her, twining his hand with hers. "Yes, Aunt, it went well."

"I imagine Jonathon is at the meeting hall?"

"Yes, the men needed to unload supplies."

"If you will excuse me, I need to speak with him."

"Of course." Angel hoped her eagerness to get rid of Eleanor wasn't apparent in her voice. "I mean, we'll hold down the fort."

Eleanor chuckled. "I'm sure you will." Then she left.

Matthew pulled Angel close, nibbling on her neck.

"Are you thinking what I'm thinking? We have the house to ourselves for fifteen whole minutes. Maybe even twenty. I was able to shake Jonathon long enough to buy more condoms."

Angel responded with a noise of frustration. She wanted nothing more than to make love with Matthew. "We can't."

His breath was warm on her ear. Taking her lobe in his mouth, he suckled gently.

Heat pooled in her belly and need tugged at her breasts.

"Are you sure we can't? You'd be amazed at what I can do in thirteen minutes."

She placed her hands on either side of his face to make sure she had his full attention. "Matthew, my love, I'm always amazed at what you do. But we have business in the study."

"Business, right." He grinned.

"Seriously. Listen to me." She told him about the disks she'd found.

Sighing, he said, "Not the kind of business I'd hoped for but a gift all the same. Don't think you're getting off easy, though. I intend to continue our interlude this evening. I just hope Ruth has plenty of earplugs."

"I'll hold you to it. Now come on. Let's get into the study." She pulled away, but he grasped her arm.

"One thing first. You called me your love. Am I?"

The longing in his eyes surprised her. "Do you really need to ask?"

"Yes."

She closed the distance between them and touched his face. "Matthew, I've never missed anyone as much as I missed you today. I love you with my whole heart."

"Good. Because I love you."

Angel's eyes misted. It was a moment she would treasure forever. When she wasn't working against the clock. "We'll continue this tonight?"

"Absolutely."

"Then let's go see what's on those disks."

"After you, my love." Matthew gestured gallantly.

Angel quickly picked the lock to the study. Matthew flicked on the computer while Angel retrieved the fabric sack from the waistband of her briefs.

Matthew raised an eyebrow.

"Don't say a word," Angel warned, wishing she wore something sexy rather than serviceable. She withdrew the disks from the bag and handed them to Matthew.

He glanced at his watch. "Twelve minutes. Keep an eye on the time, okay?"

Angel nodded, reading over his shoulder. "Plans for a hydroponic garden—fruits, vegetables and herbs. No pot, though, unless it's in code."

Matthew ejected the disk and went on to the next. *Death at Zion's Gate.*

"Yes, apparently Jonathon is a frustrated novelist. I don't think there's much there."

Matthew scrolled through the pages. Then slowed.

"What is it?"

"It's about a fire in the barn."

"Do you think it has anything to do with your father's death?"

"I'm not sure." He frowned, scanning the pages.

Angel glanced at her watch. "Less than five minutes. Wrap it up."

Matthew didn't seem to hear her. He continued scanning.

"Matt, we've got to go."

He glanced up from the screen, his gaze wide and unfocused.

"What is it?"

"Padlocks. The doors were padlocked."

"Oh, Matt. We don't know any of it's true."

"I do. I remember my mother had bandaged hands the night my father died. She said she burned them grasping a cast-iron skillet without mitts. But she was *always* careful in the kitchen."

Looking at her watch, she said, "Let's discuss this later. We don't want to get caught in here."

Nodding, he closed the file and ejected the disk. He shut down the computer and handed her the disks.

The sound of the front door opening prodded her to shove the disks in the pocket of her dress.

"Go!"

She twisted the lock tab and shut the door behind them. They were a few steps away when Eleanor came around the corner calling, "Matthew? Angel?"

Matthew took the lead. "Yes, Aunt Eleanor?"

"Jonathon has asked you to spend the rest of the evening in meditation. Angel, I won't require your help in the kitchen tonight. I'll call you when supper is ready."

"Are you sure, Eleanor?"

"Positive. Now go."

Angel glanced at Matthew. He shrugged.

Sliding her hand into his, she followed her husband up the stairs. Hadn't she been dying to have time alone with him?

But something in Eleanor's manner bothered her. She just wished she could put her finger on the problem.

CHAPTER TWENTY-ONE

MATTHEW FOLLOWED Angel down the stairs, wanting nothing more than to persuade her to return to bed. To seek a few more moments of forgetfulness in her arms.

But Angel insisted on checking on Eleanor. She was worried about his aunt for a reason she couldn't name.

She stopped short when they entered the kitchen.

Eleanor had her back to them, chopping carrots. Her shoulders shook. They heard muffled sobs.

Angel ran to her. "Eleanor, what's wrong?"

"Nothing, dear." She wiped her eyes with her sleeve. Picking up a peeled onion, she cut it in half, then proceeded to dice it. "Onions."

Even Matthew knew enough about cooking to know an uncut onion wouldn't make Eleanor cry.

Angel took the knife from Eleanor's grasp and placed it on the counter. Touching her arm, she said. "Tell me what's wrong."

Eleanor squared her shoulders. "Nothing you should worry about, dear. I'll be fine. Now why don't you and Matthew sit on the porch while I finish preparing dinner. Think of it as my gift to you."

"I couldn't—"

"Please, do it for me?" Eleanor's voice contained a note of pleading Matthew had never heard her use.

"Come on, Angel. Don't refuse a gift."

Angel frowned but gave in. "Okay. But if you change your mind and decide you need help, just let me know."

"I will." Then she turned her back and chopped with a vengeance.

They went outside and sat on the porch steps.

"I sent your e-mail while I was in town," he murmured.

"Good."

"I didn't think I was going to be able to get away from Jonathon at first. It seemed he wanted to spend quality time with me. Until I made the wire transfer, that is."

"Mmm."

Angel was unusually quiet.

"Eleanor will be fine."

"I hope so. She tried to cover, but I could tell she was really upset."

"Probably just some sort of tiff with Jonathon."

Sighing, she said, "You're probably right. I wonder if she knows about the disks? It almost seemed too easy for her to leave me in the office alone."

"What reason would she have?"

Angel shrugged. "I don't know. There's something going on with her, though."

"Like I said, there's probably some simple explanation. Oh, I almost forgot to tell you." He lowered his voice. "Jonathon has a laptop he leaves in his truck. Since his truck is locked in the garage, he probably feels it's safe. I bet his records are on that laptop."

"Any chance you can get your hands on it?"

"I'd have to have the key to the garage and the key tab to disable the truck alarm. As far as I know, Jonathon has the only tab."

"I can probably get us into the garage. Jonathon has

to have a spare set of keys. Tomorrow, find out where Jonathon keeps them. We can try to access the laptop when everyone's asleep tomorrow night."

"Sounds like as good a plan as any."

Nodding, she picked at a loose thread on her sleeve. "You don't think Eleanor's ill, do you? Cancer, like your mother?"

"I hope not."

"Me, too." She slipped her hand into his and rested her head on his shoulder. A wave of protectiveness washed over him. He'd do anything for Angel.

They talked quietly until Eleanor called them for supper. She seemed anything but upset, her mood almost overly cheery.

"Sit down, everyone. I made Matthew's favorite fried chicken and the garlic mashed potatoes Angel likes."

"Thank you, Eleanor. You shouldn't have gone to all this trouble," Angel murmured.

"Nonsense." She smiled widely, but the smile didn't quite reach her eyes.

Supper was a surreal affair, with Angel unusually quiet and Eleanor unusually talkative. And Ruth... well, Ruth was just Ruth. Oblivious to anything that didn't directly affect her.

There was a knock at the door as they finished their peach cobbler.

Eleanor's hands fluttered about her throat. "I wonder who that could be."

She went to the front door and answered. Matthew could hear the murmur of voices but couldn't distinguish words.

When Eleanor returned to the kitchen, Raphael and two other men came in.

"We're sorry to interrupt your supper, Matthew. But Jonathon has called an emergency meeting of the elders. He wants you at the meeting hall now."

Uneasiness settled in his gut. "Yes, I'll go right away."

"Jonathon wants Angel and Eleanor to come, too."

"Why?"

Raphael shrugged. "I don't know."

Raphael hadn't known a lot of things since Matthew had returned. Matthew had to wonder when his brother's memory had gotten so selective.

"Ruth, you can clean up from supper while we're away," Eleanor commanded.

"I want to go, too." Ruth pouted prettily.

Raphael shook his head. "No. You stay here."

Ruth huffed and flounced out of the room. If Jonathon thought Matthew could ever marry someone like Ruth, he was sorely mistaken. Even if he didn't have a wonderful wife and Ruth were the last female on the planet.

Could the emergency meeting have anything to do with his betrothal to Ruth? Matthew wiped his mouth and carefully set his napkin on the table.

"Angel, let's go."

She nodded and rose.

"I'll be along in a moment," Eleanor said, not quite meeting his gaze.

He had a bad feeling about this. And it was getting worse by the second. His hand at Angel's elbow, they left the house.

Raphael and the men followed close behind. An escort or unarmed guards?

At least Matthew assumed they were unarmed.

Partway down the path, he turned to Raphael. "Rafe, what's this about?"

Raphael, typically so open, shrugged again, his face impassive. "I told you I don't know."

"Yes, well, you've told me that about a lot of things. And now I have to wonder if you remember you're my brother."

Emotion flashed briefly in his eyes and was gone. "I do what I must, Matthew. Things have changed since you lived with us."

"So talk to me. Help me understand."

Raphael inclined his head toward the other men. "You will understand when Jonathon wants you to understand."

His brother's reserve, combined with the cryptic statement, sent chills down Matthew's spine. Something was wrong, very wrong. It went beyond that of a group of people living their religious tenets apart from mainstream society. There was too much fear, too much secrecy.

The elders were assembled in the meeting room next to the great hall where Sunday services were held. Folding chairs were assembled, Jonathon was at the podium, waiting. His expression was grim.

"This will be a closed meeting," he said.

Raphael turned to the two other escorts and whispered. They turned and left the room, passing Eleanor as she entered.

Raphael closed the door behind her.

It was odd seeing women in the elders' meeting room. Eleanor and Angel appeared slightly uncomfortable, as if they realized how unwelcome they would have been at any other time.

Matthew thought it was sad that Jonathon used less than fifty percent of the skills and abilities of the group.

By excluding women, he was depriving Zion's Gate of untold riches.

"Eleanor, you may sit here." Jonathon indicated a chair in the front row.

Matthew guided Angel to two remaining chairs near the back.

"I have asked you to assemble this evening regarding a very serious matter that has been brought to my attention." Jonathon's voice boomed in the small room. "A matter involving a betrayal of our trust."

The ache in Matthew's stomach increased. This was not good.

"As you all know, we invited Brother Matthew to return to the one true way of life. We were overjoyed when he accepted our invitation and we greeted him with open arms."

"Yeah, right," Angel muttered under her breath, so low only he could hear.

He nudged her in the ribs with his elbow, frowning at her. Surely she could feel the animosity in the room.

Her expression was sober. Yes, she understood the gravity of the situation.

Matthew heard hinges squeak and turned to see who had entered the room. Jumping to his feet, he said, "Rebecca."

He moved toward her, but one of the men stepped between them, his manner threatening.

Rebecca nodded to Matthew but moved to the front of the room. Jonathon guided her to the seat next to Eleanor.

After all these years, Matthew was finally close to his sister but couldn't go to her, couldn't touch her to reassure himself she was real. The only other time he'd felt this powerless was the night he'd left his home of fifteen years.

Clearing his throat, Jonathon expounded, "As I said, we welcomed Brother Matthew with open arms. We also accepted his bride, Angel. Eleanor took her into her home and treated her as if she were her own daughter."

Matthew grasped Angel's hand. Whatever was coming, they were in it together.

"Eleanor, please tell the elders what you discovered." He gestured for her to come forward.

Eleanor's back was straight, her chin raised as she approached the podium. She turned, her expression grim. "I have had my doubts about Angel from the start. But I tried to accept her as Matthew's wife. Tried to befriend her. Today, I found out she has betrayed my trust. Betrayed all our trust."

Angel stiffened. "Eleanor—"

He squeezed her hand.

"Angel is here under false pretenses."

Whispers filled the room.

Angel's fingernails dug into his palm.

Matthew stood. "You must be mistaken, Aunt Eleanor."

"Silence," Jonathon boomed, sounding like the wizard in *The Wizard of Oz*. But this was no bumbling, benign man masquerading behind a velvet curtain. This man really thought he was omnipotent.

"Please go on, Eleanor," Jonathon encouraged.

Matthew longed to wipe the benevolent smile from his uncle's face.

Eleanor nodded. "I allowed Angel access to every area of the house but Jonathon's study. I've watched her, I've tried to learn her heart. I...I thought I knew her. So today I allowed her to use the computer in Jonathon's study. We worked on a genealogy study, a project close to my heart. Then I remembered I'd promised to take some honey to our dear, sweet Rebecca."

Rebecca made a low noise of dismay.

"Angel worked on the genealogy program I'd started. She also started one for her ancestors. It wasn't until I was tidying up that I found this." Eleanor unfolded a sheet of white paper and held it aloft, then handed it to Rebecca.

Rebecca read for a few seconds, gasped and passed the paper to the next person.

"It appears to be a page from a manuscript. You'll notice *Harrison* is the name in the header. It's not unusual for a woman to use her maiden name as a pen name. Harrison is also the name she input in the genealogy program."

Matthew frowned. What was she getting at?

"As some of you know, Jonathon allowed me to take a computer class, so I have a very basic amount of computer knowledge. I did an Internet search on Angel Harrison."

Holy crap. Then Matthew exhaled, remembering there wasn't a thing anyone could find out about Angel simply by Googling her name.

"Angel is an aspiring writer of young-adult novels," Eleanor announced. "She's writing a book about two young girls who escape a polygamist sect and solve mysteries along the way."

Matthew smothered an incredulous laugh. Eleanor's story was so removed from the truth it was ludicrous. But, glancing at the faces around him, obviously believable.

"It's evident she used poor Matthew to gain access to our community. And equally as evident she abused our hospitality and intends to exploit us in the most heinous manner."

Angel snagged the sheet of paper from the elder sitting in front of them. Her mouth thinned as she scanned it quickly. Jumping to her feet, eyes blazing, she said, "I did *not* write this. I love my husband, and for you to imply anything different is wrong."

Eleanor's cheeks flamed. Her eyes were bright with the light of battle. "Are you calling *me* a liar? I have lived in this community all my life. I have been a good wife, mother and neighbor. I love our Lord and want nothing but the best for our people. How dare you call me a liar. You, you, you…Jezebel. Fornicating day and night until decent people can't stand to look at you."

Eleanor's attack shocked him so badly he barely noticed Angel begin to tremble.

He chafed her cold hand in his. Her face was pale, her eyes wide and unfocused, as if she inhabited another world.

"It's okay, Angelina. I know she didn't mean it. She couldn't mean it." Because he'd loved and trusted Eleanor. And so had Angel.

"Jonathon, you must put a stop to this foolishness," Matthew challenged. He chose his words carefully, trying to convey the truth without lying about Angel's vocation. "Surely you don't believe my wife would hurt the people of Zion's Gate."

Jonathon stepped behind Eleanor and rested his hands on her shoulders. "Eleanor is a good and righteous woman. If she says these things, they are surely true." He gestured toward the chair. "Please sit down, Eleanor."

She complied, her movements slow, as if she were too tired to move.

"Matthew, it is my decision Angel must leave Zion's Gate."

"No," Angel murmured, her eyes still glazed.

"If Angel leaves, I leave."

"No, you won't. You will obey God's will and marry Ruth. Then you'll train to assume leadership of Zion's Gate when I am no longer able. Many wives and sons will be yours, ensuring an enviable place in heaven."

Jonathon dangled a sizable carrot, especially for a man raised to believe the principle of plurality. Wealth, power, as many women as he wanted and the promise of a prime spot in heaven. It didn't get much better than that.

But it wasn't a scenario that appealed to Matthew. All he wanted was a life with Angel and a safe, happy home in which to raise their children.

"I appreciate your confidence in me, Uncle. And while I think I could be a good leader for our people, I refuse to consider life without Angel."

Matthew felt Angel's hand relax in his.

Jonathon paced. "You mean to tell me you choose a woman who has deceived you over your own family?"

"No, Uncle, you are forcing me to choose between the woman I love and my family."

"If you leave, you will never see your sister again." The venom in Jonathon's voice was staggering. "And what will you tell your dying mother? That you let your lust for this woman override your good sense? That you betrayed your family?"

Anger burned hot and bright in Matthew. How dare Jonathon speak of his mother. He didn't care about her. It was a desperate shot designed to push Matthew's buttons. And he'd almost succeeded, damn it.

Matthew managed to keep silent.

Rebecca stood. She reached her hand to Jonathon. "My mother is dying?"

"Tell her, Matthew."

Turning, Rebecca's eyes were huge, the dark circles beneath them a stark contrast to her pale face. "Is our mother dying, Matthew?"

"She's undergoing treatment for cancer. We don't know her prognosis."

"I imagine a visit from her daughter would be the best possible tonic." Jonathon's tone was oily. The man really was a snake. He was holding Rebecca and his mother's very life as hostage, gambling that Matthew hadn't broken all contact with his mother to rejoin the group.

"I'm so sorry, Matt," Angel murmured.

He looked at her. Looked at Rebecca. His shoulders slumped. "You leave me no choice. But I will ride with Angel to town to ensure her safety."

Angel's heart ached at the thought of being separated from Matthew. What if something happened? He'd be here alone, without her to watch his back. "No, I won't leave you."

Jonathon's face flushed. Righteous anger made him look larger than life as he raised his fist. "To accept your role as an elder and leader-in-training, you will publicly denounce evil. Right here, right now. As our Lord shouted out Satan, you will shout out the she-devil who wormed her way into our midst, took advantage of your good nature and sought to harm us."

"I can't."

Jonathon grabbed Rebecca and jerked her to his side. He might as well have had a gun to her head, his intent was so clear. He had to subjugate Matthew completely and publicly, intimidation designed to remind the elders who was boss. And to remind Matthew not to challenge his authority.

Angel understood this intellectually. But it didn't prepare her for the assault she knew was coming.

Remorse was written in every line on Matthew's face. Before the mask dropped and his face became a stern visage. A man she had never seen before.

"Get out!" he shouted. "She-devil, you are not welcome here."

Matthew stepped closer, towering over her. Much as Kent had towered over her before he vented his rage.

"You must proclaim her crimes against you and our community." Jonathon's voice was loud, too, as if attempting to incite a riot.

Angel tried to keep her mind firmly on the job. To detach emotionally from what was happening. But the Angel she once was kept getting in the way. The bitter taste of fear was an unwelcome reminder that she *was* emotionally involved.

"Angel Harrison." Matthew's use of her maiden name inflicted almost as much damage as his intimidating yell and the fury in his face.

Intellectually she knew Matthew was acting. Knew he would never hurt her. But memories of Kent surfaced. Memories of learning that the man she loved wanted to kill her. Angel stepped back, knocking over a folding chair. It made a harsh clatter as it hit the concrete floor, each bounce, each echo, stabbing at her nerves.

"You have deceived me. Taken my trust and twisted it. I loved you, cared for you and accepted you as my celestial wife."

"Matthew, no." The denial fell from her lips as she instinctively reacted, uncaring that these were the words Jonathon wanted Matthew to say. The words wounded the same as if they'd come straight from his heart.

"You lured me with your wanton sexuality. Blinded me with visions of your naked breasts and thighs."

One of the women gasped. It could have been Eleanor or Rebecca. Another time, Angel might have found their naiveté amusing. But now it simply underscored how powerful Matthew's attack was.

It took supreme effort to raise her chin and look him in the eye. "I don't care what you say. I'm not leaving without you."

"Whore!" he yelled, pointing his finger in her face. "I can't stand the sight of you. You aren't fit to kiss my feet."

His face was thunderous. Barely restrained rage rolled off him in waves, containing an electricity that was terrifying to behold.

She knew he could move with lightning speed once the unholy tirade touched off an explosion inside, releasing evil. Kent was always that way before he hurt her.

Angel shook her head, trying to clear it.

"Be gone. Get out of my sight. Or so help me…" He raised his clenched fist above his head.

The instinct to survive had her fleeing before he completed the sentence. She ran from the room, nearly tripping over her own feet but not slowing.

Once outside, she glanced wildly from side to side. The gate. She'd run back to town if necessary.

Before she could take another step a hand closed on her arm.

CHAPTER TWENTY-TWO

ANGEL TURNED, prepared to fight for her life.

"It's Rebecca. I won't hurt you. Neither will Matthew. He's not that way."

"How would you know?" Angel was relieved Rebecca was alone. "You haven't seen him in years."

Rebecca's eyes filled with tears. "You're right. But the Matthew I knew was always a gentle boy. I—I guess I just wanted things to be different."

"For Matthew? Or with Jonathon?"

"Both." Rebecca's voice was soft, without inflection. As if Matthew's diatribe had sapped what little hope she had left. "Jonathon said he'd drive you into town tomorrow. I'd so wanted to get to know you."

Angel took a shaky breath. "Me, too. Matthew and I wanted to see you, but Jonathon said you were too ill."

"He…exaggerates about my health."

"Is it something Matthew should know about? He'll get you the best doctors—"

"No! That's not necessary. I simply lose my appetite when I'm tense or sad. It worries Jonathon that I don't eat."

Anorexia? For a woman who couldn't control much in her life, controlling the food she ate was almost understandable. It would explain her thinness and ashy skin tone.

Angel touched Rebecca's arm. "If there's ever anything I can do, just ask."

"But you won't be here." Tears welled in the woman's eyes.

Angel swallowed hard. It pained her to turn her back on a woman in need. A woman no doubt victimized by her husband. How many other women like Rebecca were there at Zion's Gate?

"I don't have a choice. I'd stay if they'd let me. Could you persuade Jonathon?"

"No. It doesn't matter what I say. He's made up his mind." Rebecca glanced over Angel's shoulder. "I better go," she said and quickly walked away.

Angel turned to see Jonathon and Matthew approach. She clenched her hands so hard her nails bit into her palms.

"Matthew will escort you to Eleanor's house." Jonathon's tone was terse. "You shall remain in your room until we leave at sunup tomorrow."

"Isn't there somewhere else I can stay?" Eleanor's betrayal hurt more than she could have imagined. And Matthew's words, though orchestrated by Jonathon, still stung.

"No." He addressed Matthew. "See that she behaves. She duped you once. Don't let it happen again. I'll hold you responsible."

"Yes, sir."

Jonathon nodded and followed Rebecca. Angel hoped she hadn't gotten the woman in trouble by talking to her.

Matthew grasped her arm. "Come, Angelina."

"Don't call me that." She pulled away from him.

"Angel, I hope this is an act," he whispered. "You know I didn't mean any of it."

"I need time to think."

"We'll talk when we get home."

But it wasn't home. The place where she'd come to feel a part of the family was now a facade.

MATTHEW WOULD HAVE found the routine sound of running water soothing, knowing Angel readied herself for bed. But everything was different. He sat on their bed, unwilling to lie down. He knew sleep would be out of the question.

Squeezing his eyes shut, he tried to block out the images of Angel as he'd hollered at her. How small and scared she'd looked, as if she'd wanted to make herself disappear. And he'd been the cause.

Angel exited the bathroom, brushing by him without saying a word.

"We have to talk."

"I'm not sure what there is to say."

He grasped her by the shoulders. "It wasn't true. I didn't mean a word of it."

"Don't you understand, Matthew? It doesn't matter. What matters is in here." She tapped her chest. "Whether it's logical or not, you hurt me... Not only did I go to a place in my head I swore I'd never go again, but I forgot the reason I was here. I endangered myself and the people I came to help. All because of my feelings for you."

He grasped her arms. "I love you. And you said you loved me. Yes, it's crummy that we fell in love when we did. But it happened for a reason. If it causes problems for you, we'll deal with it. The last thing I intend to do is interfere with your job."

"You don't intend to, but you already have. You

believe we met and fell in love for a reason. Well, I believe things happen for a reason, too." She hesitated. "When I was in the hospital, I tried to figure out why God had allowed Kent to do those things to me. And sometimes in the middle of the night, I'd wonder why I survived. Finally I realized I survived to help other people. If I don't have that, what do I have?"

"This was an isolated incident. It won't happen again."

"How can you be sure?" Her eyes were dark with pain.

He couldn't. But he couldn't face losing her, either. "There are no sure things, Angel. I'm willing to fight for us, to do whatever it takes. All I ask is that you don't make any snap decisions."

Angel shrugged off his hands and turned away. "I'll try not to. That's the best I can do."

His instinct was to hold on to her. But he knew he would drive her away if he did. His voice was husky when he said, "I guess I'll have to accept that."

She nodded.

"Under the circumstances, do you mind if I still sleep on the floor here?"

"The floor's fine." Because she'd already shut him out.

"Sleep tight, Angelina."

Pulling the blankets and pillow from the closet, he piled them on the floor. He turned off the light and lay down. But there were too many memories. Particularly vivid was the memory of the first time he'd made love with Angel.

Matthew tossed and turned for almost two hours and knew he couldn't stay in the same room with her. His emotions were too raw.

Listening to Angel's even breathing, he decided to do something, anything, to feel like he was the master of his own fate.

Maybe he could break into the study and find something they'd overlooked before? Matthew stood and quietly pulled on a pair of jeans and a T-shirt. He exited the bedroom and carefully shut the door behind him. Glancing at Ruth's door, he was grateful no light showed beneath. She was one problem he wasn't ready to face.

When Matthew reached the study door, he was surprised to see a strip of light. He turned the knob slowly and stepped inside.

Eleanor was at the computer, so engrossed in the screen she didn't seem to hear him.

"Aunt Eleanor."

She started. "Matthew, what are you doing up?"

"I imagine the same as you. I can't sleep."

Eleanor sighed, rubbing her temples. "Yes, it's been a difficult day."

"Why'd you do it?" His voice was low, full of pain and confusion.

"I didn't feel I had a choice. I did what I thought necessary to protect Angel."

"To protect her? Hardly."

"Do you want to tell me what her real occupation is?"

"No."

"I didn't think so. That's why I came up with the story about Angel being a writer. Enough to get her sent away but not threatening enough that she'd be harmed."

"You think Uncle Jonathon would hurt her?"

"There are things happening at Zion's Gate you don't understand."

"Raphael said the same thing. So tell me what's going on."

Eleanor shook her head. "I can't. It's not that simple. I won't knowingly harm Jonathon."

"You're still loyal to him? You realize he probably engineered my father's death, don't you?"

"I suspected. But I have no proof. Yet."

"What's that supposed to mean?"

"Matthew, I'm very tired. Can we continue this conversation in the morning?"

"No. I need to know tonight whether I threw my whole life away on a whim."

"You're not going to let this alone, are you?"

"No."

"You always were a headstrong boy." The affection in her voice made him hope she had an explanation for turning his life upside down. Because he really did love her.

"Maybe I take after my aunt."

She smiled. "Why don't we discuss it over a dish of ice cream? I remember us having quite a few talks over ice cream when you were young."

He nodded stiffly, reluctant to remember his fond childhood memories of her.

She shut down the computer and stood. He led the way out the door, stopping to allow her to twist the lock and close the door behind them.

Matthew followed her down the hallway. He bumped into her back when she stopped suddenly.

Turning her head, she raised her finger to her lips.

Then he heard Jonathon's voice coming from the kitchen. "We need to go. Are you sure you have everything you need?"

"Yes, Jonathon, I do." Ruth's voice was husky. "I can hardly believe I'll be your celestial wife. Your one and only legal wife."

Eleanor made a keening sound low in her throat. She slapped her hand to her mouth, silencing her grief.

Fortunately Jonathon and Ruth were too focused on each other to hear. Jonathon grasped Ruth's shoulders. "You deserve it. You're the only woman to truly understand me. And you've proven to be a devoted confidante. It would have pained me to see you married to Matthew, but I needed to test his loyalty."

"I was still able to keep an eye on things, even from next door."

"Yes. You did fine." He leaned closer, intent on kissing her.

But she held up her hand to stop him. "Not now. I want to leave this second. It's been a nightmare staying in this house, little more than a servant."

Jonathon smiled. "As you wish."

Matthew figured that meant they were headed for the front door. And would pass through the hallway where he and Eleanor stood.

He grasped Eleanor's arm and pulled her back, jerking his head toward the hallway.

She nodded, following close behind him. When they reached the study door, Matthew almost collided with Angel as she came around the corner.

Matthew pressed his finger to his lips.

She nodded, just as Eleanor whisked a key from her pocket and unlocked the study door.

Matthew grabbed Angel's hand and pulled her inside behind him. All three pressed against the door, easily able to hear Jonathon. "I'll treat you like a princess. You'll never have to lift a finger."

Their whispered conversation faded. Then Matthew heard the front door click shut.

"That horrible man." Eleanor's voice vibrated with anger. "How could he betray me so?"

"I'm sorry, Aunt. I'm sure that was quite a shock."

"It simply confirmed something I'd already suspected. I'd anticipated he'd add her as a sister wife. But he's promising things he can't deliver. There can only be one celestial wife, and I'm it."

"What's going on?" Angel asked.

"Uncle Jonathon was here with Ruth. Sounds like they're running away together. And he's promised her Aunt Eleanor's place in his life."

A position Aunt Eleanor hadn't yet vacated. An uncomfortable suspicion formed. Could his uncle be that cold-blooded?

Aunt Eleanor spoke his fears aloud. "He'd be free to take another legal wife if I were dead. That may explain why he's been downloading information on his laptop about explosives. He underestimated my abilities to find things on the computer."

"You copied those disks and made sure I'd find them?" Angel murmured.

"Yes, I'd hoped you'd carry them to the authorities when you left."

"Which is why you made up that story."

Eleanor nodded. "Come, children, we're following Jonathon. Everyone in the settlement might be in grave danger."

"Do you have any idea where he's going?"

"The tunnel underneath the meeting hall. It leads to

an unpatrolled stretch on the Mexican side. Unpatrolled by *Federales,* that is. Our landlord has plenty of his own men there, I'm sure. But knowing my dear husband, I'm positive he has a plan."

"Let's go then."

"Wait." She unlocked the desk and removed two cell phones from the middle drawer. From the bottom drawer she withdrew a lethal-looking handgun. "Here are your cell phones."

Matthew flicked his cell phone open. "It's charged."

Angel opened hers. "So's mine."

"A precaution. I've kept them charged since your arrival."

"Aunt Eleanor, you are an exceptional woman." Matthew gave her a quick hug.

"I'm not that exceptional, Matthew. I'd like nothing better than to dissolve in a puddle of tears. But I refuse to let Jonathon hurt innocent people."

"*I* think you're exceptional."

"So do I." Angel's voice was warm.

He held out his hand to Eleanor. "Now give me the gun."

"Sorry. I'm keeping it." She tucked it into the pocket of her dress and folded her arms over her chest. He'd have to wrestle it from her, a move that could be dangerous.

Angel stepped forward. "Eleanor, I'm a law-enforcement agent. Please give the gun to me."

"I figured as much. But this is *my* battle and I intend to be prepared. Don't try to take it away from me."

Angel hesitated, then nodded.

"Is it loaded?" he asked.

"Of course. It's no good to me if it isn't loaded."

Shaking his head, Matthew said, "Remind me never to tick you off. Let's go."

CHAPTER TWENTY-THREE

ANGEL ASSUMED THE lead, motioning for the others to drop back and take cover behind a building when she saw guards approach.

The guards greeted Jonathon. They were too far away for Angel to hear distinctly, but it sounded as if Jonathon was dismissing them for the evening. Something was definitely up.

Eleanor started forward, but Angel motioned for her to wait. They needed to follow from a safe distance.

Eleanor frowned, impatience evident in her stiff movements.

A few minutes later Angel signaled for them to follow. Eleanor was right—he was headed for the meeting hall.

When they reached the meeting hall, Eleanor grasped her arm. "Let me go first," she whispered. "I know where Jonathon is."

Angel nodded and followed. Matthew was right behind.

They entered through the rear door, then Eleanor went to the storage room next to the men's meeting room. Inside were a couple brooms and a dustpan. But the metal shelves were empty of anything save cobwebs. The storage room obviously hadn't been functional for quite some time.

Eleanor grasped one shelf and pulled. It moved silently, revealing a metal door. Slowly she released the latch.

Matthew reached for the door, but Eleanor shook her head. Placing her finger on her lips, she whispered, "They're down there."

Eleanor opened the door a crack, peering inside. Then she slipped through the door and quickly descended a metal ladder.

Angel followed right behind, trying to process their surroundings. She saw a large anteroom connected to a concrete tunnel, bending sharply to the right. The drug tunnel?

She heard Mathew's steps on the rungs above her head. She should insist that the civilians stay safely aboveground. But with Eleanor carrying the only weapon, her choices were limited. Holding up her hand, Angel signaled them to stay quiet. They moved toward the bend, where the tunnel continued out of sight.

There was silence. Then Ruth's voice. "Are you sure we won't get caught?"

"Positive. The fire will burn so hot all traces of explosives with be eliminated. It will confuse my enemies on both sides of the border long enough for us to establish new identities. They might even think we perished in the fire."

"Isn't there another way? It's hard to think of all those people dying. Maybe the vision was wrong."

"No, my love. My visions are *never* wrong. The community is to be destroyed by fire, to burn away the sins of those left behind."

"It's so horrible."

"God's will is not to be questioned. He has great

plans for our new community in Mexico. I will bring salvation to many."

Eleanor murmured, "He intends to kill everyone. I can't let that happen."

"Neither can I." Her heart lurched at the thought of all the innocent women and children he could murder.

Angel and Eleanor rounded the corner, moving in tandem.

"What the…?" Jonathon stepped forward.

Eleanor withdrew the pistol and aimed it at his chest.

Angel rapidly assessed the situation. If Eleanor was remotely accurate, she had a good kill shot. Too high, she shot Jonathon in the head. Too low, he was gut shot or emasculated. Either way, he would probably bleed to death before help could arrive.

Would that be a bad thing?

"Ruth, you go sit on that chair in the corner." Eleanor's voice echoed in the room fortified by concrete on all sides.

Not as bad as metal but still too great a chance for ricochet.

The girl lost no time scuttling out of range. Jonathon was apparently on his own.

And he realized it, too. He reached out his hand in appeal. "Now, Eleanor, there must be some misunderstanding."

Eleanor released the safety and cocked the hammer. "Go sit in that chair."

He hesitated, his gaze straying to the pistol. The damn fool was considering charging Eleanor.

"Eleanor, give me the gun." Matthew stepped closer. "Somebody might get hurt."

"That's exactly what I intend." Her voice was cold and deliberate.

Fear flashed in Jonathon's eyes. "Eleanor, think of our life together. Our history, our children."

"Don't bother, Jonathon. I heard your plans for me. For all of us. Now sit in that chair or I'll shoot you."

Ruth stood, as if thinking of going to Jonathon. "Ruth, you little twit, sit down." Eleanor barely glanced in the girl's direction.

Angel held her breath until Jonathon complied.

Ruth raised her chin. "Jonathon doesn't love you. He loves me. I'm going to be his celestial wife."

"Shut up, Ruth," all three said in unison. Jonathon and Matthew because there was a real possibility someone would get shot. Eleanor because she could.

"Now stand over there, Matthew. I'll trust you to let me know if either of them looks as if they're trying anything stupid."

Angel stepped forward. "Eleanor, you can't take the law into your own hands, much as I know you want to. Give me the gun and I promise Jonathon will pay for his crimes."

Eleanor hesitated. "You're like a daughter to me, Angel. I'd hoped to get you out of here. I had no idea the extent to which Jonathon was prepared to go. But this is between Jonathon and me. It's something I have to do."

She took another step closer. "I understand, Eleanor. I really, really do. I've been hurt by a man. My first husband. He terrorized me until there was very little left."

"First husband? You were married before?" Eleanor asked.

"Yes. He was killed. I was grateful for being rescued from him. But a part of me has been so angry. My power was taken from me. I thought I could regain that power if I'd just had the chance to do to him what he'd done to me."

Eleanor nodded. "I felt a connection with you from the start. Knew you'd understand."

"I *do* understand. But I also know you have to reclaim your power another way."

"No. He has to be made to suffer like I've suffered."

"No, Eleanor, your healing depends on two things. Justice, which I *promise* will happen if you give me the gun."

"What's the second?"

"You will have to help others. Once you open your heart to women who've been hurt as you have, Jonathon will no longer have any power over you."

"Angel, I wish that was true. But I'm not a young woman." Eleanor's voice broke. "I can't take care of myself in the outside world, let alone help someone else."

"Yes, you can. And you will. Because I'll be there beside you every step of the way. And by allowing me to do that, you will be healing me."

The gun wavered in Eleanor's hands, and tears ran unchecked down her face.

"You promise?" she whispered.

"I promise."

Eleanor lowered the gun and handed it to Angel. Angel kept it trained on Jonathon while she gave Eleanor a quick, reassuring hug.

Everything would be all right. Suddenly Angel knew it was true. For Eleanor. For Angel.

Matthew's throat grew scratchy as he watched Angel comfort his aunt. He was grateful to her for stopping Eleanor before she could destroy her life. He also suspected Angel's discussion with Eleanor had helped Angel as much as Eleanor.

But frustration made him want to scream. He couldn't allow his uncle off the hook this easily. He had to find out what had happened the night his father died.

Angel murmured something to Eleanor and his aunt nodded, moving next to Matthew.

Angel stepped close to Jonathon, pressing the barrel of the gun to his temple. Her voice was very soft. "No worry about ricochet this way. Is this how you want it to end, Jonathon?"

"You promised you'd leave my punishment to the justice system."

"No, Jonathon. Listen carefully. I said justice would happen if Eleanor gave me the gun. The kind of justice you receive is up to you. If you tell me what I want to know, I'll turn you over to the authorities and you might get a vacation at the federal prison, complete with television and tennis courts."

His eyes flashed with impotent anger. "And what if I don't cooperate?"

"Then I will shoot you. I know exactly where to place a bullet to cause excruciating pain but not kill you. My choices are endless." She shrugged. "It could be hours, maybe even days before I get around to calling the authorities. It would be your word against ours."

"Who are you?"

"Angelina Harrison. I'm a detective with the Department of Public Safety."

"Bitch."

Matthew stepped forward, but his aunt grasped his arm. "No. Don't interfere."

"Jonathon, the last man who called me a bitch died on my kitchen floor in a puddle of blood." Her tone was so matter of fact, only an idiot wouldn't believe her.

And Jonathon was no idiot. He raised his chin. "What do you want to know?"

"How and when is this fire to happen?"

"Explosives. Tonight."

Matthew shifted uneasily, but Angel barely blinked. "What's the status?"

"The explosives are armed and ready."

Angel's tone was conversational. "Are they on a timer?"

"No, the detonator is in my briefcase." He nodded toward the corner.

She turned. "Eleanor, we need to get an explosives team in here right away. We'll use the land line from your house. I don't want anyone getting hurt. Can you dismiss the guard at the gate for the evening? Tell him it's Jonathon's directive?"

"Yes. They'll believe me."

"Good. Otherwise, I'll have to incapacitate him."

"What do you want me to do?" Matthew hated feeling as if all his options were held by another. All he needed was a few minutes alone with his uncle.

Angel held his gaze. Could she trust him? The question was plain as day without being uttered.

He nodded.

"You can count on me."

She handed him the weapon. "I trust you."

His heart ached at his deception. She might not ever trust him again. It was a chance he'd have to take. Because he owed it to his father to see that Jonathon was held accountable for his murder.

He was careful to keep his face bland while he accepted the gun. "I'll make sure he doesn't go anywhere."

"Whatever you do, don't use your cell phone," she instructed. "We don't want to take the chance Jonathon has lied about the method of detonation and inadvertently set off an explosion."

"How will you call for help?"

She smiled grimly. "Prearranged signal—glow sticks. Low-tech, but effective."

"You smuggled those in, too?"

"Yes. You sure you're okay guarding Jonathon?"

"Positive." He wanted to prepare for a confrontation he'd anticipated for years. Revenge no longer seemed right, though his uncle deserved it. But he'd learned to expect the unexpected with Jonathon. "Will the explosives go off if the gun discharges?"

"Not unless Jonathon is suicidal and that's not the case, in my opinion. This is his escape route. But if I'm wrong, I'm sure he'll be very careful not to give you cause to shoot him. I'll bring rope back to tie him up."

MATTHEW EYED Jonathon for a long moment after Angel left.

"I could kill you before she returns. Say you tried to escape."

Jonathon licked his lips. "Now, son, you know I only wanted what was best for you."

His uncle went into a long discourse on the things he'd done for his brother's children, recounting stories of old times.

Matthew allowed him to talk, hoping he might let important information slip. When he could stand no more of his uncle's self-serving speech, he asked, "How was killing my father best for me?"

"I didn't kill your father." Jonathon straightened, the epitome of affronted dignity.

"You removed the blankets and water from the barn that day. When he went out to check on the animals, you tossed a Molotov cocktail in the straw and padlocked both doors shut."

"That's preposterous. I did nothing of the kind. Your mother lied."

Matthew almost lost control. He wanted to kill the man with his bare hands. He took a deep breath to regain his equilibrium. At one time, he'd thought he might be able to avenge his father's death. But his father had taken the ten commandments very seriously and it would have been obscene to defile his father's memory in that way.

"My mother never said anything about it. It's all in your manuscript. The one you kept on your laptop."

"How did…?"

"Eleanor is a smart, resourceful woman. You underestimated her."

"She'll come around. She knows the pressure I've been under."

Angel clambered down the steps. Her cheeks were red and she was out of breath. "Eleanor will direct the team here."

He wanted to take her in his arms and calm the agitation he could feel simmering beneath the surface. But he knew she wouldn't let him past her barriers without a fight.

"There was no need to run, Angelina. Don't you trust me?"

"I—I don't know what to think."

"You know I love you."

She nodded. "It's not enough, though."

"It's enough to make me want to do things differently. Do you remember the first night we were here? The Bible passage I read?"

"You read from First Corinthians. 'Love is patient, love is kind.'" She held his gaze.

"You remembered." Hope sparked somewhere deep inside him. He wished they were having this conversation at another time and place. As it was, he had to keep an eye on Jonathon during what might be the most important discussion of his life.

"I memorized it. I wanted that kind of love in my life. And I thought if I repeated it to myself enough, I might believe it was true."

"I offered you that kind of love." His voice was husky.

"You did. And I thought for a while we might have a chance. Before I let things get out of control."

Matthew felt her slipping away, losing herself to the danger of the past. "There's also a part of First Corinthians about love not keeping a record of wrongs."

"I remember."

"Yet you've kept a record of wrongs. Not mine, but Kent's. And you'll punish both of us because of them."

"I don't want it to be that way." Her eyes were wide and dark. "I tried, Matthew, I really did. It just wasn't meant to be."

Her anguish resonated through him. "I won't push, Angelina. I love you too much."

She shook her head. Her tone was professional when she asked, "Did you find out anything else from Jonathon?"

"Tell her, Uncle."

Jonathon's mouth twisted. "How stupid do you think I am? I'm not going to admit murder to a law-enforcement officer."

Matthew tightened his finger on the trigger. It would be so easy.

"Don't do it, Matthew." There was an edge of desperation in Angel's voice.

"I won't. But I will tell Jonathon that my mother has proof even if he doesn't confess in front of you."

"Impossible."

"Mom has a hunk of twisted metal she keeps hidden. I always wondered what it was, but didn't ask after the first time because it upset her so much. Now I know. It was one of the padlocks from the barn."

"That's just wild conjecture based on some harmless piece of fiction."

"How could you do that to my father?" His voice was bleak, as if his last ounce of emotion had evaporated. "How could you do that to my mother?"

"I loved Abigail. I did it for her own good. Joshua was a weak leader, a weak man. Abigail should have been mine." Jonathon's eyes blazed with passion.

"You're insane." Angel shook her head in disbelief. She advanced on Jonathon. "You claim you did these horrible things in the name of love. You don't love anyone. You possess and degrade until there's nothing left."

Matthew wondered if he should intervene. Angel might as well have been talking to her late husband.

Jonathon raised his chin. "It was my right to take her as my wife."

Angel stiffened. "She was a human being with

thoughts and feelings that you couldn't own, no matter how twisted your soul. Thank God she got away from you."

"She was allowed to leave because I had already found her replacement. Rebecca was a much better fit in my household anyway."

"You possessed an innocent young girl." Angel practically spat the words. "Tell me what you've done to her. Why is she sick? Why can't she associate with anyone but you?"

The hatred in Angel's voice stirred the anger Matthew had managed to keep in check. This man had murdered his father and tried to destroy his mother. And now, he seemed to be bent on destroying his sister, too.

He stepped toward Angel, but she motioned him to stay back.

"I don't have to answer that. She's my wife," Jonathon said.

"You say that as if you own her. She was young and carefree when you married her. And you did your best to destroy her. Just because you could. Because it made you feel powerful."

"You don't know what you're talking about."

"I know all too well what I'm talking about. Someone very like you almost destroyed me once. But I survived. I made a life for myself and I help other victims."

Angel stopped as if to catch her breath. Her eyes widened. "And I can have what you never will. Love without intimidation."

Turning, she walked toward Matthew, stopping a few feet away. She held out her hand to him. "Matthew?"

He scarcely dared breathe.

"I really messed things up between us." Her eyes filled with tears. "I'm so sorry."

Making a noise low in his throat, he grasped her hand.

She squeezed his hand as if she'd never let go. "I wasn't afraid of you. I was afraid of me. I—I thought maybe I wasn't capable of seeing a man's true character once my emotions were involved. I felt so safe with you, so…whole. Then things went topsy-turvy when Jonathon made you say those awful things. I was so afraid I was turning back into what I used to be."

"You'll never be a victim again."

"How can you be so sure?"

"Because I know you. I know your heart and your courage. I admired your strength, then I grew to love the whole package. That you've managed to keep a tender heart is a testament to your compassion. You'll continue to help others. No one can take that away from you. Not me and not him." He nodded toward Jonathon.

"I thought it was only love that could bring me to that place where all I knew was fear.… But I've found hate can take me back, too. I'm awfully tempted to destroy Jonathon the way I fantasized about destroying Kent. To reduce him to a pitiful wreck. I could do it."

"I could, too. I could shoot him in revenge. But my mother and father gave me a strong foundation of love—they raised me to be a better man than that. I want to be a better man for you, too. I'll leave it up to the authorities and God to punish him."

"I want a chance to grow old with you, Matthew." Tears trickled down Angel's face. "I don't want the Kents and Jonathons of this world to win."

"Then accept the love I've offered."

"It can't be that easy." Her voice held a note of hope.

"It can be that easy if you choose it to be."

She touched his face. "I love you, Matthew. I want to try."

He released a shaky breath. "I love you, too, Angelina. And we'll do more than try. We'll make it happen."

The sound of boots reverberated above their heads. Angel glanced at the ceiling. "I think we're going to be okay."

Matthew wrapped his arm around her waist and pulled her close, keeping the gun trained on Jonathon.

"I know we are."

EPILOGUE

Three months later

THE ONE PERFECT white rose shook slightly in Angel's hands.

"Who gives this woman in marriage?" the pastor asked.

"Her mother and I do." Angel's father's reply was deep and sure.

Tears blurred Angel's eyes as her father kissed her on the cheek. Then her mother kissed her.

"Do not cry, *mija*. This is a joyous day."

"I know, Mama."

Isabella took her seat with Angel's father in the front row. Next to them sat Matthew's mother, Abigail. And next to her was Eleanor, smiling every bit as proudly as Angel's mother.

"Angelina, you may join Matthew."

She stepped forward, her heart a jumble of emotions. Joy, awe, protectiveness and a bit of fear. Because they were embarking on a journey bound to be challenging and intense. But a journey she wouldn't miss for the world.

"Angelina and Matthew have gathered their friends and family here today to witness a recommitment ceremony. As many of you know, they were married in a civil ceremony several months ago. Now they would like to seal their marriage before God."

Matthew held her gaze. He knew this ceremony was her gift. An acknowledgment of how important his beliefs were to him. And an admission that she might someday forgive his God.

"Angel and Matthew have chosen a passage for me to read. 'Love is patient, love is kind…'"

The pastor's words washed over Angel. She placed her palm on her stomach, smiling to herself. The rest of the ceremony passed like a lovely, lovely dream, culminating in a tender kiss from Matthew.

The reception took place in their Houston home. Spacious and light, it was everything she'd dreamed of. Maybe because her life was everything she'd dreamed of.

"There's got to be something I can do," Angel insisted, glancing around her kitchen.

"No, dear, we've got it under control. Don't we, ladies?" Angel's mother asked Eleanor and Abigail.

"We most certainly do." Eleanor bustled around the kitchen.

"Yes, please sit down, Angel." Abigail hugged her quickly before placing the bride and groom figurines on the cake.

"You absolutely must tell me all about your trip to the islands," Isabella said. "You both look so relaxed and healthy."

Both women looked fabulous. Tanned, happy and, for Abigail, in remission.

Eleanor made a joke about the handsome island men.

Abigail blushed.

Angel's mother made an off-color comment in Spanish. All four women laughed.

"Hey, what's going on in here?" Matthew stepped up behind Angel and wrapped his arms around her.

"Just girl stuff. And talking about Abigail and Eleanor's trip."

"Ah. And how were the Caymans?"

Eleanor smiled. "Lovely. As was the cruise ship. We didn't lift a finger the entire time."

"You deserve to be pampered," Angel declared. "Especially after you helped the U.S. authorities gain access to Jonathon's Cayman accounts."

"We received a most generous reward, so it was a win-win situation. Isn't that what they call it?"

Angel patted Eleanor's hand. "Yes, definitely a win-win situation. Are you still planning on breaking ground next month on Austin's House?"

"Yes, and we've got the perfect couple lined up to run the place. We'll be able to give many displaced boys a new start and the tools they'll need to build a life outside polygamist sects." Abigail's face lit with enthusiasm. "And still have time to travel a bit ourselves."

Eleanor said, "We hope to open Rebecca's House in one to two years. By then, my Austin should have his bachelor's degree and be ready to oversee the charitable foundation."

Matthew shook his head. "You two are a couple of dynamos. Remind me to ask you if I ever need anything done."

Eleanor patted his cheek. "We're just trying to give back, dear. Right a few wrongs. And heal."

Angel's eyes misted. "You seem to have done that in spades."

"I had an excellent coach."

"No more mushy stuff. You're going to make me cry and my makeup will run." She snagged a stuffed mushroom from one of the platters. "I hear Rebecca went to visit Jonathon in prison. Closure before her marriage."

"Rebecca is much too forgiving a creature." Eleanor placed another mushroom on the tray. "Harlan will be good for her. He absolutely adores her. And she'll be treated like a princess."

Angel sighed. "I wish she would've tried Houston. Matthew and I would have loved for her to stay with us."

Abigail patted her hand. "Ellie's right, Angel. Rebecca is better off in a world familiar to her. She has every intention of being an integral part of creating a new Zion's Gate. With Raphael as their new leader, I think they'll do fine. I do wish I could see my grandchildren more often, though."

Matthew nudged Angel and smiled. "When you ladies are ready, I'd like everyone to gather in the great room for a toast."

Angel grabbed the plate of mushrooms. "I'll carry these."

Her mother touched her shoulder. "Thank you, *mija*. Are you going to give me a hint about Matthew's announcement?"

"He didn't say anything about an announcement, Mama." She widened her eyes innocently. "Just a toast."

"I thought perhaps there was…news." Isabella glanced at Angel's waist.

But Angel was too smart for her trap. "You'll have to wait, like everyone else. Because if I tell you, you'll tell the other grandmothers before Matthew gets a chance."

"Other grandmothers? I knew it." Isabella smiled. "But I won't spoil Matthew's moment."

Angel went to her husband. "Better make it quick, Matt, my mother guessed. And if she knows, all three of them will know—they're thick as thieves."

Matthew tapped his wineglass filled with sparkling cider. "Angelina and I want to thank you for being here to share our happiness. When we went to Zion's Gate we found much more than we anticipated. Love and family. And in the spring we'll add a new member to our family. Angel and I are expecting a baby. Our child will be very blessed to have so many loving influences in his or her life."

The three women converged on Angel, showering her with hugs, kisses and congratulations. A few minutes later they moved on, gushing over the father-to-be.

"I'm very proud of you, Angel." Her father enfolded her in a hug. "You deserve every moment of happiness."

"Oh, Daddy, I *am* happy."

"I can tell. And, believe me, I've watched this relationship very closely. I will never forgive myself for abandoning you to Kent."

"Daddy, you didn't abandon me. You gave me space to grow. Unfortunately someone evil took advantage of that space. I only hope I'll have the courage to allow my daughter to live her own life once she's old enough."

"So it's a daughter?"

Angel grinned. "I'm not telling. It might have been a slip of the tongue. Or I might be teasing you. Because those three won't be content until they know for sure." She nodded toward her mother and the two Cooper sisters, as they referred to themselves.

Her father grasped her shoulders. "I know it's been difficult for you to be on desk duty, but I have to admit I'm relieved now that the baby's coming. You don't need to be on the streets while you're carrying a child."

Angel made a face. "I don't like it, but it's what I need to do. Zion's Gate taught me that if I don't deal with the stuff from my past, it might come back to bite me later. I don't want to put myself or anyone else in danger. The DPS counselor has been great."

"I think you learned many things at Zion's Gate."

She grinned. "I've accepted that I can't be in the thick of the action all the time. Eleanor showed me there's a rhythm to life and sometimes I need to slow down."

"A good lesson."

"Besides, I'll be able to sneak in some research for Abigail and Eleanor during the slow times."

"Research?"

"Yes, for their book about the intrepid Cooper sisters, girl detectives. I'm brainstorming ideas with them."

Her father shook his head and laughed. "You remind me more of your mother every day. You will definitely keep Matthew on his toes."

Matthew walked over to them. "I wouldn't have it any other way."

* * * * *

*Experience entertaining women's fiction for every
woman who has wondered "what's next?" in their
lives.
Turn the page for a sneak preview of a new book from
Harlequin NEXT,
WHY IS MURDER ON THE MENU, ANYWAY?
by Stevi Mittman*

On sale December 26, wherever books are sold.

Ambience is everything. Imagine eating a foie gras at a luncheonette counter, or a side of cole slaw at Le Cirque. It's not a matter of food but one of atmosphere. Remember that when planning your dining room design.
—Tips from Teddi.com

"Now that's the kind of man you should be looking for," my mother, the self-appointed keeper of my shelf-life stamp, says. She points with her fork at a man in the corner of The Steak-Out Restaurant, a dive I've just been hired to redecorate. Making this restaurant look four-star will be hard, but not half as hard as getting through lunch without strangling the woman across the table from me. "*He* would make a good husband."

"Oh, you can tell that from across the room?" I ask, wondering how it is she can forget that when we had trouble getting rid of my last husband, she shot him. "Besides being ten minutes away from death if he actually eats all that steak, he's twenty years too old for me and—shallow woman that I am—twenty pounds too heavy. Besides, I am *so* not looking for another husband here. I'm looking to design a new image for this place, looking for some sense of ambience, some feeling, something I can build a proposal on for them."

My mother studies the man in the corner, tilting her head, the better to gauge his age, I suppose. I think she's grimacing, but with all the Botox and Restylane injected into that face, it's hard to tell. She takes another bite of her steak salad, chews slowly so that I don't miss the fact that the steak is a poor cut and tougher than it should be. "You're concentrating on the wrong kind of proposal," she says finally. "Just look at this place, Teddi. It's a dive. There are hardly any other diners. What does *that* tell you about the food?"

"That they cater to a dinner crowd and it's lunchtime," I tell her.

I don't know what I was thinking bringing her here with me. I suppose I thought it would be better than eating alone. There really are days when my common sense goes on vacation. Clearly, this is one of them. I mean really, did I not resolve less than three weeks ago that I would not let my mother get to me anymore?

What good are New Year's resolutions, anyway?

Mario approaches the man's table and my mother studies him while they converse. Eventually Mario leaves the table with a huff, after which the diner glances up and meets my mother's gaze. I think she's smiling at him. That or she's got indigestion. They size each other up.

I concentrate on making sketches in my notebook and try to ignore the fact that my mother is flirting. At nearly seventy, she's developed an unhealthy interest in members of the opposite sex to whom she isn't married.

According to my father, who has broken the TMI

rule and given me Too Much Information, she has no interest in sex with him. Better, I suppose, to be clued in on what they aren't doing in the bedroom than have to hear what they might be.

"He's not so old," my mother says, noticing that I have barely touched the Chinese chicken salad she warned me not to get. "He's got about as many years on you as you have on your little cop friend."

She does this to make me crazy. I know it, but it works all the same. "Drew Scoones is not my little 'friend.' He's a detective with whom I—"

"Screwed around," my mother says. I must look shocked, because my mother laughs at me and asks if I think she doesn't know the "lingo."

What I thought she didn't know was that Drew and I actually tangled the sheets. And, since it's possible she's just fishing, I sidestep the issue and tell her that Drew is just a couple of years younger than me and that I don't need reminding. I dig into my salad with renewed vigor, determined to show my mother that Chinese chicken salad in a steak place was not the stupid choice it's proving to be.

After a few more minutes of my picking at the wilted leaves on my plate, the man my mother has me nearly engaged to pays his bill and heads past us toward the back of the restaurant. I watch my mother take in his shoes, his suit and the diamond pinkie ring that seems to be cutting off the circulation in his little finger.

"Such nice hands," she says after the man is out of sight. "Manicured." She and I both stare at my hands. I have two popped acrylics that are being held on at weird angles by bandages. My cuticles are ragged and there's marker decorating my right hand from measuring carelessly when I did a drawing for a customer.

Twenty minutes later she's disappointed that he managed to leave the restaurant without our noticing. He will join the list of the ones I let get away. I will hear about him twenty years from now when—according to my mother—my children will be grown and I will still be single, living pathetically alone with several dogs and cats.

After my ex, that sounds good to me.

The waitress tells us that our meal has been taken care of by the management and, after thanking Mario, the owner, complimenting him on the wonderful meal and assuring him that once I have redecorated his place people will be flocking here in droves (I actually use those words and ignore my mother when she rolls her eyes), my mother and I head for the restroom.

My father—unfortunately not with us today—has the patience of a saint. He got it over the years of living with my mother. She, perhaps as a result, figures he has the patience for both of them, and feels justified having none. For her, no rules apply, and a little thing like a picture of a man on the door to a public restroom is certainly no barrier to using the john. In all fairness, it does seem silly to stand and wait for the ladies' room if no one is using the men's room.

Still, it's the idea that rules don't apply to her, signs don't apply to her, conventions don't apply to her. She knocks on the door to the men's room. When no one answers she gestures to me to go ahead in. I tell her that I can certainly wait for the ladies' room to be free and she shrugs and goes in herself.

Not a minute later there is a blood-curdling scream from behind the men's room door.

"Mom!" I yell. "Are you all right?"

Mario comes running over, the waitress on his heels. Two customers head our way while my mother continues to scream.

I try the door, but it is locked. I yell for her to open it and she fumbles with the knob. When she finally manages to unlock and open it, she is white behind her two streaks of blush, but she is on her feet and appears shaken but not stirred.

"What happened?" I ask her. So do Mario and the waitress and the few customers who have migrated to the back of the place.

She points toward the bathroom and I go in, thinking it serves her right for using the men's room. But I see nothing amiss.

She gestures toward the stall, and, like any self-respecting and suspicious woman, I poke the door open with one finger, expecting the worst.

What I find is worse than the worst.

The husband my mother picked out for me is sitting on the toilet. His pants are puddled down around his ankles, his hands are hanging at his sides. Pinned to his chest is some sort of Health Department certificate.

Oh, and there is a large, round, bloodless bullet hole between his eyes.

Four Nassau County police officers are securing the area, waiting for the detectives and crime scene personnel to show up. They are trying, though not very hard, to comfort my mother, who in another era would be considered to be suffering from the vapors. Less tactful in the twenty-first century, I'd say she was losing it. That is, if I didn't know her better, know she was milking it for everything it was worth.

My mother loves attention. As it begins to flag, she swoons and claims to feel faint. Despite four No Smoking signs, my mother insists it's all right for her to light up because, after all, she's in shock. Not to mention that signs, as we know, don't apply to her.

When asked not to smoke, she collapses mournfully in a chair and lets her head loll to the side, all without mussing her hair.

Eventually, the detectives show up to find the four patrolmen all circled around her, debating whether to administer CPR, smelling salts or simply call the paramedics. I, however, know just what will snap her to attention.

"Detective Scoones," I say loudly. My mother parts the sea of cops.

"We have to stop meeting like this," he says lightly to me, but I can feel him checking me over with his eyes, making sure I'm all right while pretending not to care.

"What have you got in those pants?" my mother asks him, coming to her feet and staring at his crotch accusingly. "*Baydar?* Everywhere we Bayers are, you turn up. You don't expect me to buy that this is a coincidence, I hope."

Drew tells my mother that it's nice to see her, too, and asks if it's his fault that her daughter seems to attract disasters.

Charming to be made to feel like the bearer of a plague.

He asks how I am.

"Just peachy," I tell him. "I seem to be making a habit of finding dead bodies, my mother is driving me crazy and the catering hall I book two freakin' years ago for Dana's bat mitzvah has just been shut down by the Board of Health!"

"Glad to see your luck's finally changing," he says, giving me a quick squeeze around the shoulders before turning his attention to the patrolmen, asking what they've got, whether they've taken any statements, moved anything, all the sort of stuff you see on TV, without any of the drama. That is, if you don't count my mother's threats to faint every few minutes when she senses no one paying attention to her.

Mario tells his wait staff to bring everyone espresso, which I decline because I'm wired enough. Drew pulls him aside and a minute later I'm handed a cup of coffee that smells divinely of Kahlúa.

The man knows me well. Too well.

His partner, whom I've met once or twice, says he'll interview the kitchen staff. Drew asks Mario if he minds if he takes statements from the patrons first and gets to him and the wait staff afterward.

"No, no," Mario tells him. "Do the patrons first." Drew raises his eyebrow at me like he wants to know if I get the double entendre. I try to look bored.

"What is it with you and murder victims?" he asks me when we sit down at a table in the corner.

I search them out so that I can see you again, I almost say, but I'm afraid it will sound desperate instead of sarcastic.

My mother, lighting up and daring him with a look to tell her not to, reminds him that *she* was the one to find the body.

Drew asks what happened *this time*. My mother tells him how the man in the john was "taken" with me, couldn't take his eyes off me and blatantly flirted with both of us. To his credit, Drew doesn't laugh, but his smirk is undeniable to the trained eye. And I've had my eye trained on him for nearly a year now.

"While he was noticing you," he asks me, "did *you* notice anything about him? Was he waiting for anyone? Watching for anything?"

I tell him that he didn't appear to be waiting or watching. That he made no phone calls, was fairly intent on eating and did, indeed, flirt with my mother. This last bit Drew takes with a grain of salt, which was the way it was intended.

"And he had a short conversation with Mario," I tell him. "I think he might have been unhappy with the food, though he didn't send it back."

Drew asks what makes me think he was dissatisfied, and I tell him that the discussion seemed acrimonious and that Mario looked distressed when he left the table. Drew makes a note and says he'll look into it and asks about anyone else in the restaurant. Did I see anyone who didn't seem to belong, anyone who was watching the victim, anyone looking suspicious?

"Besides my mother?" I ask him, and Mom huffs and blows her cigarette smoke in my direction.

I tell him that there were several deliveries, the kitchen staff going in and out the back door to grab a smoke. He stops me and asks what I was doing checking out the back door of the restaurant.

Proudly—because, while he was off forgetting me, dropping by only once in a while to say hi to Jesse, my son, or drop something by for one of my daughters that he thought they might like, I was getting on with my life—I tell him that I'm decorating the place.

He looks genuinely impressed. "Commercial customers? That's great," he says. Okay, that's what he *ought* to say. What he actually says is, "Whatever pays the bills."

"Howard Rosen, the famous restaurant critic, got her the job," my mother says. "You met him—the good-looking, distinguished gentleman with the *real* job, something to be proud of. I guess you've never read his reviews in *Newsday*."

Drew, without missing a beat, tells her that Howard's reviews are on the top of his list, as soon as he learns how to read.

"I only meant—" my mother starts, but both of us assure her that we know just what she meant.

"So," Drew says. "Deliveries?"

I tell him that Mario would know better than I, but that I saw vegetables come in, maybe fish and linens.

"This is the second restaurant job Howard's got her," my mother tells Drew.

"At least she's getting *something* out of the relationship," he says.

"If he were here," my mother says, ignoring the insinuation, "he'd be comforting her instead of interrogating her. He'd be making sure we're both all right after such an ordeal."

"I'm sure he would," Drew agrees, then looks me in the eyes as if he's measuring my tolerance for shock. Quietly he adds, "But then maybe he doesn't know just what strong stuff your daughter's made of."

It's the closest thing to a tender moment I can expect from Drew Scoones. My mother breaks the spell. "She gets that from me," she says.

Both Drew and I take a minute, probably to pray that's all I inherited from her.

"I'm just trying to save you some time and effort," my mother tells him. "My money's on Howard."

Drew withers her with a look and mutters something that sounds suspiciously like "Fool's gold." Then he excuses himself to go back to work.

I catch his sleeve and ask if it's all right for us to leave. He says sure, he knows where we live. I say goodbye to Mario. I assure him that I will have some sketches for him in a few days, all the while hoping that this murder doesn't cancel his redecorating plans. I need the money desperately, the alternative being borrowing from my parents and being strangled by the strings.

My mother is strangely quiet all the way to her house. She doesn't tell me what a loser Drew Scoones is—despite his good looks—and how I was obviously drooling over him. She doesn't ask me where Howard is taking me tonight or warn me not to tell my father about what happened because he will worry about us both and no doubt insist we see our respective psychiatrists.

She fidgets nervously, opening and closing her purse over and over again.

"You okay?" I ask her. After all, she's just found a dead man on the toilet, and tough as she is that's got to be upsetting.

When she doesn't answer me I pull over to the side of the road.

"Mom?" She refuses to meet my eyes. "You want me to take you to see Dr. Cohen?"

She looks out the window as if she's just realized we're on Broadway in Woodmere. "Aren't we near Marvin's Jewelers?" she asks, pulling something out of her purse.

"What have you got, Mother?" I ask, prying open her fingers to find the murdered man's ring.

"It was on the sink," she says in answer to my dropped jaw. "I was going to get his name and address and have you return it to him so that he could ask you out. I thought it was a sign that the two of you were meant to be together."

"He's dead, Mom. You understand that, right?" I ask. You never can tell when my mother is fine and when she's in la-la land.

"Well, I didn't know that," she shouts at me. "Not at the time."

I ask why she didn't give it to Drew, realize that she wouldn't give Drew the time in a clock shop and add, "...or one of the other policemen?"

"For heaven's sake," she tells me. "The man is dead, Teddi, and I took his ring. How would that look?"

Before I can tell her it looks just the way it is, she pulls out a cigarette and threatens to light it.

"I mean really," she says, shaking her head like it's my brains that are loose. "What does he need with it now?"

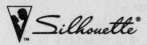

In February, expect *MORE*
from

as it increases to six titles per month.

What's to come...

Rancher and Protector

Part of the
Western Weddings
miniseries

BY JUDY CHRISTENBERRY

The Boss's
Pregnancy Proposal

BY RAYE MORGAN

Don't miss February's
incredible line up of authors!

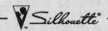

SPECIAL EDITION™

Logan's Legacy Revisited

THE LOGAN FAMILY IS BACK WITH SIX NEW STORIES.

Beginning in January 2007 with

THE COUPLE MOST LIKELY TO

by

LILIAN DARCY

Tragedy drove them apart. Reunited eighteen years later, their attraction was once again undeniable. But had time away changed Jake Logan enough to let him face his fears and commit to the woman he once loved?

REQUEST YOUR FREE BOOKS!

2 FREE NOVELS PLUS 2 *FREE GIFTS!*

HARLEQUIN®

Super Romance®

Exciting, emotional, unexpected!

YES! Please send me 2 FREE Harlequin Superromance® novels and my 2 FREE gifts. After receiving them, if I don't wish to receive any more books, I can return the shipping statement marked "cancel." If I don't cancel, I will receive 6 brand-new novels every month and be billed just $4.69 per book in the U.S., or $5.24 per book in Canada, plus 25¢ shipping and handling per book and applicable taxes, if any*. That's a savings of close to 15% off the cover price! I understand that accepting the 2 free books and gifts places me under no obligation to buy anything. I can always return a shipment and cancel at any time. Even if I never buy another book from Harlequin, the two free books and gifts are mine to keep forever.

135 HDN EEX7   336 HDN EEYK

Name _____ (PLEASE PRINT) _____

Address _____ Apt. _____

City _____ State/Prov. _____ Zip/Postal Code _____

Signature (if under 18, a parent or guardian must sign)

Mail to Harlequin Reader Service®:

IN U.S.A.
P.O. Box 1867
Buffalo, NY
14240-1867

IN CANADA
P.O. Box 609
Fort Erie, Ontario
L2A 5X3

Not valid to current Harlequin Superromance subscribers.

Want to try two free books from another line?

Call 1-800-873-8635 or visit www.morefreebooks.com.

* Terms and prices subject to change without notice. NY residents add applicable sales tax. Canadian residents will be charged applicable provincial taxes and GST. This offer is limited to one order per household. All orders subject to approval. Credit or debit balances in a customer's account(s) may be offset by any other outstanding balance owed by or to the customer. Please allow 4 to 6 weeks for delivery.

HSR06

nocturne™

WAS HE HER SAVIOR
OR HER NIGHTMARE?

HAUNTED
LISA CHILDS

Years ago, Ariel and her sisters were separated for
their own protection. Now the man who vowed
revenge on her family has resumed the hunt, and
Ariel must warn her sisters before it's too late.
The closer she comes to finding them, the more
secretive her fiancé becomes. Can she trust the man
she plans to spend eternity with? Or has he been
waiting for the perfect moment to destroy her?

On sale December 2006.